Lost Weekend in May

Stuck in Huwabola, a small Indiana town, incoming high school sophomore Tyler Puspoon's world has turned upside down. His parents are newly divorced, and they worry him to no end. His dad, a Marine Corps Recon Ranger, is 10,000 miles away, getting shot at in Vietnam, and his mom, Twyla, a CCU nurse, is being wooed by a slaggy traveling salesman who wishes Tyler was old enough for the draft.

To make matters worse, the Summer of Love is three years in the past, and Tyler's afraid the sexual revolution will be over before he gets to enlist. But he's got an even bigger problem looming. After a weirdly wonderful make-out session with Darlene Wantel, who he barely knows, he finds a wallet loaded with cash and gets kidnapped by a gang of murderous bank robbers while trying to open a savings account.

Tyler's abduction sparks a statewide manhunt by a joint state and federal task force led by FBI Special Agent Carol Kramer. When Kramer finally catches the break she needs, she bucks agency regulations to team with Tyler's dad, Lieutenant Jack Puspoon, to attempt a rescue and maybe capture the gang.

Lost Weekend in May

Darrell V. Poer

Lost Weekend in May

ISBN: 978-1-711381-55-8

Cover Design and Illustrations by Caleb Poer
Interior Book Design by Maureen Cutajar
Media Marketing by Patrick Ford and Caleb Poer

for my mother,
Geraldine Ann Swager, a nicer person never lived

Lost Weekend in May

SOME FIFTY YEARS AGO, over a span of five days surrounding Memorial Day weekend, I had an experience that changed my life forever. When the FBI questioned me, I told the truth and nothing but the truth, but I didn't tell them the whole truth. This is the complete story, and it's all true.

Chapter 1

Friday, May 29, 1970

"WHERE THE HELL HAVE YOU BEEN, TYLER?" Frank shouted. He leapt off the front porch and headed toward the side door to cut me off. My throat knotted up, tight as a noose.

"Just hanging out with friends," I said guardedly. Mom banged open the front door, saw the broken glass, and glared at me, hands on hips. Summer vacation had taken a sudden bad turn.

Frank bent forward, so we were nose-to-nose. "Just hanging out with friends," he said, mimicking me with a prissy tone.

"We were—"

"YOU SHOULD'VE BEEN HOME HOURS AGO!" I jumped backward with my head hunched beneath my shoulders, but he took a long step forward and again shoved his face in mine. He had one jagged eyebrow shooting down his nose like a hairy lightning bolt and the other arced like a furry rainbow. I hated that look.

"WHAT THE HELL'S WRONG WITH YOU?"

My mouth was frozen in teeth-baring fear.

"ANSWER ME!"

"S-s-sorry," I mumbled in a small, quiet voice.

"SORRY? WHY DIDN'T YOU CALL?"

"I don't know," I lied. "I guess I forgot," I lied again.

I was in it up to my eyebrows. After weeks of warming weather, school was finally out for the summer. I should've been home at four o'clock, which was when bus 88 braked to a stop at our house, but I'd stayed behind to make out with Darlene Wantel.

Frank was Mom's boyfriend. He started nosing around after my folks split up. Early one Friday morning, he telephoned from his hotel room on the road somewhere. I was eating a bowl of cereal and cramming for a test I'd spaced. Mom was across the table, chatting away like a teenager; she had her knees at her chest and her feet on the seat and she was twirling the telephone cord around her index finger. Occasionally, she looked at me and smiled. Mom looked happy, which made me happy, but I hated Frank all the same.

"Tyler?"

"Yeah?" I looked up from my notes. She had her palm over the mouthpiece.

"Frank wants to eat at Oscar's Big Boy tonight. You want to go?"

"Uh, no, thanks." *I'd rather drink bleach.*

"Okay, he can come over then. We'll order a pizza and watch a movie. How does that sound?"

It sounds like pure fucking torture. "Sounds like fun, but I'm going over to Randy's after school to watch *Dark Shadows*, and then we're going to the movies."

"I didn't know you had plans."

I didn't have plans. I didn't even know anyone named Randy. I just wasn't going to spend Friday night at home with Mom and Frank cozied up on the couch.

She got back on the phone, and they talked a little while longer. After she hung up, she sat down beside me.

"What's wrong?" Mom always knew when something was up.

"It's weird seeing you with somebody besides Dad."

"I know," she said. Grandma didn't remarry after Grandad died, never even dated. "It's a big change for me, too. Are any of your friends' parents divorced?"

"Oh, yeah."

"Have they remarried?"

"Yeah, Alan Schieber's mom. One of my teachers, too. Wait, you're not marrying Frank Beetz, are you?!"

"Noooo," Mom laughed. Then she snapped her fingers and frowned.

"What's the matter?"

"He didn't give me a time. I better call him before he heads out."

"I've got to get ready for school," I said, seizing the opportunity to ditch the conversation.

After a quick shower, I tugged on my jeans and rooted around for a clean T-shirt. Carrying my black Chucks, I walked barefoot to the basement and grabbed a pair of socks from the dryer. After lacing up, I went upstairs. Mom was at the sink, staring out the window.

"What's wrong?"

"Nothing," she said. Her tone suggested otherwise. "Just thinking."

"About?"

"I called Frank." She turned around and leaned back with her hands on the white Formica countertop. "The desk clerk put me through to his room, and a woman answered." Mom paused and looked at me. "So, I said, 'Is Frank there?' and she said, 'He's in the shower!' Just like that, very nasty, and then she slammed the phone down!"

"Uh-oh."

"Mm-hmm, that's not all. He called back not five minutes later with a story about the maid showing up to clean his room and slipping her five bucks to field business calls while he showered."

"Yeah, right," I said, wondering what else he slipped her.

Mom, frowning, cupped her chin with her thumb and index finger along each side of her jawline, thinking. Then she nodded her head, almost imperceptibly, over and over, apparently acknowledging something. I broke the silence.

"You don't believe him, do you?"

"Hardly. Maids don't start cleaning rooms at six in the morning, and who gets business calls that early?"

"So, the woman?"

"She was jealous."

They didn't go to Oscar's, and Frank didn't come by for pizza and a movie either. So, I told Mom that Randy flaked on me and we ate at Doc Caccamo's and then saw *A Bullet for Sandoval* at the drive-in.

A month passed, Frank stopped coming around. Mom didn't mention him, and I didn't ask. But then one Saturday, I came home sick after spending the night at Tim Brooks' house. His mom made tuna casserole for supper, and I hated tuna casserole. I planned to grab a bucket and go to bed. It was early, cool, and still dark outside when I walked through the side door. The kitchen light was on. Frank was just shutting the fridge. He was naked.

"Awww, no!" I said.

"What the hell are you doing here?!"

"What am I—?! I live here! What're you do—wait, where's Mom? Whoa . . . are you two, oh, no!" I bolted for the bathroom with my hand cupped over my mouth, gulping mouthfuls of air to buy time.

"Frank, what's wrong?" Mom called from the bedroom. She flipped on the hall light but shielded herself behind the door when she saw me coming.

"Tyler! You're supposed to be at Tim's house!"

I shot past her, banged open the bathroom door, and dove for the toilet.

"Gaawaht!" I yakked the casserole in one long stream and hung there, hunched over the bowl, staring at the offending ingredients.

"Are you okay?" Mom was tapping on the door, still in the hall. She poked her head inside and flipped on the light.

"Yeah," I panted, flushing the toilet. I was not okay. My stomach was roiling. I rose, rinsed my mouth, and brushed my teeth.

Mom slipped on her blue-striped robe and hovered nearby, looking worried.

"Sorry, Mom, I just came home to change clothes."

"Tyler . . ."

"No, it's fine. I'm going back to Tim's."

"Are you sure you feel okay?"

"Yeah, I'm all right. I'll be back tomorrow after Frank's gone."

"Okay, we'll talk then. I love you."

"Me, too." When I reached the kitchen, Frank was leaning against the counter, looking smug. Thank God he'd put on his boxers. I passed by without a word or glance, but his eyes were all over me.

"Next time call," he said. "Don't just pop in like that."

I opened the door and looked back at him. "Next time don't be here when I do."

When Frank came sniffing around, my Dad, a Marine Corps lieutenant, was finishing his fourth straight tour in Vietnam. By then, he was all scarred up—souvenirs, he called them—from bullets and shrapnel. Mom kept all of his medals—a Navy Cross, two Silver Stars, six Purple Hearts—locked in her jewelry box. Dad was coming home soon, and although I looked forward to seeing him, it was going to be weird with Frank hanging around.

By May 1970, everyone was fed up with the Vietnam War, and they'd taken to the streets to show it. Protests and marches occurred nearly every day throughout the country, and they were getting more violent as the war dragged on. On May 4, Ohio National Guardsmen opened fire on students at Kent State. When the smoke cleared, there were four dead and nine wounded. Eleven days later, Mississippi Highway Patrolmen, armed with shotguns, killed two people and injured twelve more in response to rioting at Jackson State University. All across the country, demonstrators were being clubbed, cuffed, and carted off to jail, although not necessarily in that order.

America was brimming with so much hate and anger. The Weather Underground declared war on the federal government and embarked on a bombing campaign. South Carolina's governor blamed the Black Power movement for the Orangeburg massacre. Then the Black Panthers started ambushing cops, leading J. Edgar Hoover, the legendary FBI Director, to call them the "greatest threat to the internal security of the country." Well, maybe to some, but the Panthers had support in inner cities where people seethed about unemployment, rundown schools, substandard housing, discrimination, and crime. Of course, there was always racial violence in the south while out west, Charles Manson was about to go on trial for the Tate-LaBianca killings. Meanwhile, here, in Indiana, there was a gang of murderous bank robbers terrorizing the state. America was one big crime scene.

The Vietnam War overshadowed it all. A year ago, when Dad came home after his third tour, he promised us it was his last. Mom and I danced in the front yard. He would've, too, but he was still on crutches. The Corps assigned him to a recruitment center in Fort Wayne, so we got to stay in Huwabola.

It was perfect except Dad hated it. The driving, dingy motels, and greasy food got old quick, and he likened recruiting during the war to selling blast furnaces in Hell. Students on campuses couldn't wait to harass him. He got cursed, flipped off, and spat at everywhere he went. The Corps' olive drab sedan got its share of abuse, too. It went back to the motor pool after every trip to fix dents, replace broken windows, and get a good washing.

Dad lasted a month. He decided to resign his commission until he learned Bravo Company was down a platoon commander.

I was hitting rocks with a cracked baseball bat when he got home. Mom was weeding the garden. She took the news well.

"ANOTHER TOUR? WHAT THE HELL DO YOU MEAN 'ANOTHER TOUR?' ARE YOU OUT OF YOUR GODDAMN MIND?" Mom snatched my bat and went after him.

"No, Twyla, don't.... Put it down," Dad said, backing away. She swung at his head, but he ducked. Strike one. He kept backpedaling, trying to explain. She was having none of it.

"Listen here, you son of a bitch, you've done more for your

country than a hundred Marines, and you've put us through hell doing it!" Mom took another swing, this time at his knees, but he jumped out of the way. Strike two.

"The Colonel needs me."

"I don't care if the Commandant of the United States Marine Corps needs you! We need you!"

"I have a duty—" That was as far as he got.

"You're damn right, you do! It's to Tyler and me, not ten thousand miles away in some fucked-up jungle!" Mom choked up on the bat. Down in the count, she was determined to make contact. Dad noticed and darted to the other side of the car.

"The battalion's deploying in two weeks and they need a platoon commander," he said, looking over the roof at her.

"And there's no one else in the entire Marine Corps who can do it except you? Give me a break!" Mom stepped back and swung a third time. She connected, and the front passenger window exploded into a million pieces. She regripped.

"I'll get my silver bar. We'll have more money."

"NO!" Mom brought the bat down hard on the roof, leaving a deep dent for emphasis.

"I already signed the papers."

Mom's shoulders sagged, but then she straightened right up. "You son of a bitch!" If you go back to Vietnam, those won't be the only papers you sign!" She turned and walloped the sedan's side mirror, shattering it.

"C'mon now, Twyla."

"No, you promised!" Mom wheeled around, threatening him with the bat. "You don't know what it's like to wake up and spend the day wondering if you're dead or alive! Every time a car door slams, I rush to the window, hoping it's not a Navy chaplain! I'm through with it! And it's not fair to Tyler either, he needs you now more than ever!"

Dad slept on the couch after that. Mom gave him the silent treatment, but she made her anger clear by slamming doors, banging pots and pans, and ramming the vacuum cleaner into table legs, chair legs, and Dad's legs.

I hardly slept the night before Dad left for Vietnam. The next morning, Mom served him the divorce papers alongside his bacon and eggs. He grew quiet and paged through them while he ate, nodding occasionally. When he finished reading, he sipped his coffee, wiped his mouth, and signed the last page. Then he kissed Mom and me goodbye and left for the airport. That was early fall 1969.

Dad wrote every two weeks. His letters read like a travel brochure, though. He never mentioned the war, writing instead about lush jungles, endless rice paddies, and long, pristine coastlines. He complained of monsoons and the heat and humidity but not of gunfire, grenades, or booby traps. He always ended with "Take care of Mom and don't worry," but worrying was the one thing I never stopped doing. I saw footage of gaunt, weary soldiers getting shot at or diving for cover before a mortar exploded. I watched the injured being carried to hovering helicopters. The dead, too, but with less urgency; they were on a long journey home to lay in flag-draped coffins on the tarmac at Dover Air Force Base. I watched nightly, not knowing if Dad was among them.

Mom and I carried on as always in his absence. She woke me up in the morning, fixed breakfast, and went to work while I waited for the bus. We came straight home at the end of the day unless I had ball practice, or she had errands. Once in a while, we went out to eat or picked up a pizza. At night, I did homework, and then we watched television or played a game until bedtime. On weekends, we took care of the laundry and yard work, usually together, but sometimes we split things up and raced to see who got done first. It all seemed familiar, but Frank was an ongoing reminder that everything had changed.

Chapter 2

Friday, May 29, 1970

Huwabola, Indiana, was a law-and-order town in a law-and-order state. There were no marches or protests, and the only weathermen were on the news. There was no racial violence either since everybody was white. In addition to the local public school system, Huwabola had a small, private, divinity college—Huwabola Bible College—where the focus was Revelations, not revolutions. Students at HBC, unlike their contemporaries in Berkeley, Madison, and Ann Arbor, bathed daily, wore their Sunday best to class, and had the absurd notion that sex was solely for procreation. I knew better, of course, although not from personal experience.

I was seven when I discovered I had a way not with girls. That's when I fell in love with Erin Cussler, a pretty, blond-haired, blue-eyed first-grader. My love for Erin was deep and true. It was also one-sided. Still, I relentlessly pursued her with untiring vigor and always with a broken heart since she had boyfriend after boyfriend during grade school and not one of them was me. Every night before going to sleep, I analyzed the day with longing in my heart, examining those few occasions when Erin looked my way or, rarer, spoke to me. I replayed our every interaction over and over, trying to interpret looks she gave me or dissecting her words, twisting and turning them to find something—anything—to give me the hope and optimism I needed to start chasing her again in the morning. Bloodhounds couldn't have found anything. I did, though, and it fed my inane fantasy that Erin and I would one day marry, a delusion I maintained for six years through mirror-dodging denial.

Things got tougher at Crescott Junior High. On the first day of school, all the good-looking girls paired off with the good-looking guys. Not only was Erin gone forever, but my circle of friends instantly shrank. It got uglier, too. Girls kept picking, though, and boys kept dropping from our ranks. No one chose me, although I occasionally sent Brooks to find out if a certain girl "liked" me. He returned each time having been jeered or beaten. Eventually, there was no circle. Nor a triangle. It was just Brooks and me, and neither one of us could get a date off its tree. I was finally forced to acknowledge that I was that scrawny, four-eyed kid with a round head, weak chin, and crooked front teeth staring at me in the mirror.

So, Joe Vaughn had a stranglehold on my attention when he sidled up to me that last Monday before summer vacation and asked if I wanted to go to "The Weeds" when school let out on Friday. The Weeds, you see, was a legendary make-out spot in Crescott schoolboy lore. Every kid who went there had a cousin who was best friends with a guy who knew someone who got laid in The Weeds. People called it The Weeds because it was an empty lot overgrown by sorghum, foxtail, milkweeds, and, as I was soon to discover, poison ivy.

Joe was a "hood," the kind of kid parents told their children, especially their daughters, to avoid. He had half a billion freckles and long, greasy, red hair that his dad styled with hedge trimmers. His clothes were worn and tattered, veteran hand-me-downs from his two older brothers. Joe smoked, drank, and cussed. He also knew everything about sex. We became fast friends.

The Vaughns lived on the southeast side, outside city limits. Locals called the area "S.E." or "Essie." Crescott sat a few blocks further east. Essie succumbed to crime and neglect decades earlier. Boarded-up, abandoned houses made up entire neighborhoods. Homes were run-down even by Great Depression standards. Dirt front yards and potholed streets were separated by crumbling cement sidewalks. Main routes in and out looked like they'd been buzz-bombed. Town residents hastened Essie's reverse gentrification, converting vacant lots into dumpsites for broken appliances and discarded mattresses. Sheriff deputies responded to calls in Essie, but they refused to patrol the streets. Older residents stayed in at night. It was how they got old.

Essie was the guts of Huwabola's economy, though, explaining the close proximity of the sewage plant. The electrical grid was also in Essie, and so were factories, trucking companies, and an enormous limestone quarry, all of which deputies routinely patrolled at night. They had to; everybody in the county worked there or, like the government, depended on those who did. Very little of that money found its way back to Essie. Crescott, of course, was a rare exception since Huwabolans wanted to keep the poor kids where they belonged, i.e., away from their children.

Joe's dad worked at the quarry. He toted a sledgehammer, turning big rocks into small rocks and small rocks into dust. His mom worked at the laundromat, washing, drying, and folding clothes. They were a family of five cramped in a one-story house with crumbling, gray shingles for siding. The front yard was hard-packed dirt except for patches of crabgrass and dandelions. Toys, long outgrown and abandoned by the Vaughn brothers, lay scattered in the yard. A car battery leaked acid in the flowerbed. Around back, the frame of a child's bike rested against a rusted swing set corroded to brown, grainy fuzz. The place reeked of the Florida Panhandle without the salty air.

The first time I knocked on the Vaughns' front door, Joe invited me in, but what I saw over his shoulder sent shudders through me, so I told him I'd wait outside. He insisted, though, and somehow maneuvered me to the other side of the threshold while I was still groping for a reason to stay glued to the porch.

The house had five small rooms: two bedrooms and a kitchen, living room, and bathroom. The kitchen and bathroom had stained, cracked linoleum tiles best described as unhealthy. Everything else was covered by a filthy-looking carpet that probably witnessed a few felonies. Beer cans and cigarette butts littered the front room. Fist holes in the walls documented mood shifts. The house was overrun with noxious vermin: furry brown mice took off under the oven and refrigerator when Joe flicked on the kitchen light; cockroaches disappeared from the countertops while others scrambled over, under, and around a pile of rotting trash, most of it in torn, grease-stained paper sacks; ants marched between the mountain of garbage and the baseboard while squadrons of flies strafed its peaks and summit like attack jets.

The stench was overpowering. I held my breath to avoid getting sick, risking permanent lung scarring. My eyes were on fire. I fell to my knees, rubbing them frantically, and expelled the foul air. Then, cupping my mouth and nose with one hand, and waving the other for balance, I crawled on my knees toward the front door, promising God I'd never return if allowed to live. When I finally burst outdoors, I collapsed on the porch, coughing and choking and trying to draw a breath in between. I've kept my end of the bargain.

I figured Joe would go to The Weeds with Beverly Ruddles, and not for the first time either. Bev moved to Huwabola from the hills and hollers of Kentucky after school started last fall. She just sashayed into class one day and the boys started gawking. Of course, Bev's early development had a lot to do with it. Most girls had what would politely be referred to as "budding breasts," but she had tits! And to our great enjoyment, she saw no need to harness them in a bra!

Beverly was the definition of cute. Her brown eyes, dark as chocolate pudding, hinted at the sort of mischievousness that led to teen pregnancy, and her hair, which she wore in a short bob with bangs, was as black and shiny as the keys on Liberace's piano.

Everybody loved Bev. She was bright and cheerful, always smiling, and she loved to laugh, even at herself. Her colorful clothes reflected her personality, especially when she dressed up like it was

Derby Day and tittupped about in a big, wide-brimmed hat adorned with flowers.

I quickly came to my senses.

"I wish," I said with a sigh.

"What's the problem?" Joe smelled of cigarettes. Beer, too. It was first period.

"I don't have anyone to go with." No prospects either.

"That's 'bout to change."

"What's that supposed to mean?"

"I know someone who likes you." My heart rate doubled, then tripled. Then it slowed to a crawl.

"Who?" I asked warily, thinking he'd say Holly Thalshart or Ginny Hamstole, two stout freshmen who the varsity football coach prayed had brothers.

"Darlene Wantel," he said.

"Darlene?!" I looked at Joe in disbelief. He looked back and giggled like a five-year-old hearing his first fart joke before busting out laughing. I just stared at him. He was doubled over, hands on his knees, with tears streaming down his cheeks, coughing and wheezing like an end-stage emphysema patient. He finally caught his breath, and after wiping his eyes, stopped laughing. Then he looked up at me and started all over again. I turned to leave, but Joe grabbed my forearm, stopping me, and tried to pull himself to his feet. I shook him off, and he lost his balance, falling to his hands and knees, giggling again.

"Man, that ain't cool!"

"No, it's the truth, I swear," Joe wheezed, completely gassed, "but you should've seen the look on your face!"

"C'mon, Joe, Darlene? Really?"

"Really," he said, still struggling to catch his breath.

"Waaaait a minute," I said. Suspicion replaced disbelief. "How do you know?"

"Bev, how else?"

It was plausible. Bev and Darlene lived on the same block and hung out together. Surprisingly, she confirmed it.

"She shore daay-id, Taah-lur! Ah wunt bay puttin' on witch ye. Nawt 'bout sumpin' lahk tha', nossiree. Tha' bay maain!"

If Bev had a flip side, Darlene would be it. She was as quiet as snowfall. She didn't volunteer in class or spend time chatting in the hallways like the other kids. She always sat by herself at lunch, studying or reading, and she never participated in any school activities. Darlene was gorgeous, though. Her olive complexion favored a Mediterranean ancestry as did her long, flowing black hair, fleshy red lips and dazzling, emerald eyes. I was amazed she even knew I existed.

About then I had a second reality check. Mom wasn't going to let me hang out in Essie after school for anything short of a national emergency, and me getting laid did not qualify, at least not to her.

"Man, I wish I could, but there's no way my Mom's going for that. I wouldn't have a way home anyway."

Joe looked at me like I was crazy. "Lemme tell you something," he said, "there're things worth gettin' in trouble for, an' makin' out with Darlene Wantel in The Weeds is one of 'em. So, just do what I do."

"What's that?"

"Ask for forgiveness, not permission." Clearer sense had never been made, and when Joe said he'd haul me home on his bike afterward, I agreed on the spot.

I avoided Darlene like church the rest of the week, figuring she couldn't back out if she couldn't find me. Thursday night, I drew a chart, dividing the last day of school into eighty-four five-minute blocks. Friday was torturous, easily surpassing the nerve-racking times I took tests without cracking a book. I kept an eye on the clock and shaded each block as its time passed.

When the final bell finally rang, I joined the screaming horde of deliriously happy students storming the hallway. Joe caught up with me and said he and Bev would meet me at my locker. Bev, he said, had ducked inside the girls' locker room to change clothes, and he was heading out back for a quick smoke. I walked to my locker with my head on a swivel, scouring the crowd for Darlene, intending to introduce myself.

The hallways thinned. Kids fanned out in different directions or boarded buses for the last ride of the school year. I still hadn't seen Darlene, and I had a growing fear she'd ditched me. I was emptying my locker when I heard footsteps behind me. I turned, hoping it was her, but it was only Joe.

"What's goin' on, man?" he said.

"Not a whole lot. Have you seen Darlene?"

"Yeah, 'bout ten minutes 'go. She was headed home. What's the deal? Ain't you two meetin' up?"

"What're you asking me for?!" I whispered loudly. "You set it up!" I was gutted. Red-faced and mad, I spun away and pretended to rummage around in my locker.

"Sorry, dude, my bad," Joe said without a hint of sincerity.

"No biggie," I squeaked in a helium-laced voice, "but I've got to catch the bus." I grabbed my rucksack and threw it over my shoulder, completely dejected. I trudged down the hallway toward the parking lot.

"Have a good summer," Joe said, cheerily.

I grit my teeth, but before I could respond, Bev came bopping around the corner.

"Howdy, Taah-lur, whar ya goin'?" Her halter top halted nothing and her cut-off jeans looked like a belt with pockets.

"Hey," I said, glumly.

"Yer shore lookin' a might puny. Wha's wrong?"

"Nothing," I said, voice cracking, "but Joe said Darlene already left, so I'm going to catch the bus."

"Yep, we jes' gawt done talkin' to 'er nawt too long 'go. She wen' on home to worsh up an' change clothes, so yer s'posed go by thar' in fif-tane minutes. Din't Joe tale ya?"

"Uh-uh." I looked back. Joe was bent over, laughing, and slapping his hands on his knees.

Bev shot him a dirty look. "JOE VAWN! Ah swar yer as rotten as roadkeel, teasin' poor Taah-lur lahk tha'! Ya otter be 'shamed yerself!"

I ran the three blocks to the Wantels' house and knocked on the side door right on time. Kent, Darlene's brother, answered.

"Tyler? What brings you nosing around?"

"Oh, hey, Kent. I'm looking for Darlene. Is she here?"

"Yeah, yeah, don't play dumb. C'mon in, I know what's going on." He pushed the screen door open.

"Thanks." I puzzled over that comment as I slipped indoors. Kent disappeared around the corner and up a short flight of stairs.

"DARLENE! TYLER'S HERE!"

Darlene came downstairs within the minute, but I have no idea how long I stared at her.

"Tyler? Hey, Tyler? Tyler!" Darlene waved a hand in front of my face. "Are you okay?"

"What? Oh, sorry. Wow!" I looked around. Somehow, we'd wound up on the sidewalk.

"Wow?" She looked at me quizzically.

"Yeah, you look fantastic!" She really did, too. Until then, she could've passed for a student at HBC, but she'd slipped on a thin cotton tank top and shorts so short they were probably illegal in most states.

"Oh, how sweet, thank you," Darlene said. She put her hands in mine and rose on her tiptoes to kiss me on the cheek. She brushed against Tyler Jr., looked down, and giggled. Then she pivoted so we were side by side. Holding hands, we set off down the street.

"So, where are we going?"

WHAT? She doesn't know about The Weeds? I kept my cool. "I thought we'd hang out with Bev and Joe."

"Oh, okay," Darlene said, a small smile forming. "That sounds like fun. Where're we meeting them?"

Now what? "Uh, they didn't say."

"Didn't you ask?"

"No, I forgot."

"So, what do you want to do?"

"I don't know. Want to head over to Crescott and goof around on the playground?" I groaned. *What are we, six-year-olds?*

"The playground?"

"Wait, I know, have you got a Frisbee? Or do you want to go for a walk?" I was babbling and not at all prepared for what she said next.

"Let's go to The Weeds."

Chapter 3

Friday, May 29, 1970

The police blocked off the courthouse square after the murder and bank robbery, forcing traffic, including the tractor-trailer rigs, onto Teymore's narrow side streets. Two firetrucks, an ambulance, and a dozen squad cars from state, county, and city law enforcement sat at odd angles with their revolving red, white, and blue lights reflecting off the façades of the buildings fronting the square. Police officers, firemen, and emergency medical technicians milled in the streets near the double doors of the First National Bank. Reporters and television crews had set up on the courthouse lawn. When locals started gathering, the police looped yellow tape around parking meters and streetlamps, cordoning off the entire square block. The scene looked surreal in the shadows of the western sun.

FBI Special Agent Carol Kramer watched it all from her car. She spotted the detour on SR 42 when she pulled into Teymore and ducked into an alley two blocks from the bank, guessing correctly there'd be no barricades. She crept to the square, switched off the ignition, and rolled to a stop between a tavern and a lawyer's office. She had a clear view of the bank and spotted the black hearse parked discretely at the rear. Kramer had been an FBI agent for nearly a year, and she been without a partner for most of that time, a violation of agency policy. She neither complained nor asked why, though. Her job was difficult enough without opening new fronts.

Kramer, wearing a white blouse between a gray jacket and slacks, climbed out the new Polara Pursuit she'd been assigned in somebody's moment of mismanagement and walked up Main Street with her badge cupped in the palm of her hand. She bumped and nudged through the crowd of emergency personnel, gently jostling those blocking her path, and apologizing in response to stern looks. She did a lot of apologizing. Unfortunately, she also caught the attention of a volunteer auxiliary policeman, a handyman sporting a pot belly and handlebar mustache. His uniform, a freshly-pressed dark blue cotton blend with shiny gold buttons and stitching, appeared new, but it wasn't. He'd last worn it five years earlier while directing traffic at the Teymore SausageFest. He'd caused a fatal accident.

Called into action and standing inside the tape at the corner by the mailbox, the buddha-bellied handyman had been admiring a motorcycle and missed the Polara's sudden appearance on the square. The theatrics began when he spotted the tall, fit, young black woman in braids weaving a path through the crowd toward the bank. *No, no, no, not in Teymore! Not on my watch!*

Kramer side-eyed him, expecting something similar to what happened next.

"Annh!" The handyman's nasal tone sounded feeble and sheep-like. He knew it lacked authority, but it angered him beyond endurance when people ignored him. Kramer ignored him.

"ANNH!" he bleated, louder this time, attracting the attention of the barflies who'd gone back to drinking and shooting pool. They scrambled over, under, and around each other, fighting for position at the front window.

The mouth-breathing handyman, limping like a peg-legged pirate, finally got in front of Kramer, but he had to backpedal to stay there because she neither broke stride nor changed direction.

"FBI," she said, flashing her badge. Down went the handyman in a tangle of his own legs and feet. The bar exploded in laughter. Everyone outside did, too. Somebody said his coordination was no better than his money-handling skills. Kramer, suppressing a smile, kept walking. She crossed the street and stopped before a man dressed in tan slacks and a blue and white dress shirt open at the collar.

"Hi, I'm Agent Kramer, FBI. Are you Detective Reed?"

"Last time I looked, yeah," the man said tiredly.

Lowell Reed was in his late thirties, deeply-tanned, and at 6'3" and 210 pounds, trim and fit. He had a full shock of wavy blond hair and a strong jaw beneath deep-set sapphire eyes. Reed spent fifteen years with the LAPD, the last dozen as a homicide detective. He was a Hoosier, though, born in Corunna, and when he heard the Teymore Police Department planned to hire its first detective, he sent in his resume. After a brief telephone interview, he got the job.

The Midwest's heat and humidity wore on Reed, and it wasn't even summer yet. He'd ditched his sportscoat as soon as he got to the office, and he'd unbuttoned the top button of his shirt and loosened his tie shortly after. By nine o'clock, Reed's shirt sleeves were at his elbows and his tie was in his desk drawer, but even casually dressed, he stood out in the small farming community where men wore scruffy blue jeans, sweat-stained T-shirts, and boots caked in animal feces.

"Have you ever handled a murder investigation?" Kramer asked.

"Too many."

The three-story limestone building's ceiling was open to the roof. The wall facing Main Street had four large rectangular windows at each level. With its double doors, white rococo wood trim, and green and white, gold-flaked marble floor, the bank, light and airy, lacked the starched, stuffy formality of most banks. Reed stopped in the lobby and faced the doors. Kramer kept pace, her low black heels echoing throughout the hall-like bank. Behind them, the coroner knelt over a body face down on the floor, making notations in a black journal.

"This case has DTK all over it," Reed said for the coroner's benefit. The press had dubbed them "Dressed to Kill" because of their natty attire and penchant for murder. Reed knew the reporters would pump the coroner for details, probably while paying for lunch.

Reed crooked his finger, motioning Kramer to follow him. He walked to the lead teller's station and pulled a small, green notebook from his back pocket. Leaning against the polished blond wood, he flipped to a page and nodded toward the front doors.

"Just before two o'clock, two men, Laurel and Hardy look-a-likes, burst in."

"Wait, hold up. Laurel and Hardy?"

"Comedy duo. You never heard of them?"

Kramer shook her head.

"Before your time, I guess."

"I guess."

"Okay, so, Stan Laurel was a skinny guy. Oliver Hardy was fat. Two white men in black suits with matching hats and ties."

"All right, I get it. They fit the profile."

"Am I the first to make that connection?"

"So far as I know."

"These two carried guns and wore sunglasses and gloves, though."

Kramer wrote it all down.

"So, Ollie comes straight here," Reed said, tapping the counter. "He's a slob—rumpled clothes looking like he'd slept in them, stained shirt, spots on his tie, that sort of thing."

"Hmm," Kramer murmured, still taking notes.

"Early fifties, six feet tall, and even wider around. He's got black, curly hair, no visible scars or tats. He shows Theresa ...Theresa Clark, she's the lead teller, he shows her his gun and tells her to keep her hands where he can see them. Then he handed her a big, black, heavy-duty cloth bag and told her to fill it with large bills, twenties and up. He made the other two tellers do the same thing. Then he marched everybody to the safe."

"And...Laurel, is it?"

"Yeah, Stan, he's the killer." Reed turned to a marked page. "He was a different character altogether. Bit taller than Ollie, very thin, close-cropped gray hair, and a lot better dressed. Older, too, apparently. 'Wrinkly-faced' is how Theresa described him."

Kramer scribbled in her notepad again. Reed paused and scratched his cheek with his thumb.

"All right, Stan heads straight to the bank manager's office." Reed pivoted and lead Kramer to the hallway but stopped abruptly. Looking around, he spotted a bald, middle-aged man in black suit trousers and a blood-stained white dress shirt holding an ice bag to his face. Reed nodded toward him.

"That's the manager, Donnie Cole," he said and then walked the length of the hall before stopping again. "This is his office here." Reed stood in the doorway, leaving Kramer in the hall. "Stan breezed past his secretary without a word; he just gave her a big, friendly, smile and waved. When he got to Donnie, he stuck out his hand as if to introduce himself, but instead popped him on the nose."

"That's dirty," Kramer said. She looked at Donnie, who had his hand out, palm up, while a medic shook a couple of pills from a small, white bottle.

"Yeah, broke it, too," Reed said, wincing. "Then he marched Donnie to the safe." Reed set off down the hallway and opened a door leading to the vault and the teller stations beyond. "Careful where you walk, there's blood everywhere." Kramer sidestepped and tiptoed around the black spots and smears, wondering if Donnie was a hemophiliac. Reed stopped at the vault. "He made Donnie load his bag—same heavy, black cotton—with bundles of twenties, fifties, and hundreds. A few seconds later, Ollie showed up with the tellers, herded them inside, and made Theresa do the same."

"Any idea how much they got?"

"A lot. Donnie thinks over eighty grand, but that's just a guess. It could be more. Auditors will pin it down."

"That much for a town this size," Kramer mused.

"I know. There was a Brinks delivery this morning since Social Security and VA checks arrive on Monday."

"Not to mention it's a holiday weekend and the '500's tomorrow."

"Exactly."

"These guys knew when to hit. I bet that Brinks is on a set schedule. What about security?"

"None. No guard, no video. Teymore's just a little farming community. There's never been a bank robbery, let alone a murder."

"Yeah, tell me about that," Kramer said quietly.

"Ray Olivero," Reed said. "Real nice guy." He swung the gate open and walked toward the lobby, completing a circuitous tour of the bank. "He and his wife, Shawn Marie, own the hardware store across the street. Wrong time, wrong place. Ray got to Theresa's station, saw everyone in the vault, and took off running. Stan ran after him and shot him in the back."

"Cold."

"Yeah, the wound's bad. That's a .45 with hollow points."

"You sound pretty confident."

"I've seen a lot of bullet wounds," Reed said, shrugging. "I'm not always right, but I'm seldom wrong."

"I believe you," Kramer said with an amused smile, "but I'll wait for ballistics."

"Suit yourself."

"What about the car and driver?"

"Nothing on the driver, but people saw a green station wagon going north on Zunis in a hurry. That's kind of interesting."

"How so?"

"Zunis dead ends at a field after a mile, but there's a trail across it that lets out on Mission Road. From there, it's a straight shot to the highway. It's not mapped, but the kids around here use it for a shortcut. These guys knew about it, too."

Chapter 4

Friday, May 29, 1970

Bev and Joe were nowhere to be seen when we reached The Weeds, but their moaning, punctuated by gasps and grunts, gave us a general idea of their whereabouts. Darlene finally pointed them out, nodding to a spot in the thicket where the bushes were moving rhythmically. I pulled her in the opposite direction and started searching for a quiet place of our own. I was tramping about, looking this way and that, but having no luck and growing increasingly frustrated. After combing the same ground for the third time, Darlene, sensing my aggravation, quietly pointed in a different direction and suggested we follow the path. Before long, she was leading me by the hand down a series of trails that took us deeper into The Weeds. We passed a hollow log and plunged through a narrow gap in the brush. Darlene seemed awfully familiar with the real estate, and eventually we came upon a flattened pile of brush just big enough for two people.

Darlene wasted no time. She reached out, grasped my shirt, pulled my head down, and mashed her mouth against mine in a bruising lip-lock. Then she slid her hand behind my neck to keep me there. Her tongue came to life, frantically darting back and forth across my lips, trying to snake its way in between. I yielded to its insistence, and Darlene immediately thrust it past my front teeth, after which it set about exploring the crooks and crevices of every tooth between my canines and molars. I had to wrestle myself free when her tongue, now well beyond my back teeth and into my esophagus on its apparent mission to my upper intestine, began choking me.

I came up coughing, sputtering, and gasping for air. I sucked in a lungful, bringing me back from the edge of collapse, but only just because Darlene pulled me to the ground atop her and started up again, kissing, licking, and running her lips and tongue all over my cheeks, chin, nose, and forehead. I whipped my head around, trying to find her mouth, but she was moving at speeds I hadn't anticipated. I never thought making out was like *this.* I pictured us laying together, our legs intertwined, gently caressing each other, and exchanging slow, soft kisses—like the movies. I should've watched peep shows.

After a brief lull, Darlene rolled over, putting me on my back, and hopped astride my hips. She looked down and, smiling wickedly, leaned forward with her outstretched arms on either side of my head, so her long, dark hair fell all around us. Then she lowered her lips to mine and teased me with her tongue, flicking it in and out of my mouth and running it all over my lips. I gasped when she grabbed ahold of Tyler Jr. and gave him a few tugs. Darlene winked and shifted her hips to straddle my shin. She threw her head back and started dry humping it, moaning softly while gliding back and forth. She moved slow and easy at first, but she soon picked up the pace, and, grunting and groaning, began breathing in short, ragged gasps.

I was mesmerized. Darlene's eyes stared without seeing. She arched her spine, bent backwards at the waist, and rolled her head from side to side, sweeping her thick black hair back and forth on the ground like a broom, collecting bits of debris, until, suddenly, without warning, her upper body whipped forward like an unstrung bow and she flattened her mouth against mine again. Darlene wrestled my tongue for control, and when she got it, she sucked hard, nearly collapsing my lungs, and creating a vacuum-packed seal with our lips. She sent her tongue off on another journey, this one even more adventurous, and the trip was lasting way longer than my oxygen supply. I tried breaking free for a quick breath, but Darlene, oblivious to the changing colors of my now lavender face, kept my head pinned to the ground.

I tapped out or at least tried to, first by politely patting Darlene's shoulder and then by franticly thumping her on the back. She ignored me. I grabbed her head to pry our mouths apart, but it was no use. I started kicking my legs and beating the ground with both hands. Birds took flight. Small animals scampered for safety. Everything was going gray. I was dying.

That's when my will to live kicked in. I slid my foot back, wedged my knee between us, and raised my leg, prying our bodies apart and lifting Darlene off the ground. That put more pressure on her crotch, which, if her grunting was any indication, she enjoyed immensely. Waving her arms for balance, she wobbled on my shin, all the while keeping her lip-lock on me. My vision blurred. The world grew dark. Desperate for air, I grabbed Darlene by the shoulders and wriggled my leg violently back and forth, up and down, trying to break our kiss. That just made her hotter, though, and she arched her back and tossed her head around, finally freeing my mouth. I sucked in lungfuls of air while Darlene, shaking violently, ululated like a keener. Then she stiffened and collapsed.

I lay there on my back, gasping and staring at the blue sky and white, fluffy clouds. Darlene was inert. Her head hung lifelessly over my shoulder and her limp arms lay outstretched beyond my head. I waited for her to say or do something, anything involving movement, but she was as still as a graveyard. I whispered her name and stroked the back of her head. No response. I weaved my hand through her hair—nothing. I said her name loudly—same thing. I thrust Tyler, Jr. against her—no response. I tried not to take that personally.

Frowning, I grabbed Darlene by the shoulders, raised her off my chest, and gave her a little shake. She was dead weight. Now I was scared. I shook her some more, and then again vigorously while shouting her name. *Nothing!* That's when it hit me. *Darlene's dead and I killed her with my shin!* Panic-stricken, I tried wriggling out from beneath her.

"Where're you going?" she asked groggily.

"To get help! I thought you were dead!"

"Oh, I'm okay; I just passed out there for a moment."

"Passed out? Passed out?! You're kidding, right?"

"No, it happens sometimes when I get really excited. My blood pressure drops, and I get woozy. I've had all kinds of tests done, but the doctors don't know why."

"That's unbelievable! You pass out, and no one knows why?!"

"Oh, it's no big deal. It doesn't happen very often. That was an incredible orgasm, though!"

"Yeah?" My ego ballooned.

"Yeah, nobody's ever made me come like that!"

Pop!

I figured Darlene would take off for the ER after her near-death experience, but she was eager for round two. She slid off me and rolled to my side with her leg between mine. Then, starting at my chest, she pantomimed a sexy walk with her index and middle fingers all the way down to the waistband of my jeans. Looking me in the eye and smiling suggestively, Darlene brought her index finger back to her thumb and "kicked" my belt buckle.

"This won't do at all," she said in mock seriousness while unfastening my belt and unsnapping my jeans. "This, too," she whispered, unzipping my fly halfway. Then she leaned back. "Can he get out on his own?" Tyler Jr. was extended lengthwise with my zipper and partially visible. I made him jump and twitch. Darlene laughed, her hands flying to her face and covering her mouth.

"I don't know," I chuckled, "but he's trying." Darlene stared with wonderment as Tyler Jr. jerked up and down.

"He's getting angry," she said. "I better free him." Holding the top of my jeans, she eased my zipper down the rest of the way. Tyler Jr. sprang forward like a catapult and slapped against my stomach. Darlene, laughing, rocked back, and clapped her hands in delight.

"Nice! And you don't wear underwear either!"

"No, it feels like my dick's in a straitjacket." I raised my hips, and Darlene grasped both sides of my jeans and tugged them down, fully exposing the team. Then she moved back up and, thrusting her tongue in my mouth, grabbed hold of Tyler Jr., who, in a moment of betrayal, exploded on contact.

"SHIT!" I said angrily. I sat partway up with my elbows propped behind me.

"It's no big deal," Darlene said, wiping her fingers on my pants leg.

"Shit!" I said again, this time dejectedly.

"Hey, it happens. Now we get to find out your downtime."

"Downtime?"

"Yeah, you know, the time it takes before you're ready again."

"Oh, yeah, right." *What doesn't she know?*

"Maybe this will help," Darlene said as she leaned back on her haunches and, without a hint of self-consciousness, whipped off her tank top, exposing her amazing breasts.

"WOW!" I didn't know which opened wider, my eyes or my mouth, but, yeah, it helped! Tyler Jr. went to full attention! Darlene grasped him again, and then she leaned forward, thrusting an erect, wine-red nipple toward my mouth. Suddenly, there was rustling outside our little nest.

"I'm tehwen," a small voice squeaked. Darlene immediately let go of Tyler Jr. and yanked down her top. I kicked and bucked to get my ass off the ground and yanked my jeans over my hips. When I turned around, I saw a little boy, about six years old. He had vanilla ice cream all over his face, and he was peeking at us from behind the bushes. He looked a lot like Darlene and Kent—same skin color, hair, and eyes.

"Get out of here, you little brat!" Darlene snarled with startling viciousness.

"I'm tehwen mawm, Dawween," the little boy repeated without a hint of fear. "You not s'posed to be here."

"You do and I'll pound you!" She lunged for him, but he jumped out of reach.

"You in big twouble, Dawween."

Darlene scrambled to her feet, but he was already running away. Giggling, too.

"He must've followed us. Sometimes I hate having a little brother."

"No biggie."

"Yeah, it is. I've got to get to him before he tells mom."

"Oh," I said disappointedly. Darlene kissed me, tenderly for a change, and turned to leave.

"Hey, wait a sec."

"Yeah?" she replied, looking back.

"Will you be my girlfriend?"

"Of course, Tyler. Do you think I'd come out here with just anybody?" Then she was gone.

Joe was waiting on his Stingray with a wide grin on his face when I emerged from The Weeds. He wanted all the details, of course, but I said we didn't do anything except talk. He snorted derisively, but I just shrugged and climbed on the back of his bike. Joe wasn't letting me off that easy, though, and said he had time to wait even if I didn't, and he knew I didn't. So, he sat there, hands on the handlebars, one foot on the ground and the other on the pedal, waiting for me to start talking. It was only after he threatened to make me walk home that I conceded we'd kissed a couple of times. Joe swore and muttered something about knowing Darlene better than that. Then he pushed off the curb and started pedaling. We rode a long ways in silence.

"Kissin'? That's all? No fuckin' way," Joe finally said. We were still in Essie and Joe was pedaling slowly, weaving around the potholes. We crossed into city limits. The streets were clean and smooth.

"That's all we did."

"Stop lying. I ain't stupid. I know Darlene better'n that."

"That's the second time you've said that. What do you know?"

"Nothin', forget it."

"No, you brought it up!"

Joe, standing on the pedals, slowly coasted to a stop and straddled the crossbar. I kept one foot on the hub and stretched the other one to the curb. He turned halfway around and looked back at me with his mouth in a firm line. I stared back, attempting my own hard look.

"Look, let's just say Darlene an' I know the same people, all right?"

"No, let's not just say that. What do you mean?"

"Just drop it."

"No, let's hear it!" I dreaded what Joe was about to say. My gut felt like a rollercoaster flying off its tracks.

"I know more 'bout Darlene than you do. A lot more."

"Go on." Now I felt sick.

"She's had some boyfriends, okay? I know 'em all, an' they like to brag if you catch my drift."

"If they're anything like you, then, yeah, I caught it."

"I guess I deserve that," Joe said, grinning sheepishly.

"You're saying Darlene's a slut. Is that why you and Bev fixed me up with her?"

"I ain't saying that at all!"

"Well, what then?"

"An' we didn't fix you up neither. Darlene told Bev you're cute. I sure as hell don't see it, but that's what Bev said."

"But you think she's a slut, don't you?" I didn't know my fists were clenched.

"I didn't say that! I've just heard some things. I don't even know if they're true!"

"That didn't stop you from saying them, though, or calling me a liar. Did you ever think they might be lying?"

Joe studied my face a short while. He could see I was mad, but we both knew he could kick my ass three different ways in under three minutes. His silence evinced an understanding of my confused emotions that I lacked. Joe considered his response and chose his words carefully, trying to walk back the cat.

"You're right. I'm sorry for sayin' all that. Now get on, an' lemme take you home."

Neither one of us said anything for miles, and I used it think about Darlene. I finally broke the silence while we coasted down the Bryant Street hill,

"This seat sucks!" The banana seat on Joe's Stingray was torn where I was sitting, and my balls were resting against bare metal where the foam rubber had worn away. I felt every bump.

"I know, I hate . . ., wait a sec! I've been standin' on the pedals this whole time, an' you're bitchin' 'bout sittin' on a seat?!"

"Well, my nuts hurt!"

"That ain't the seat! You got blue balls!"

"What're blue balls?"

"It's when your balls ache because you didn't get off after havin' a boner."

It was the seat.

We were barely halfway up the hill on Lynwood Drive, and Joe, red-faced and grunting like hogs at feeding time, was standing head over handlebars, pedaling so agonizingly slow he had to keep whipping the front wheel back and forth just to stay upright. I steadied myself, bracing for a crash, but Joe was determined to get to the top. He threw his entire body weight down on the left pedal and then the right, over and over, pounding up and down. We barely moved.

Sweat streamed from Joe's face and ran down his neck, leaving his sopping wet red T-shirt skintight against his chest. His head and shoulders rolled left and right in time with the pedals, and his oily hair became a wet whip. I had to lean back to avoid getting flogged, but I didn't complain. It relieved the pressure on my nuts.

When we finally crested the hill, Frank was on the front porch in Dad's rocking chair, reading the Huwabola Gazette. Joe's grunting apparently piqued his curiosity because he lowered the newspaper and stared at us. Frank couldn't see me, but I could see him. He leaned back in the rocker for a better look, craning his neck and twisting and turning his head as if dodging a bee. He spotted me when Joe swung into the driveway.

Frank shook the paper angrily and jumped out of the chair while Joe, oblivious to the looming shitstorm, smiled and triumphantly thrust his fist in the air like Eddy Merckx on the Champs-Élysées. The rocker smashed into the storm door on its backswing, shattering the glass. Scowling, Frank bounded off the porch just as I pushed off the back of the bike. We both headed for the side door. He intercepted me.

"You forgot?" Frank said sarcastically. He bent forward, so we were face to face. "Tell me something, just one thing."

"Okay," I said cautiously.

"Why're you so *stupid?*" He poked my forehead with his index finger for emphasis.

That was it. I'd had it. Frank and I had exchanged lots of insults, but he'd just crossed a line. I turned sideways, dropped my right foot back, and put up my fists.

Frank just laughed, exposing his gray gums and yellow teeth. "Oh, so now you're a tough guy, huh, Pussypoon?"

I hated that nickname. "I don't know, Frank," I replied, "you tell me, does a tough guy stand up to someone twice as big or pick on someone twice as small?"

I saw it coming but had no time to react. Frank's right fist arced east out of Huwabola headed for Bronson. It looped around and swooped down toward Cortville, where, picking up momentum, it shot through Newburn and smashed into my mouth at 424 Lynwood Drive. I dropped like a lemming. For a brief instant, I saw the blue sky and white, fluffy clouds again. Then the back of my head hit the sidewalk, and my brain launched into the drum solo from *In-A-Gadda-Da-Vida*.

I laid there, dazed. Drool dripped off my chin and ran down my neck, or at least that's what I thought it was until my shirt started turning red. Just then, my upper lip felt like fire, as if someone had jabbed me in the face with a hot poker. I began coughing, expelling bright red specks skyward that dropped and dotted my face. I tried to breathe but sucked down a mouthful of blood instead, choking off my air supply and setting off another spasmodic coughing fit. I spit blood between hacks and then desperately sucked in a lungful of air. Then another.

I propped myself up on my elbows. My eyes were blurry from tears. My mouth tasted like pennies. I gently probed my upper lip with my tongue, assessing the damage. Frank's ruby ring had split it from top to bottom and my bottom teeth had cut it side to side. I traced and retraced the inverted T, exploring the depths of both channels. Blood continued to flow from my mouth, dripping off my chin and onto my shirt. I rubbed the knot at the back of my head. More blood. Woozy, I struggled to my feet and dropped back into a fighting stance. Frank looked on, amused, until he reached the angry conclusion that I wasn't backing down. Then his grin flipped upside down, and he curled his lip, ready to dot my eyes.

"NO, FRANK, DON'T!" Mom had come back outside with a broom and dustpan. Frank stopped, but not because of her. Something off to his left caught his eye. He turned, and a look of irritated inquisitiveness crossed his face. Joe was leaning with his forearms on the handlebars, hands dangling, with one foot on the ground and the other resting on the top pedal, watching us. A half-spent cigarette hung off his lower lip. The two of them locked eyes. Joe openly smirked.

"GET THE HELL OUT OF HERE, YOU SON OF A BITCH!" Frank yelled. Joe didn't move, not an inch or a muscle, and not until enough time passed for Frank to realize he wasn't going to do a goddamn thing until he felt like it. Eventually, Joe took a long, slow drag on his cigarette. Then he pinched the butt and flicked it. It bounced off Frank's shoe and smoldered in the grass.

"Fuck you, asshole," Joe said, underscoring the sentiment with his middle finger. Then, laughing, he popped a wheelie on his way out the driveway, dropped it, and slowly coasted down the hill to Bryant Street with his middle finger up. Frank stood there, watching until Joe disappeared from sight. Then he turned toward me, ready to pick up where we left off. I looked at him.

"Yeah, fuck you, asshole." I flipped him the bone and went the other way, a bit quicker than Joe.

Chapter 5

Friday, May 29, 1970

My parents grew up in Wester, not far from Huwabola. They started dating in high school and got married in 1954, when they were sophomores at Indiana University. I came along sometime later. They both earned degrees at IU, Dad's in political science and Mom's in nursing, and we stayed in Bloomington so he could keep working for Congressman Bowden while pursuing a graduate degree in international relations. Dad had his eyes set on the U.S. Diplomat Corps. Mom took a job at Bloomington Hospital, working as an RN in the CCU to keep us afloat. Two years later, Senator Hartke hired Dad to run his reelection campaign, so we moved north to Huwabola. Mom stopped working for a few years since keeping me in line was a full-time job by then.

Growing up, we did the usual things families do, like backyard barbecues, camping trips, swimming, and an occasional Tigers game in Detroit. Then one day, Dad joined the Marine Corps. Mom threw a shit fit! She expected him to apply for a parental deferment or, if necessary, get Hartke to pull some strings, but he said it was his duty to serve, so, except for their ongoing squabbling, that was that.

Dad left for Officer Candidate School at Quantico and returned as Second Lieutenant Jack Puspoon with orders to the First Division at Camp Pendleton. There, with the Third Battalion, Seventh Marines, he underwent more infantry training before heading to Vietnam with a brief stopover in Okinawa for jungle warfare school. Dad arrived in Da Nang in mid-January 1967. A month later, he led a platoon of Marines during Operation Desoto, a search and destroy mission in Quảng Ngãi Province during which the 3/7 and 3/12 killed nearly 400 enemy soldiers.

A year later, Dad was with the 3/5 as part of Task Force X-Ray at the Battle of Huế during the Tet Offensive. That's when he drew the attention of Major Wheeler Baker, the commander of First Reconnaissance Battalion.

Toward the end of the battle to recapture the city of Huế, the cultural and religious capital of Vietnam, there was a lull in the fighting while the 3/5 awaited reinforcements and supplies. There'd been fierce clashes in the streets with both sides suffering heavy casualties. The 3/5 had penetrated the Citadel days earlier in a bloody daytime attack. They were preparing for a final assault on the Imperial Palace where the NVA were headquartered.

2nd Lt. Wilson Caspry, a platoon commander in First Recon Company, code named Slayer Sam, was leading an understaffed fireteam in the southern sector, a good distance from the palace, when they took fire from the ground floor of an outlying administrative building. Caspry wore no insignia, but his sidearm revealed him as an officer, and the NVA were intent on capturing him. The ambush was brief, but effective. Caspry was struck by AK-47 rounds in his right shoulder and left leg, but it was a Soviet-made RGD-33 grenade that left him lying motionless in a growing puddle of blood. Searing-hot shrapnel had peppered his right side, and some of it had cut deep. The lieutenant was concussed, knocked senseless by the blast wave. Next to him, shocked and covered in blood, sat his radioman, Lance Corporal Helton, who'd taken most of the blast. He was alternately looking where his right knee used to be and the hemorrhaging stump of his left wrist.

Nobody was unscathed. One Marine, Sergeant Rose, was cut and bleeding up and down his right side from nonlethal shrapnel wounds while Kimbrough, furthest from the grenade, had taken a round through his left side from a ChiCom-80 machine gun. He wasn't gut shot, but he had a gaping wound that was bleeding profusely. Rose dragged him by the collar to the burnt shell of an ARVN tank and went to work, staunching the flow with battle dressings. Kimbrough stabilized quickly and then laid cover fire for Rose's repeated attempts to reach Caspry and Helton, but his M16 was no match for the ChiCom, and Rose was driven back each time. Rose refused to give up, though, and he made one last attempt during which he managed to grab the PRC-25 radio.

Combat units at Huế monitored the same radio frequency, and when Rose radioed for help, 2nd Lt. Puspoon was several blocks away with his own undermanned team. In the time it took to reach the courtyard, two NVA soldiers, covered by the ChiCom and AK-47s, broke from the building, shooting on the run and leapfrogging each other toward Caspry and Helton. Rose and Kimbrough barely slowed their advance against the stream of automatic weapons fire, and eventually they couldn't risk shooting at all. They watched in helpless anguish while the soldiers dragged Caspry by his wrists across the courtyard and into the building. Several quiet moments passed. Then the ChiCom let loose a short burst that made Helton jerk as if electrocuted. He slumped backward in the dirt, dead.

Bullets kicked up dirt and ricocheted off the tank tread. Kimbrough hemorrhaged again. He flitted with consciousness, blinking his eyes slowly and nodding out for seconds at a time. During a lull, Rose heard his unintelligible grunts. He went to work, repacking his side with sulfa, talking to him, trying to keep him awake. Puspoon's team picked up the slack, taking positions around the tank and returning fire. Puspoon stripped off his rucksack and crawled to the right front tread, snuck a look, and spotted the ChiCom's muzzle flash in the middle window.

The smell of blood, dirt, and nitrate propellants hung in the air. Tension and fear, too. Kimbrough stabilized again. He inserted a fresh magazine and crowded up against the tank tread. Rose stood over him, straddling his body while the 3/5's Sgt. Watts and Pvts. Kelso and Dandridge swapped bullets with the enemy. Puspoon grabbed Watts' M60 machine gun. He leapt atop the tank tread and scrambled behind the turret. After eyeing the building, he directed their gunfire at the middle window.

On three, Puspoon lobbed a grenade as far as he could toward the building, arcing it high across the courtyard. It landed several yards short of the window and exploded. The Marines in position around the tank followed with a blistering pace of fire while Puspoon, finger pegged on the M60's trigger, leapt to the ground to storm the machine gun nest. Bullets—Russian, Chinese, American—flew back and forth. The Marines, well hidden behind the tank, never let up. Rounds pinged and kicked up dirt and stone around them, but their outpouring of lead demolished the shutters and blasted the wall in a whirlwind of splintering bamboo and crumbling stone. Within seconds, the machine gunner and his ammo feeder were dead.

The Marines' gain was short-lived. A nearby enemy squad, probing lines in a residential area, responded to the gunfire and took positions inside the admin building. Minutes later, the ChiCom opened up from the corner window with an ear-hammering barrage of rounds that ricocheted off the tank and street. Three NVA soldiers emerged from the building's rear, attempting to outflank the now outmanned Marines, but Kelso and Rose saw them and forced them back with multiple bursts from their rifles. The Marines continued to engage the NVA reinforcements, coordinating their fire to produce a continuous stream of lead that gave them a brief advantage again. They used it to find better cover behind the wreckage of an overturned M422 Mighty Mite.

Puspoon had made it to the wreckage of the middle window, but with projectiles streaming all around him, he wasn't going anywhere. He was safe, but stuck. Then he heard the hollow thump of the bloop gun and grubbed the rubble. The 40 mm grenade exploded on impact, sending chunks of stone flying in all directions as the entire corner of the two-story building collapsed. The ChiCom was silent again.

Although shielded by debris, Puspoon felt the shockwave pulse through him. Dazed, he rose unsteadily to a knee and leaned against the wall. He tried to get to his feet, but fell, so he crawled to what was left of the corner. There, he pushed aside rocks and stones until he got his arm though a small hole. He surveyed the room with a small mirror, spotting two dead NVA soldiers and a trail of blood leading out the door.

Puspoon pushed himself up. Lurching clumsily, he staggered to the end of the block. He saw Caspry being dragged toward the Palace and started for him, but heavy boots thudded from behind, forcing him to duck in a doorway. Puspoon watched as a half dozen enemy soldiers ran past and fanned out at the end of the block. He stepped out and raked them with the machine gun.

An NVA sniper perched on a nearby rooftop recognized the sound of the M60 and searched through the scope on his Mosin Nagant M91/30. He located Puspoon, centered the crosshairs over his heart, and fired, but a sudden tailwind made the bullet track a fraction higher than he intended. It slammed into Puspoon's left collarbone, shattering his clavicle. The sniper cursed, quickly chambered another round, and repositioned for a better shot, but Watts spied him from the hospital a block away and emptied his magazine. The sniper fell from the rooftop, clutching his midsection, and landed in the middle of the narrow street. His rifle clattered on the stones a few feet away.

AK-47 rounds blasted bits and pieces of stone right above Watts's head. Kelso and Dandridge, who'd repositioned across the street from the hospital, spotted the NVA muzzle flashes. The three Marines let them have it, emptying one magazine after another, and when Rose and Kimbrough saw their outgoing tracer rounds, they zeroed in as well.

Bullets streamed back and forth between the Marines and the NVA. Puspoon, bleeding heavily and still woozy, had crawled back to the doorway. He was trapped with bullets whizzing past within arm's reach. The hospital took a pounding; a corner window was gradually made larger and larger while bullets ricocheted off medical equipment, pierced metal pans, and shattered beakers and bottles. Neither side gained ground, or an advantage.

Kimbrough was bleeding again. Rose saw his head droop and applied a new dressing, finishing just as a sniper put a bullet through his heart. He fell backward, eyes open, dead. Enemy soldiers suddenly broke from the rear of the admin building, falling back to regroup. Puspoon stood, left arm limp at his side, and grabbed a grenade from his vest. He bit the pull ring and safety pin. Then he relaxed his grip, allowing the striker lever to disengage. The cap ignited, and the delaying chemical started its slow burn. He counted to three and let fly. The grenade bounced once ahead of the fleeing soldiers and exploded. They fell like bowling pins.

Three more soldiers crept from the building, but M16 gunfire sent them scurrying back inside. Watts made it to Puspoon and stripped open his blood-stained camouflaged jacket, exposing what was left of his shoulder. He sloshed water over the wound, washing away metal fragments, dirt, and other debris. Then he packed it with sulfa and taped three dressings in place.

The NVA had troops on both sides of the bridge spanning the moat to protect the palace. If the soldiers made it across, Caspry, if not already dead, would die a slow, torturous death. Puspoon got to his feet, intent on rescuing him. He looked up the street; several NVA soldiers advanced, blocking his path.

"Frag 'em and cover me." He took his M16 from Watts. "On three. One, two, three!"

Watts popped up and sent a grenade skittering down the street. The soldiers saw it and dropped flat on the stones, escaping most of the shrapnel, but catching the full effect of the blast and shockwave. They lay stunned, leaving Dandridge and Kelso a canned hunt.

Puspoon ran parallel to Caspry a block off the main street. His shoulder began bleeding almost immediately. He ran several blocks before stopping to listen. The bandages were soaked through, but he was running on pure adrenaline. Puspoon was about to take off again when a bullet smacked the wall an inch from his head, spraying his face with small bits of stone. He threw up his arms and turned away while diving headfirst into a doorway. He landed on his right side and slid from one side of the transom to the other, banging his helmeted head against the jamb.

The sniper swore, but he knew his prey was trapped, and, if he was patient, he'd get another shot. Puspoon realized a waiting game had begun, but he didn't have time to play. He tried the latch on the door, but it was locked, so he pressed his back against the jamb and pushed himself to his feet. Puspoon removed his helmet and wiped his face with his sleeve. Sweat beads immediately reappeared on his forehead and dripped off his brow, stinging his eyes. He gripped his helmet firmly and thrust it at eye level beyond the transom. The sniper fired, piercing the metal pot. When the bullet ricocheted off the stone transom, Puspoon angle his mirror, training it on the rooftops to his southwest. Suddenly, gunfire erupted all around him.

"Go, Lieutenant! Go!" Watts yelled. He'd led Kelso, Kimbrough and Dandridge up the street, a block at a time, in a running gun battle. They covered Puspoon, and he took off again, ducking around corners, darting through buildings, trying to catch up to Caspry. He ran several blocks before stopping to listen. There was distant gunfire, but no other sounds. He ran on, and as he neared the next corner, he heard scuffing and caught a brief glimpse of the three men before they disappeared from view.

B-1 bombers droned overhead, leaving explosions echoing in their wake. Puspoon's shoulder, limp at his side, throbbed. The bandages, soaked in blood, had come unraveled, so he pulled them off. Then he pushed on, unsnapping the sheath on his KA-BAR as he ran. When he got to the corner, he drew his Browning and, barrel up, back against the wall, he side-stepped toward the opposite corner.

Puspoon heard them coming just before he saw them. When they passed, he shot the nearest man in the head. The other man, eyes wide, let go of Caspry and unslung his rifle. Puspoon fired again, but the gun jammed. The soldier raised his AK-47, but Puspoon advanced and wedged the barrel in his left armpit, sending burning pain through his shoulder. Enraged, he hammered the Browning's butt against the man's head again and again and then kneed him in the midsection. Puspoon let go the .45 and grabbed his KA-BAR as they fell to the street. He scrambled atop the soldier and, right arm overhead, buried the wide, razor-sharp metal blade in the man's chest. Then he did it twice more.

Puspoon, face twisted in pain, rolled off the dead man and attended to Caspry, probing his mouth with a finger to clear his airway. He checked for a pulse. After several anxious seconds, he felt one, but it was very faint. Puspoon sliced open Caspry's bloody camouflage jacket, exposing the shrapnel wounds on his side and his splintered shoulder joint. His neck was swollen and already bruised where the bullet was lodged. The lieutenant's leg wound was clean, though, having struck only muscle. Although neither injury was fatal, Caspry was in shock from blood loss. He might survive with a transfusion, but he needed it quick. Puspoon did, too.

Up the street, several enemy troops broke from the bridge, firing on the run. Puspoon grabbed one of AK-47s and flipped it to automatic. Then, shielding Caspry's body, he emptied the banana clip. The soldiers scrambled for cover. Puspoon tossed the rifle aside and gripped the lieutenant's faded, blood-stained jacket in his right fist. He squatted and, grunting, slung Caspry across his broad shoulders with his one good arm. A piercing pain shot down his left side, forcing him to a knee.

Puspoon snatched the other AK-47. He rose, firing from the hip in three-round bursts and backtracked toward the corner. Rounds ricocheted off the stone street in front of him. Puspoon's uniform was soaked in blood—his and Caspry's. He stumbled and dropped to a knee again. The bullets kept getting closer, whizzing past his head and body. Puspoon flipped the rifle to automatic and squeezed the trigger, emptying the magazine of its last dozen rounds and forcing the soldiers to drop to the street. It bought him just enough time; Watts rounded the corner and cut loose with his M60, killing three men before they could get up. The last man, furthest from everyone, took off running. Kelso chased him down a side street. There was a gunshot, and then it was quiet. Moments later, Kelso emerged at the head of the block and joined Watts, who was helping Puspoon and Caspry to safety.

After a bloody battle lasting four weeks, the Marine Corps finally liberated Huế. Caspry and Puspoon were evacuated to the *USS Sanctuary*, a Navy hospital ship. There, Maj. Baker, who'd made a special trip from Da Nang, asked him to join Slayer Sam. Despite having a ticket home, Puspoon agreed on the spot. Mom went berserk.

Chapter 6

Friday, May 29, 1970

Mom went back inside, and after staring at me for a short minute, Frank did, too. I didn't have anywhere to go. I was on my own with a split lip and a knot on my head. I inventoried my pockets, finding my keys, fifty-nine cents, and an eraser. Not exactly a doomsday survivor's kit. There was barely enough for a Big Murphy Burger. Then it hit me! Frank kept spare change in a plastic container under the front seat of his car! All I needed was a handful, and I'd be set for the weekend!

Frank drove a pearl 1962 Oldsmobile Starfire 88 convertible with the high-performance version of the ultra-high-compression 394-cubic-inch Skyrocket V8. It had a center console with a floor shifter for the Hydra-Matic transmission, red and pearl leather bucket seats, and a custom-made white top with red piping. The car was in as pristine of condition as the day it rolled out the factory. Mom kept her Toyota outdoors because, as Frank explained, it was a "piece of shit" while his car was an investment that couldn't be exposed to the elements or the temptations of "your troublemaking son." Frank kept the garage locked, thinking the only keys were on the hook by the fridge. He was wrong.

I crouched by the gate at the edge of Dan McGuire's backyard, planning to cut across it to the field running the length of our block. Old Man McGuire hated everyone, especially me. He was the sort of neighbor nobody really knew much about. He had a long, drawn face full of deep creases, changing lines, and overlapping skin like a shar-pei, as well as an end-of-life look about him. McGuire was lanky and his gray hair was buzzed close. His eyes, dull and lifeless, were dark with even darker circles beneath them. Thick blood vessels twisted and turned up his forearms like a winding blue river. At the other end, huge, calloused hands, nicked and cut from pruning roses, hung off thin, hairless wrists.

Kids took shortcuts through Old Man McGuire's backyard for the pure excitement of it. We'd heard stories growing up about how mean he was, so it was scary fun because he'd get mad and chase us. Old Man McGuire kept a .22 Winchester handy, and every so often, late at night, the neighborhood would be jolted awake by a gunshot. Sure enough, someone's dog or cat would turn up missing. Everyone knew McGuire was responsible, but nobody knew it better than me.

It happened after Dad shipped out for his first tour in Vietnam. I was bumming big time, so Mom, trying to cheer me up, said I could have a dog. I'd been bugging her for one for the better part of a year, but she kept saying I was too young and she didn't want to get stuck with the responsibility of taking care of it. One Saturday morning, we drove to the dog pound south of town. The barking and howling carried all the way to the parking lot. Inside, the attendant, a cute blond chick, about seventeen, smelling of patchouli oil and wearing bell-bottoms, a green and white tie-dyed T-shirt, and round, yellow-tinted sunglasses, looked up from her copy of *Teen Beat.*

"Can I help you?"

"My son wants to adopt a dog," Mom said over the din. The girl flicked her eyes dismissively at me.

"The ones available for adoption are in the kennel, straight down that hallway," she said, cracking her gum and pointing over our shoulders with a bored look. "They've all had their shots and been de-wormed."

"How much is it to adopt one?"

"Three dollars, one for the license, one for the shots, and one for the shelter."

"Wow! That's steep just to give a dog a home, isn't it?"

"I don't know." Nor did it appear she cared.

"I hadn't planned on spending that much." Mom looked at me. "We still have to buy bowls and food, you know."

"Oh, c'mon, Mom, please," I said with an unintentional whine. The girl snickered.

The hallway dead-ended, becoming a glass-enclosed kennel in equal measure left and right. When the dogs saw us, their barking intensified and they jumped, danced, or stood with their paws pressed against the glass. I walked back and forth from one end to the other, unable to decide which one to choose. Dogs followed my every step, and when I stopped, wet noses and twice as many paws swelled in number. The bigger dogs just hung out in back, tongues hanging, tails wagging.

"Look at all these dogs!" Mom said. "You've sure got a lot to choose from."

"No kidding! Which one should I get?"

"Whichever one you want."

I sat on the floor opposite a cage of German shepherd puppies, planning to adopt the first one to come to me. That was Hakie. He fell out when Mom opened the door and then stumbled on over. He was six weeks old and black and tan with a droopy ear and brown eyes. The girl didn't know anything about him except he was part of the litter born at the kennel.

Hakie was around six months old when he woke me up way too early one summer morning, needing to be let out. I tried ignoring him, but he kept jumping on and off the bed and jolting me awake with his cold nose. I finally gave up on sleeping and got up, groggily slipped on a pair of shorts and flip-flops, and stumbled down the hall to the rear of the house with Hakie dancing excitedly beside me. When I cracked open the screen door, he pushed past me and raced outside whereupon he sniffed every blade of grass to find the ideal spot for his business. I plopped down in a lawn chair to wait him out and, within seconds, dozed off.

I couldn't have been asleep more than a few minutes when the crisp crack of a rifle jolted me awake. I shot upright, looking for Hakie, but he wasn't in the backyard. Up the block, someone slammed a car door. Moments later, the motor fired up. I scrambled to the front yard and looked down our street in time to see red taillights disappear around the corner, up Gurley Street. I walked to Old Man McGuire's house. His garage door was up, the overhead light was on, and his car was gone.

I searched for Hakie all day, afraid he was dead, but not prepared to acknowledge it. I must've walked five miles, calling his name and knocking on doors. I slogged home, hoarse from yelling, and filled with dread. The only house I hadn't gone to was McGuire's. I had to confront him. He jerked the door open when I reached his porch. A cigarette hung limply off his lower lip. He squinted at me through the smoke.

"What do *you* want?"

"I'm looking for my dog. Have you seen him?"

"I don't know." McGuire took a deep drag and exhaled the smoke straight at me. "Describe him."

"You know what he looks like," I said, fanning my face and coughing, "he's a black-and-tan German shepherd puppy with a droopy ear. He's wearing a red collar with tags."

"Hmmm, let me think," McGuire said, looking skyward as if deep in thought. He rubbed the grayish-black stubble on his chin. "Is there any other red on him?"

I looked at him, confused. "No, like I said, he's black and tan."

"You sure?" McGuire's top lip curled, revealing his nicotine-stained teeth. "What about a round red spot on each side of his neck?" He slipped his thick calloused thumbs behind the suspenders of his bib overalls. Then he chuckled with a grin that made his grizzled cheeks look like corduroy. I got a cold chill.

"You shot Hakie," I said in a low, menacing voice. McGuire's eyes narrowed. He stepped back inside, closing the door, but then stopped.

"Was he a good dog?" He tried to shut the door, but I wedged my foot in the jamb.

"I'll get you for this," I said quietly. "I'm going to make your life hell on earth."

"Get off my property!" McGuire spat. "If I see you on it again, I'll shoot you like I shot your fucking dog!" He kicked my ankle and slammed the door. I stood there, stunned. Hakie was dead. I went home, crawled into bed, and cried. I woke up hours later and, just for a second, thought I'd dreamt it all. When I realized I hadn't, I hatched a plan.

It was nearly midnight. The neighborhood was asleep. I dressed entirely in black—T-shirt, sweatpants, and Chucks. Then I slipped out the side door and ran through the field to McGuire's backyard. Along the way, I grabbed two rocks, one big, the other small.

It was spookily quiet. I climbed the fence and then the steps to the back deck. I peeked through the window over the kitchen sink. It was dark inside, but the moon at my back shined bright.

I held the small rock against the window's lower right corner and tapped it with the big rock. Nothing. I tapped again, harder. Still nothing. My heart pounded. I took a deep breath and gave it a good, hard rap and the glass splintered in a thousand directions. I plucked out a few shards, enough to make a small opening. Then I brought up the garden hose and fed a good ten feet of it inside the house. I went back down the stairs and slowly opened up the spigot, gradually increasing the water's flow until it was going full blast.

I went home and slept for five hours, returning before dawn. The entire upstairs of McGuire's house was flooded. Water had soaked through the carpet, padding, and subflooring, causing a rainstorm in the basement. I went downstairs, shut the water off, coiled the hose, and snuck home and back into bed. McGuire called the police, but I had a solid alibi; Mom had to wake me up to ask about it.

One year to the day, I snuck over to McGuire's house in the dead of night and popped the lock on the side door of his garage with a putty knife. Inside, I eased open the hood of his gold Dodge Dart, removed the oil cap, and poured a mixture of dirt, sand, gravel, and water into the motor. After wiping off the dribbles, I quietly closed the hood, and went home.

I slept like a stone, and when the alarm went off at six o'clock, I was already dressed. I slipped out the back door and crept from yard to yard, staying in the shadows, avoiding streetlamps until I got to McGuire's house. I didn't have to wait long. He came down the deck steps, opened the overhead garage door, and got in his car. A few moments later, the morning calm was shattered by a loud, violent clacking like ice cubes in a blender amplified through a bullhorn. McGuire cut the motor, got out, and raised the hood. While he was checking belts, hoses, and all else, I leaned against the streetlamp at the end of his driveway. He climbed behind the wheel again, keyed the ignition, and got the same ear-splitting noise, only louder with the hood up.

Cursing, McGuire shouldered the door open and slammed it shut with so much force the whole car shook. Then he stomped back to the front and stood over the engine bay with his hands on his hips.

"Hey, dog killer!" I yelled. McGuire popped his head around the hood and stared at me. "Having car trouble?"

"You did this!"

"Brilliant deduction, Mannix."

"I'll get you for this!"

"No, you won't, dog killer. You're not going to do jack shit to me, but I'm going to fuck with you until you're dead. Probably afterwards, too." I turned to leave, but stopped and turned around. "Did you ever get flood insurance?"

The police had Mom bring me downtown. A detective advised me of my rights, took me into a room without her, and threw question after question at me, but I told him I don't answer questions and refused to say anything else. Dad once told me, "Don't settle at an eye for an eye. That just evens the score. His other eye's for punishment." He didn't say anything about revenge, though, so on the same date last year, I snuck into McGuire's yard after dark with a can of gasoline and gave his roses a good drink. Then I tossed a match on them and hid behind the shed while he frantically ran around with the garden hose in his boxers and wife-beater, trying to douse the flames. He finally got the fire out, but the next morning awoke to "DOG KILLER!" scorched in his flower bed. He didn't even bother with the cops.

Blood was flowing from my lip like molten lava. I nudged open the gate. McGuire was nowhere in sight. Keeping low, I crept toward the gap in the hedge. I was twenty feet away when I heard the slider open. I froze. Winchester in hand, McGuire crossed the deck and headed down the steps. I was silhouetted against the hedge, easy pickings. He disappeared inside the garage, just for a moment, but it was enough time for me to hide behind the tree. He returned carrying a water can and gardening tools along with his rifle.

McGuire leaned the Winchester against the side of the garage and eased himself to his knees. While he pruned, I inched backward, keeping the tree between us, angling for the gate. I was about to make a break for it when I tripped over a tree root snaking above ground and fell flat on my ass. McGuire's head and shoulders turned toward me as he straightened up, but I was quicker and scrambled out of view. He knew he'd heard something, though, so he started to get up. That's when I took off running for the shed.

McGuire stood, rifle in hand, and eyeballed the yard, but I'd made it behind the shed by then. He knew where to go looking, though, and marched toward it. I'd rounded the back and crept to the front, kneeling, watching, and waiting for him to pass by on the other side. When he did, I lit out for the gap in the hedge. McGuire came around the back just as I got there.

"You little shit!" He raised the .22, but I hopped the fence before he got it shouldered.

"Dog killer!" I yelled as I slid down the steep bank and disappeared into the field of head-high grass and weeds.

The field separated backyards from the woods beyond. Most yards, like ours, had a hedgerow or line of trees for privacy, but a few had fences and there were one or two that had nothing at all.

When I got to our house, I climbed up the bank and lay on the dry grass beneath the hedge, craning my neck to see past its twisted, gnarled branches. Frank was stomping around the kitchen and waving his arms around. His shouts were muffled, almost inaudible, and definitely incomprehensible from where I lay. Mom just stood there with her arms folded across her chest, looking at him like he was nuts.

When they both had their backs turned, I snuck along the side of the house, keys in hand, and quickly unlocked the garage door. Inside, I turned the deadbolt and waited, listening, but it was all quiet.

The Starfire's hinges gave a long, loud groan when I opened the driver's door, so I eased it shut and hopped over, landing with both feet on the seat. I reached beneath the seat and blindly felt around and almost immediately gouged my hand. I screamed as quietly as I could and wiped the blood on my pants. I tried again, but, by the time I located the container, my fingers were slick and slipped right off. I wiped the blood off again and reached under with both hands. I got a good grip and pulled, but it didn't even move. I kept trying, first tugging, and then jerking back and forth, but the container was fixed tighter than a rusted bolt, and all I got was hotter, sweatier, and madder.

I stepped between the bucket seats and knelt on the rear floorboard. The container was wrenched between an assortment of metal rods, springs, and brackets. I worked my fingertips over the top and pushed and pulled until the plastic warmed and weakened. I finally got a decent grip and gave it a good, hard, yank. It still didn't move, but I heard the change rattle.

Frustrated, I swung my body around until I was upside down with my head, neck, and shoulders on the floorboard and my legs and feet somewhere above me on the back seat. Just then, the side door slammed! Panicked, I grabbed the container with both hands and jerked as hard as I could. Out it came! Coins exploded in my face and bounced off my chest, landing on the carpet and floormat. I flipped over and shoveled them back inside the container. Then, holding it like a football, I bounced a couple of times on the back seat, testing the springs before vaulting over the passenger door. I almost stuck the landing, but my upper body pitched too far forward. I tucked, rolled, and somersaulted and somehow came up in a squat. Hugging the container, I quickly duckwalked to the wheelbarrow and quietly huddled behind it next to the rakes and lawnmower.

There was a soft click, and the overhead lights flickered to life, flooding the garage with a harsh, fluorescent glare. Frank's boots echoed like cannon shots as he walked the length of the Starfire and rounded the front. He headed straight for the wheelbarrow while my heartbeat increased in rate and volume with every step. I was in a crouch, ready to jump out and run for the door, but Frank suddenly stopped and turned around. My heart fluttered.

The hinges groaned. There was some scraping and scuffing. I looked over the wheelbarrow but Frank was nowhere in sight. I peeked under the car. He was on his knees.

"What the . . . where the hell is it?" Frank got to his feet and stood with his hands on his hips, a confused frown on his face. Shaking his head, he gave the back seat and floorboard a quick once over before returning to the front seat for a second look. Frank, on his haunches, leaned across the console, checked under the passenger seat and ran his hand alongside the door. Then he swore and ran his fingers through his hair, which, like his patience, had thinned.

"I can't believe this is happening, not on a Friday fucking night!"

I rose, quiet as a glacier, and snuck another look. Frank had his back to me. He unlocked Dad's tool cabinet and jerked the top drawer open with the whoosh and clatter of metal on metal. He rooted around a moment and slammed it shut. Then he yanked open the drawer right below it. He grabbed a flashlight and flicked it on and off, making sure it worked, before turning back to the Starfire. He crouched, disappearing from view. There was more rustling before Frank slapped the seat.

"WHERE THE FUCK IS IT?"

I almost laughed aloud, but bit my kneecap and shook instead. Suddenly, an explosion overhead redirected my attention. Pieces of glass and plastic and four D batteries caromed off the wall. Frank stomped out the garage, slamming the door behind him. I waited for him to slam the kitchen door, and when he did, I busted out the garage and hauled ass across the field to the woods, where I collapsed in the shade, hot and sweaty, but still cradling the container.

I sat with my back against a tree until realizing I might be safer *in* the woods than on its edge, so I trudged over to the hill we used for sledding, past the spot where Frank had started dumping garbage.

The hill was steeper than I remembered. Keeping a tight grip on the container, I inched sideways, anchoring myself with my back foot while testing for a toehold with the front one. I slipped twice but dropped in the dirt and dug in my heels to keep from sliding to the bottom. I was only a quarter of the way down.

I wasn't so lucky the third time. I was at the steepest part of the hill, toeing the ground, feeling for a foothold, when I stepped on a loose rock and lurched forward off balance, head and shoulders leading the way. I struggled to stay upright, legs spinning like pinwheels, trying to catch up with my upper half. No chance. I had too much lean and too much hill. I went airborne, and so did the container. I landed face-first, ten yards from the bottom, and slid the rest of the way beneath a glittering silver and copper shower.

When I woke up, I was once again staring at the blue sky and white, fluffy clouds, but I was afraid to move, not knowing if I could, or if I could, if I should. Eventually, I had to try, though, and when I did, the pain of a thousand kitten claws shredded my skin. I'd landed smack dab in the middle of a tangle of thorn bushes. I wasn't going anywhere fast.

Ten minutes passed, and I'd dared only to blink my eyes. I knew I had to do something, or die, which, admittedly, had its appeal, so, moving one joint at a time, and as few as possible, I carefully triaged myself. It was worse than I thought. I was a pincushion.

Time moved slowly, but I moved slower. After a solid hour, and with a few hundred thorns still embedded in me, I freed myself. However, when I tried to stand, a jolt of pain shot across my lower back. I stiffened like the dead. When the pain subsided to merely excruciating, I tried again, this time with slower, more deliberate movements. I eventually cleared an area on either side of me. Then I started rocking back and forth, easy at first, but gradually gaining momentum until I rolled onto my stomach. I grabbed whatever I could—weeds, rocks, clumps of grass—and inched myself clear of the thorns like a giant slug. I collapsed. Survival still seemed iffy.

Then I remembered the container! I looked around and spotted it lying upside down in the grass. I crawled over, snaking through the brush, following a trail of coins. I mined for silver, ignoring the copper, and found a rich vein of quarters and half dollars. Before long, I had fifteen bucks, more than enough to survive the weekend. I could get a hotel room and order room service! Maybe have some friends over!

That's when I spied the wallet. Curious, I slowly squirmed over to it. It was leather, mostly brown, but black where it slid in and out of back pockets. I picked it up. It was thick and heavy, and when I opened it, I saw why—there was an inch-thick wad of bills, most of them hundreds! I found a driver's license. *Frank!* I tore it into a million tiny pieces and threw them in the air. Then, with blue and white confetti falling, I started counting.

Chapter 7

Friday, May 29, 1970

"Son of a bitch!" Frank slammed the side door.

"Why'd you hit Tyler?!" It wasn't so much a question as an accusation.

"What're you talking about? I didn't hit him."

"Oh, really?" Twyla said disbelievingly. "How'd he wind up on the ground then?" She folded her arms across her chest.

"He must've fallen."

"Sure he did. Did he land on his mouth?" Her voice was laced with sarcasm.

"How the hell would I know? Ask him."

"I will," Twyla said, staring hard, "and if I find out you hit him, you're going to be in a world of shit."

"We might've bumped into each other, but that's it."

"Oh, okay, so now you bumped into each other. Did your fist bump his mouth?"

"No!"

"You had it drawn back when I came outside."

"I was just trying to scare him. That's all."

"Sure you were. What was that noise in the garage just now?"

"I threw a flashlight against the wall. So what?"

"So what? I'll tell you so what!" You also broke the glass on the storm door! Is that a 'so what,' too?"

"Look, lay off. I'll take care of it, all right?"

"No, it's not 'all right,'" Twyla said, making quote marks with her fingers. "Now, get a piece of cardboard and tape it up before all the damn bugs get in!"

Muttering under his breath, Frank grabbed a utility knife from the junk drawer in the kitchen and stomped down the hall to Tyler's room. He dragged a large cardboard box from the closet and upended it on the bed, dumping out winter clothes, eight-track tapes, tube socks, and brick after brick of rubber-banded baseball cards. Frank, still grumbling, cut a square from the box and, leaving the mess, returned to the living room. Twyla wiped her hands on a yellow dish towel and watched over his shoulder.

"What's got you so pissed off?" she asked.

"I can't find my wallet." Frank tore four strips of duct tape, squared the cardboard, and taped it to the door.

"Where'd you lose it?"

"If I knew that it wouldn't be missing." He smoothed out the tape.

"Don't be a smartass."

"It was under the front seat in that container I throw change in."

"You sure?"

"Of course, I'm sure," Frank said irritably.

"Did you have any money it?"

"Only thirty-three hundred dollars."

"Whaaaat?" Twyla drawled, looking incredulous. "Are you serious?"

"No, I'm joking. Hilarious, isn't it?"

"You must've sold a lot of vacuum cleaners!"

"I keep telling you, they're not vacuum cleaners, they're Kirbys!"

"Whatever. How many did you sell?"

"Ten."

"TEN?"

"Yeah, I sold three right off the bat. Boom! Boom! Boom!" Frank said proudly.

"I don't know how you do it. Those things cost a mint, and I don't have the money to buy one, or the personality to sell them."

"Yeah, well, they do damn near everything from cleaning rugs to cutting wood."

"Polish shoes, too, right?"

"Spit shine! I left here with five of the beasts Sunday and had the office ship five more on Tuesday. I sold the last one after lunch today." Frank opened the door and checked the cardboard's fit from the porch.

"And now you've lost all that money?"

Frank's smile faded, replaced by a frown, and he stormed out of the room.

Twyla rolled her eyes and went back to the kitchen. She grabbed the hamburger she'd picked up on the way home and then opened and closed cabinet doors, looking for her frying pan.

Frank shook off the drops, tucked himself in, and flushed the toilet. He returned to the living room, sullen as a swamp, and flopped on the couch. Twyla started on a salad while the burgers cooked. She put some lettuce in a bowl and, after slicing a tomato, added onions, olives, and croutons. She rinsed the knife under the tap, dried her hands, and joined Frank.

"Mom used to say, 'think and remember' whenever we lost something." Twyla reached for her lotion on the end table and squirted a glob on her hand. "Give it a try."

"I don't feel like it, okay?"

"I bet you'll remember where you left it." Twyla rubbed her hands together, working the cream into her pores.

"Look," Frank said tiredly, "just leave me alone for a while."

"Oh, come on, it's easy and it'll only take a minute."

Frank shook his head firmly. "I'm not in the mood for yo—," he stopped. "Games." His voice was strained. He breathed deeply and exhaled slowly. Then again.

"Just try."

Frank stood and looked down at her. "Jesus, Twyla! Are you deaf?!" he barked. "I said my wallet was under the seat in the container, and now they're both gone! Can you hear me? Blink and nod if you understand."

Twyla didn't nod. She didn't blink either. Her back stiffened like uncooked lasagna, though, and she stared up at him, or right through him, it was hard to tell. She took a long, deep breath. Her chest slowly expanded, and by the time she exhaled, which took a good ten seconds, she was calm as could be.

"It's the first day of summer vacation and I took the whole weekend off, so I could spend it with Tyler. Then you showed up and ran him off."

"Hey, don't blame me, you were pissed at him, too!" Frank dropped to the couch and looked at her.

"I told you when we started dating that you don't discipline him!"

"He should've called, you said so yourself!"

"That's not the point!"

"Whatever, I'm through talking about it. I'm out three grand."

"And that's the other thing. I'm trying to help you find your money and getting nothing but sarcasm in return."

"I asked you to leave me alone, but you just won't let up!" Frank, elbows on his knees and his hands palms up, looked at Twyla, exasperated.

"Just give it a try. You can thank me later."

Frank slumped in resignation. "Oh, for...okay, what do I do?"

"Like I said, think and remember. Where were you when you last had it?"

"I was driving back from Valparaiso, and I stopped in Lafayette for gas. I reached under the seat and grabbed it from the container." Frank looked up, cocked his head and raised his eyebrows.

"So, keep going," Twyla said.

Frank rubbed his face. Then he shook his head as if resetting his thoughts.

"Let's see, I pulled the container from under the seat, grabbed my wallet, and waited for the attendant."

"Did he see you reaching under the seat?

"I don't know, maybe."

"Did he see your wallet?"

"He was standing right there."

"So, he saw all that money, didn't he?"

"Probably. I had to dig out a ten."

"What about the container, did he see it?"

"I doubt it. He wasn't close enough to the car."

"All right, what happened next?"

"I told him to fill it up."

"And?"

"And he headed for the pump."

"What'd you do with your wallet?"

"I dropped it in the container."

"Did he see you?"

"I don't know."

"Did you have the top down?"

"Yeah."

"Well, he put the nozzle in the tank, so he was standing right over your shoulder, wasn't he?"

"Yeah, but I had my back to him."

"Okay, maybe he didn't see it. What'd you do next?"

"I pushed the container under the seat with my foot."

"What else?"

Frank thought some more before speaking. "Oh, that's right, I had to take a leak, so I went to the bathroom."

"Without your wallet?"

"Yeah, like I said, it was in the container."

"Why didn't you put it in your pocket?"

"I don't know, Twyla, because I didn't, okay?"

"Whatever. How long were you gone?"

"Not very, only a few minutes."

"Then what?"

"I got in the car and got back on the road."

"Did you have any change?"

"Nope, he topped it off at ten bucks."

"Did you check to see if the container was still there?"

"No."

"Well, there you go! Mystery solved!"

"I don't know, Twyla, I don't think so."

"Why not? It's the only thing that makes sense."

"He was a young man, clean-cut, polite . . . He just didn't seem the type."

"They never do. He could've grabbed them from under the seat while you were gone."

"I doubt it."

"Okay, if he didn't steal them, where are they? They must be somewhere. Wallets and containers don't just sprout legs and walk off. Have you checked your luggage? Maybe your wallet's in there."

With barely a whisper of hope, Frank dumped his laundry on the floor and painstakingly went through every article of clothing, one at a time, making sure his wallet hadn't found its way inside a pocket, sleeve, or sock. It hadn't. Grumbling, he gathered his dirty clothes and dumped them in the beat-up wicker hamper. Then he opened his battered tan suitcase. He didn't really think his wallet would be in there, and he was right, it wasn't, but he swore anyway.

The garment bag was next. Frank angrily snatched it off the hanger and threw it on the bed. He started with his suit jacket, feeling the side and inside breast pockets. They were empty. He took his slacks out next, checking the front and back pockets and then feeling the legs and cuffs. Again, nothing. Lastly, he turned the bag inside out, just in case his wallet had fallen to the bottom. It hadn't.

"Damn it!" Frank sat heavily on the bed and stared at the ceiling. Then it hit him! He'd counted the contracts at the stoplight before hopping on the highway! Frank rushed down the hall to the living room. He grabbed his briefcase, tossed it on the couch, and released the clasps. The lid popped open. No wallet. It was too much.

"SON OF A BITCH!" Frank grabbed his briefcase by the handle and flung it across the room. It bounced on end, flipped twice in the air, and broke open, sending contracts flying like leaflets. The briefcase struck the wall just above the baseboard, knocking a big hole in the drywall. It laid there with a busted hinge, covered in bits of plaster.

Twyla rushed from the kitchen. "What was that?!"

"My briefcase," Frank said quietly.

"Then what's that hole in the wall?"

"Where it hit after I threw it."

"What's your major malfunction, Frank?"

"I'm out thirty-three hundred dollars!"

"And you think destroying my house is going to help you find it?" Twyla picked up a powder blue throw cushion and threw it at him.

"I'm venting."

"Venting? Is that what this is, 'venting'? Looks more like a temper tantrum, but, fine, let's call it venting. Now, listen to this, the next time I feel like venting, I'm going out to the garage and vent all over your car, and you better believe I've got experience in the area."

"Don't touch my car, okay?"

"Then stop being an asshole!"

"Oh, now I'm an asshole, huh?"

"No, you're always an asshole, and I don't know why I put up with you!"

"Well, that's just fucking great! I guess I was an asshole when you were worried to death about that son of yours, wasn't I? Hell, I bet he's the one who stole my wallet!"

"Oh my God, here we go again! You've blamed Tyler for everything since the earth cooled. Now it's your wallet. It's getting old, Frank, it's worn out. I want it to stop. Here. Now. Forever."

"You need to take your blinders off, Twyla. Tyler is trouble with a capital T."

"He's just a boy!"

"Stop making excuses!"

"I'm not making excuses, damn it! It's the truth! When did he ever have time to take your wallet anyway? He didn't get a foot in the house before you ran him off!"

"Yeah, well...."

"And why am I even having this debate with you about *my* son in *my* house? You better get over whatever problem you have with him, and I mean but quick!"

"He's a little smart-ass!"

"Give him a break! I haven't been divorced a year, and his dad's on the other side of the world fighting a war!"

"I don't care! I don't trust him!"

"Tough! Get over it, or there WILL be changes!"

"What's that supposed to mean?"

"You change, or where you spend weekends does."

"Oh, that shit again. Okay, fine, whatever. Have it your way!"

"That's right, my way or the highway, but right now, take the street out front to the hardware store and get what you need to fix my window and wall!" Twyla stalked off, but stopped and turned around. "And get a flashlight, too, so you don't get lost on the way back!"

"I'll need some money," Frank said quietly.

"You can't be serious!"

"I lost my wallet, remember?"

"So, you're broke?"

"I found a few quarters in the car."

"That's all the money you have?"

"Yes," Frank said, exasperation creeping back in his voice.

"I've had it with you," Twyla said. She turned to walk away, but Frank wrapped his arms around her and nuzzled her neck.

"Hey, I'm sorry. I'm just really mad."

"I don't want to hear it," Twyla said, struggling to free herself. "You've pissed me off now!"

"C'mon, you can't be as upset as I am. I'm down three grand!"

Frank slid his hand beneath Twyla's T-shirt and cupped her bare breast while unsnapping her shorts with his other hand.

Twyla gave him a sharp elbow and spun around to face him. "You think getting in my pants is the answer to everything, don't you?"

"Ow! Not anymore!" Frank rubbed his ribcage. "Tell you what, loan me twenty bucks, and I'll run down to the hardware store. While I'm gone, go to the grocery store and get some stuff for a picnic, you know, bread, cold meat—I like pickle-pimento loaf—cheese, chips, potato salad, beer. When we—"

"I'm not going on a picnic with you!"

"No, no, let me finish. When we get back, we'll pack up and go to the race tomorrow."

"The Indy 500?"

"Yep!" Frank kissed her cheek. "What do you say? I need to get my mind off losing my wallet."

"What about Tyler?"

"What about him?"

"I can't leave him here on his own."

"Why? The kid's what, sixteen years old?"

"Fifteen."

"Whatever. I had a job by then. Just leave him a note and tell him we'll be home tomorrow night."

Twyla thought a moment. "He's probably not coming home anyway, not after the way you acted. Oh, all right, there's a twenty in my purse."

Chapter 8

Friday, May 29, 1970

I hobbled to the north side of the woods, emerging at a cul-de-sac on a freshly paved street in a new housing edition. The street-lamps were starting to light up. Houses, too. I was caked in a mixture of blood, sweat, and gore. My clothes were dirty and torn. Adults stared at me. Children ran. Dogs barked. I was a horror movie. I walked for miles, and when I stopped, I was in Essie, so I wandered over to Darlene's house. She was sitting on the porch with a glass of lemonade, reading *Life* magazine, but looked up when I shambled corpselike down the street. She dropped the magazine and came running.

"Tyler! What in the world happened?! Are you all right?" Darlene brushed who knows what from my cheek and kissed it.

"Long story, but it started with Frank."

"Who's Frank?"

"My Mom's boyfriend."

"Okay, but how'd you get so, uh, beat up?"

"I got beat up."

"You two got in a fight?"

"Not really, one-punch knockout."

"He did all this with one punch?!"

"I've had a few other experiences since then."

"Tell me later. Let's get you cleaned up and into some clean clothes. You're not going home, are you?"

"No way."

"Where are you spending the night?"

"Uh, that's still in the planning stage."

"Great! You can stay here and go to the 500 with us."

"The Indianapolis 500? Wow! Wait, I can't. I need to go to the bank tomorrow."

"The bank can wait."

"No, it can't."

"It'll have to. Tomorrow's Memorial Day, remember? Besides, what's the hurry? They'll open back up on Monday. I promise."

"CNT's open half a day tomorrow, and I can't wait until Monday."

"Okay, tell you what, I'll ask mom if she'll stop in Indy. There's got to be a branch down there."

"That'll work, but are you sure I can spend the night? What're you going to tell your parents?"

"Well, dad's already at the track and mom's dropping off my little brother at my aunt's house. I'll get Kent to tell her something when she gets back."

"Like what?"

"Oh, I don't know, let's see . . . oh, I got it! Your mom had to go out of town because your grandma's in the hospital."

"Both of my grandmothers are dead."

"Well, I'm resurrecting one and, oh, I'll be damned, she's taken ill. C'mon, Tyler, work with me here, okay?"

"Sorry, I'm not thinking straight."

Darlene's features softened. "Oh, poor baby, is there anything I can do?" She pulled me inside the garage and shut the door. Then she snuggled up close, unzipped my pants, and grasped Tyler Jr. by the neck. "I sure hope he's okay," she purred. Tyler Jr. sprang to attention.

Kent bounded down the steps just then but stopped when he saw us. "Oh, hey, sorry. You two really like each other, huh?"

"Shut up, Kent!" Darlene growled.

"Hi, Kent," I said embarrassedly while pirouetting to zip up. Darlene's brothers were starting to get on my nerves.

"You're getting to be one of the regulars around here, aren't you?"

Darlene made her pitch before I had time to think that through. "Listen, Tyler needs a place to stay tonight. Do him a favor and tell mom you invited him to spend the night and go to the race with us, okay?"

"I don't know, I've still got a lot to do. I haven't even packed."

"Just do it! Look at him, his mom's boyfriend beat him up and he's got nowhere to go."

"That right, Tyler?"

I nodded. My appearance said enough.

"There! Happy?" Darlene challenged. "Now help him out."

"Help *you* out." Kent could smell her desperation.

"All right, knob-nose, let's deal," She pushed him back up the stairs and, grabbing my arm, dragged me along behind her.

We wound up in Kent's room. While they dickered, I called Mom to let her know I was all right and that I was staying at the Wantels. I only got half the message in before the interrogation began.

"Did Frank hit you?" I hesitated, and she caught it. "That son of a bitch! He did, didn't he?"

"No, no, we just bumped into each other, and I went down, that's all."

"Are you lying to me?"

"No," I lied without knowing why.

"You better not be."

"I'm not," I lied a third time.

"Why were you so late getting home?"

"I stayed after school to hang out with a friend." That much was true.

"Why didn't you tell me?"

"I thought you'd say no."

"You thought right, and now you're in big trouble!"

"I'm sorry, will you forgive me?"

There was a pause. She hadn't expected that. "Of course, I will," she said slowly, but quickly added, "don't go getting in any more of it, though!"

"I won't." Turned out, I was lying then, too.

Later, Darlene said her dad, Ben, was friends with Mel Kenyon, who raced midget cars but also ran the Indianapolis 500 when he had a ride. Ben and Mel grew up together in Davenport, and Ben, along with Mel's father, Everett, and brother, Don, was part of his pit crew on the stock car circuit during the 1950s.

In 1955, Ben met Darlene's mom, Olivia, at Waukegan Speedway. He proposed on the first date and every date afterward until she said yes. They were married the next day. In 1958, just before Mel started racing midgets, Ben and Olivia left Davenport so they could be closer to her family in Huwabola. Ben and Mel kept in contact, though, and when Mel entered the 1965 Indianapolis 500, he asked Ben to be on his pit crew. He'd been part of the team ever since.

Kent drove a hard bargain; Darlene agreed to take out the trash, wash the dishes, and mow the yard for a month. He left, quite pleased with his negotiation skills, while Darlene, looking less keen with the outcome, turned to me.

"I'll get you some lemonade and start the shower. There're towels and washcloths in the cabinet. When you're done, leave your clothes and I'll throw them in the wash."

"Man, I'm lucky I met you!"

"You sure? All of this happened because of me."

"Oh, right. Then I guess you're worth it."

The lemonade, cold and tangy, stung my lip, but it cut my thirst. I drained the glass in three quick gulps. Darlene refilled it, kissed me on the cheek, and went back outside to read.

A billowing cloud of steam greeted me when I opened the bathroom door. I groped blindly in the warm, hazy mist until I found a towel. I wiped the mirror and shrank in horror. My face was a war zone, mapped out in abrasions, welts, shiners, knots, scratches, cuts, punctures, and contusions.

I leaned wearily against the wall and slid to the floor, legs splayed, and rested my butt and balls on the cool tile. I could've stayed there, but I would've ended up taking a cold shower, so, sighing, I grabbed the base of the white porcelain sink and pulled myself up. I had the curtain pulled back and one foot in the tub when there was a discreet knock and the door cracked open.

"Here're some clothes to put on when you're done," Darlene said from the hallway "They're Kent's, so they should fit okay." She reached in and dropped them on the floor.

"Thanks!" I called.

"No problem." She closed the door and padded down the hallway.

I stepped gingerly over the rim of the tub and scalding hot water hit me like nitric acid, curling the top layer of skin and sizzling the next few beneath it. I twisted and turned, frantically trying to block the water with my hands and arms, protecting myself where it struck last or hurt most, all the while fumbling for the knobs, trying to get the temperature north of Hell. I eventually found a combination I could handle and stood beneath the showerhead to enjoy the hot water beating on my sore muscles.

I soaped up and washed my abused body, careful of my lip, which I gently patted with the washcloth until the blood went from black to red and, finally, pink. Unbeknownst to me, Darlene had snuck inside, and when I turned off the water and pulled back the curtain, she wrapped me in a soft, thick towel fresh from the dryer. Starting at the top, she dried me off, gently wiping my face, mindful of my lip, and then running the towel over my neck, shoulders, and back. Darlene kept working her way lower and lower, exposing more and more of me. By the time she got to my waist, Tyler Jr. was hanging there like a tree snake, ready to strike. That's when she abruptly stopped and left the towel draped over him.

"Hurry up and get dressed," she said. "Mom will be here soon."

Blue balls.

By the time I'd dressed and cleaned up the bathroom, Darlene's mom was home, and she'd fixed dinner as well. Olivia Wantel closed the fridge and pointed to the table.

"Hi, Tyler. I'm Olivia. Sit between those two, so you can help referee." It was clear where Darlene got her looks. I had a hard time keeping my eyes off her, something I later learned didn't go unnoticed.

"You about fell out of your chair staring at my mom. That's kind of weird."

"I'm sorry, but I couldn't help it. You two could be sisters you look so much alike."

"Everybody says that."

We left room for dessert, which Mrs. Wantel had enticed us to do by setting a cherry pie in the middle of the table. She was getting the ice cream out of the freezer when Kent told me they were moving to Lebanon at the end of the summer to be closer to 3K Racing. I felt like I'd been kicked in the stomach. Later, on the couch in the basement, with just the black-and-white television for light, Darlene said there'd been a big argument about it.

"I don't want to move and neither does Kent. It'd suck extra hard being at a new school and having to make new friends, but dad loves racing, and mom says it's important that he chase his dream."

"His dream's my nightmare."

"Let's not talk about it." Darlene grabbed my chin and gave me a quick kiss.

"Fine by me." She leaned back against me and I wrapped my arms around her.

"Whoa! That's not all you!"

"Uh, no, some of that's money, I said. Then, changing the subject, "Tell me about the race. What's it like?"

"Forget the race!" Darlene said excitedly. "I like walking around the infield. Music's blaring and people are dancing around, having a good time. I've seen some wild stuff down there!"

"Like what?"

"Oh, like guys surrounding girls and chanting, 'Show your tits! Show your tits!'"

"Uh-uh, no way!"

"Yeah, huh! Some of them do it, too!"

"Get out!"

"Serious biz! They flash their tits, and everybody laughs."

"That *is* wild!"

"It's even crazier in the Snake Pit!"

"What's that?"

"Inside turn one. It's where all the bikers, freaks, and heavy partiers hang out. They're all drunk or stoned or tripping or whatever. The Hell's Angels always show up and there're lots of fights, too."

"Have you ever lost?" As hard as she slugged me, probably not.

Chapter 9

Friday, May 29, 1970

The plaster on the wall was still wet when Twyla returned from the grocery store.

"It's done," Frank said. "Looks good, doesn't it?"

"Mm-hmm," Twyla grudgingly acknowledged. "You'll have to paint it."

"You think so?"

"I'm just saying, that's all."

"Should I wait for it to dry first?"

"Whatever," Twyla said curtly.

Frank, sensing thin ice, skulked off to the garage with the tools. He slunk back just as quietly and washed up at the sink.

"Did you get everything, babe?" he asked sweetly, probing.

"Yeah, the place was packed, though. Looks like a lot of people have plans."

"Hey, let's have a cookout Sunday!"

"Let's wait to see if you're still here."

It was dark when Frank finished packing the Starfire, and he still wasn't back on shore. He slumped in the chair and pulled the tab on a can of Blatz. Twyla started a load of towels and jeans in the washer. She stopped in the hallway with a basket of white clothes.

"Guess who I saw?"

"Who?"

"McGuire." She nodded her head in the direction of his house.

"Man's got to eat." Frank took a swig of beer.

"He looked like he'd just got out of church. I'd never seen him so dressed up—black suit, tie, and hat."

"Somebody's probably getting married or buried. "Let's leave tonight, want to?"

"Aren't you tired? You just got back from Valpo."

"Nah, we're packed, and now I'm pumped about the race, aren't you?"

"Not really, I've been to the 500 a few times, and I'm getting too old for all the partying."

"Oh, c'mon, let's go! We can cruise Sixteenth and Georgetown, have a few beers, and check out the freaks."

Chapter 10

Saturday, May 30, 1970

It was half one in the morning when Agent Kramer arrived at her small, cramped, one-bedroom apartment on Indianapolis's north side. She leaned against the door, kicked off her shoes, and headed for the living room where she collapsed dispiritedly on the sofa. Rufus, her big, blue-eyed gray cat, meowed insistently and hopped in her lap. He flopped on his side with a grunt and then looked up purring, demanding attention.

Kramer arched her back and yawned. Rufus stretched right along with her. The call about Teymore came in the afternoon while she was grabbing a quick bite to eat. She'd gone up there and back, but, as usual, writing the report took twice as long. Kramer raised her foot and massaged her toes one at a time. She'd worn tennis shoes from grade school through law school, so the switch to the FBI's regulation low-heeled, black pumps was murder. Rufus hopped off her lap. He dashed to the kitchen, looked back from the doorway, and meowed. Then again, louder.

Kramer padded to the kitchen in her stocking feet and opened a can of cat food. Rufus, recognizing the sound, hopped on a barstool and jumped on the counter where he knew he wasn't supposed to be. When he wasn't looking, Kramer flicked water at him and, feet in a frenzy, he leaped to the floor, seeking safety beneath the dining room table. There, he glared at her and licked his fur stoically until she set his bowl on the floor. Then he trotted right over, insult forgiven, but not forgotten.

Kramer took off her earrings and necklace and laid them on her dresser. She put her gun and holster on the bedside table and got undressed. She removed her blouse and shook out of her bra. She laid them on the corner of the bed and then did the same thing with her skirt and pantyhose. Naked, she stood before the full-length mirror.

"Not too bad for a skinny, freckle-faced girl from Detroit."

Kramer was close to six feet tall but weighed just 130 pounds. She had a runner's build, and hoped to get back into training after she closed the DTK case. The FBI had strict fitness regulations, and being a woman, and a black woman at that, in an agency dominated by white males, she intended to prove she belonged.

Kramer attended Detroit Mercy High School, where she lettered all four years in track and field. She finished second at state in the 880 as a junior and vowed to train hard and make it back as a senior. Kramer had a phenomenal senior year, winning every race heading into the sectionals. The Mercy Marlins were also undefeated in the 3200 relay.

Expected to win two state titles, Kramer's season ended in the sectionals when she finished a disappointing seventh in the 880 and later blew the hand-off anchoring the relay. The night before, a teammate showed up unannounced, wanting to party. Kramer inexplicably stayed out all night and got hammered. It was the stupidest thing she'd ever done, and eight years on, she was still embarrassed by it. She was the team captain, too! The teammate was all smiles; she'd run her fastest split ever.

The University of Detroit offered Kramer a full ride. She did well against stiffer competition, winning an increasing number of races each year. As a senior, she pulled an upset in the conference finals, winning the 880. Then she anchored the Titans' win in the 3200 relay, putting her and her teammates in the field for the

NCAA Championships. It appeared Kramer was peaking at the right time. Unfortunately, she tore her hamstring during training, and she and her teammates were scratched from the meet. Her coach wanted her to train for the upcoming Olympic trials, but she was burned out on running and wanted to get on with life, so, instead, she finished her degrees in psychology and criminal justice and went on to law school at Michigan. There, she made law review and graduated cum laude.

Kramer worked for the Detroit Police Department in between her second and third years of law school, but she also applied to the FBI, fully aware the agency had only one black woman, Sylvia Mathis, working as a special agent. Kramer was selected and headed to Quantico as one of three black people, and the only black woman, in her class. She did well, distinguishing herself in the classroom and in the field, and she finished near the top of her class. Kramer was a relentless investigator. Law school sharpened her analytical abilities, and her naturally friendly demeanor and psychology degree made her an excellent interrogator.

Kramer lifted her breasts and then let them fall. She sighed. They're okay, she thought. A bit on the small side, but she was pleased they still rode high and retained their firmness. Turning sideways, she ran her hands over her flat stomach. Then she turned her back to the mirror and glanced over her shoulder, examining her backside. It's too small, she thought, and it could be rounder. Still, she was thankful it, too, had resisted the earth's gravitational pull.

Kramer had beaver brown eyes and a disarming smile. She wore her black hair in shoulder-length tree braids, which suited her high cheekbones and conveniently required little maintenance. She got her height from her father, a French-Canadian from Quebec, but with her clear skin, scattered freckles, and full lips, she mostly favored her mother, who grew up in an upscale neighborhood in Grosse Pointe. The blend gave her just enough melanin for a Kahlua and cream complexion.

After toweling off, Kramer slipped on her thick, white, cotton bathrobe and walked to the bedroom. Rufus was already beside her pillow, eyes closed and settled in for the night. He purred when she slipped beneath the covers. Within minutes, they were both fast asleep.

Chapter 11

Saturday, May 30, 1970

Darlene and I spooned on the couch and talked past midnight. She asked about my family, so I told her the about the divorce and Dad being in Vietnam. I also told her about Frank.

"Oh, I see, he's the jolly, lighthearted type."

"Yeah, that's him."

"Your mom dates this creep?"

"Worse than that. He's practically living with us."

"What's that mean?"

"He's a traveling salesman. He comes around on the weekends."

"Ah, okay. Did your mom see him hit you?"

"Nah, she was in the house."

"But you told her, right?"

"Not really."

"You either did or you didn't."

"I didn't. I said we bumped into each other."

"You should've told her."

"I'll deal with it."

"Has he ever hit you before?"

"Nope."

"Why'd he do it? Wasn't he outside his jurisdiction?"

"I'd say so."

"Maybe he's compensating for having a small dick," Darlene said dryly.

"There's an angle I hadn't considered," I laughed. "I sure don't hear much noise coming from Mom's bedroom at night."

"Wait, you lie awake at night listening for your mom and her boyfriend to have sex? That's weird."

"No, NO! Of course not! I mean, not intentionally," I stammered, "but my room's next door."

"Whatever you say, Tyler. I'm not one to judge," Darlene said teasingly.

She had me flustered. "Look, all I'm saying is it's quiet in there, and that's a whole lot different than when my Dad was around."

"You sure keep on top of things going on in your mom's bedroom, don't you? Or not going on, I guess."

"I'm not on top of anything! I'm just trying to sleep, that's all!"

"Try counting sheep."

The television was on, and we were making out when a wave of fatigue washed over me. I yawned mid-kiss. Darlene quickly sat up.

"Am I boring you?"

"No, I'm beat. It's been a long day."

"You better get some sleep then. We're getting up early, and it's going to be another long day tomorrow." She got no objection from me, but a mutinous couch spring had other ideas; I hardly caught a wink.

At five o'clock, I gave up and just lay there, dead tired, listening to the "WOOOOOOOO!" from the television and staring at the Indian Chief on the test pattern. I finally nodded out, but not long after, an alarm went off above us, which got the dog going. She bounded down the stairs, barking nonstop. A few seconds later, Kent opened the door and hollered something about binoculars.

During a quick breakfast of cereal and toast, he filled me in on the race.

"The start's wild! Thirty-three cars come out of turn four, perfectly lined up in eleven rows of three. Everyone's on their feet, yelling, but you can't hear anything except the whine of the engines."

"It's loud," Darlene agreed.

"It sounds like a swarm of bees," Mrs. Wantel added.

"We're sitting in Tower Terrace," Kent said, "right behind 3K's pit. It's not the best seat, but it's still plenty good, and you get to see the pit action."

"Where're the best seats?"

"Oh, turn one, easy. E Stand. As high up as you can get. E Penthouse if you've got the bucks for them."

"Why're they so good?"

"They're right smack dab in the middle of the turn for one thing, and they're high up, too. You get a clear view down the front stretch as they come out of turn four, so the cars are coming straight at you. You also see them go through the first turn and short chute and then partway into turn two."

"What's the short chute?"

"It's a short, straight part of the track between turns one and two. There's another one between three and four."

"Okay, got it."

"You can't beat the price of our seats, though, right, mom?" Darlene said.

"That and watching your dad are the best parts, dear."

Darlene and her mom cleared the table and washed the dishes while Kent and I filled the coolers and loaded the family's yellow Olds 442. I was sore all over, and I tried not to think about what I looked like.

"Kenyon's starting twenty-second, so he'll be on the inside of row eight."

"How fast did he qualify?"

"About 166 miles an hour. The whole front row was over 170!"

"Intense!"

"The cars are all bunched up at the start, see, but when the green flag drops, they zig and zag, dive low or go high. The drivers are looking for gaps in traffic but trying to be careful, too. They say, 'You can't win the Indy 500 on the first lap, but you can sure lose it.'" Kent then explained everything about restarts, pit strategies, tire wear, turbulence, and drafting. He talked the whole time, stopping only to grunt when putting the coolers in the trunk.

Finally, after everything was loaded up, we all piled in. Kent called shotgun and got no argument from Darlene or me.

It was three hours to Indianapolis. I slept most of the way, but dreamed I was running around with Frank's wallet while Old Man McGuire was trying to run me down in a race car. He was about to tag me when Mrs. Wantel hit a pothole.

"Mmph?"

"You were out of it," Darlene said.

"Mmph?" I repeated.

"You were asleep before we even left town."

"I didn't sleep much last night." That drew a frown from Mrs. Wantel. I sat up, rubbing my eyes. "Where are we?"

"About twenty miles north of Indy," Mrs. Wantel said. "I've factored in a proper breakfast if you kids want to stop."

"I'm hungry," Kent said. "What about you, Tyler?" He tossed a look over the seatback.

"Yeah, a little bit."

"Okay, I'll get off at the next exit."

"Hey, what about me?" Darlene had her lower lip stuck out. "Doesn't anyone care if I'm hungry?"

"Sorry, dear," Mrs. Wantel replied. "Would you like to stop for breakfast?"

"Oh, whatever you guys decide is fine," she said sweetly.

We approached Pendleton, home to one of Indiana's state penitentiaries, but it was too dark to see it from the highway. I was about to say John Dillinger did time there when a gold Dart blew passed us. I sat upright, but it was already gone.

"Did you know you snore when you sleep?" Darlene asked.

"Uh-uh." I was still thinking about the Dart. It sure looked like McGuire's.

"Talk, too."

"What'd I say?"

"I couldn't make out much, but you said something about a wallet and an old man."

Chapter 12

Saturday, May 30, 1970

Frank took a quick shower and quietly dressed in the bathroom's light to avoid waking Twyla. He needn't have been concerned. She'd drank way too much, and he'd ended up carrying her to their room and putting her to bed. He pulled the blankets up tight around her shoulders. It was just past dawn.

"Hey, babe, I'm going out for coffee and a newspaper. I'll be back in a bit, and we'll head to the track." He bent down and kissed her on the cheek. She didn't even move.

Indianapolis was more familiar in the daylight. Landmarks were easily recognizable, and Frank could see the city skyline as he passed under the viaduct spanning I-70. Traffic was picking up. He stayed on secondary roads and pulled into a Sinclair station. The attendant dutifully approached, smiling broadly while wiping his hands on an oily shop rag.

"Nice car! Fill 'er up?" He stuffed the rag in his back pocket.

"Thanks, yeah, premium, and check the oil, please." Frank reached for the container before remembering it was gone, and got mad about it all over again. While he fumed, the attendant fit the nozzle in the tank and locked the handle in place with the gas cap. He walked to the front of the Starfire with a bottle of blue, soapy water and sprayed the windshield.

"Headin' to the track?" He wiped the glass with blue paper towels.

"Yeah," Frank said curtly. Then, in a friendlier voice. "How about you?"

"Nah, gotta work." The man squirted the windshield again and scraped off some bug guts with his thumbnail.

"That's too bad. Who do you think's going to win?"

"Hard to say." The attendant raised the hood. "There're seven or eight drivers who've got a shot." He wiped the dipstick, reinserted it, and pulled it out again. "Foyt and Rutherford will probably run up front, so will Donahue, but my money's on Unser—Al, not Bobby. He's had a really good month."

"He's on pole, right?"

"Yep," the man replied, checking the dipstick. He peeked around the hood. "Oil's fine." The pump clicked off.

Frank counted what he had left over from Twyla's twenty. "Top it off at seven bucks."

"You got it."

"Where can I get some coffee?" Frank handed him a five and two ones.

"There's a Pancake House on Washington. Head south and take a right at the second light. It's just past the used car lot on the left."

"Got it, thanks."

Chapter 13

Saturday, May 30, 1970

Shapiro's Delicatessen had been a fixture on the near south side of downtown Indianapolis since 1905. Over the years, people from all backgrounds—business leaders, politicians, and both white- and blue-collar workers—flocked there for breakfast, lunch, or an early dinner.

Mr. Wren, an immensely obese man stuffed inside a rumpled black suit with a stained white shirt and black, greased-spotted tie, dined at Shapiro's whenever he was in town. He always chose the same table, too, a large round one in the far back corner by the kitchen. Today he had to wait for it, but he didn't mind. Wren was as patient and affable as he was large, and when the family occupying it finished and left, he even cleared their dishes, wiped it down, and handed the waitress the tip. Wren had waited for that particular table because he could see the front door and everyone inside. It was also near the rear exit where he'd parked.

The cafeteria line curled toward the door. Wren lumbered to it, drawing plenty of looks, gazes, and stares. He waited patiently, advancing a few steps at a time, but when got to the serving line he grabbed plates and bowls from counters and shelves at light-speed. It took three cooks just to make his eggs. Wren headed for his table with four trays, one atop the other, each one loaded with food. He had to go back for cutlery, napkins, and coffee.

Wren covered the entire table surface with dishes, arranging them in a manner that made sense only to him. He attacked his artery-clogging breakfast of two dozen eggs, various cuts of pork, a house of home fries, a smokestack of pancakes, two plates of biscuits and gravy, a rack of toast, and six glazed donuts with all the intensity and vigor of a world class athlete.

Wren dunked a donut in his coffee and waited until it was on the verge of falling apart before cramming it in his mouth. Even when eating, he resembled a cherub with his big, rosy cheeks, button nose, and cupid's bow lip. His charcoal eyes twinkled when he was amused and his full head of thick, black, bushy hair spilled wildly over his collar and ears. Wren had a warm, friendly smile that easily broadened into a grin or gave way to low, rumbling laughter. IQ tests at school, and later, during presentencing, revealed Wren was at the sharp end of the 99th percentile.

Few people started off life with Wren's advantages. His family had old money, so he attended exclusive, private schools from kindergarten through prep school. He made it into Oberlin College, not on grades, and certainly not in sports, but only after his parents ponied up a very generous endowment. Wren spent seven fun years as a Yeoman without so much as declaring a major before his father, after so many threats, cut him off.

Even without a degree, Wren could've made important achievements in the fields of math, science, or technology—he was that smart—but fun, pleasure, and excitement were better fits with his insouciance, and he wasn't going to get his fix on a hamster wheel. Crime, on the other hand, came naturally to Wren: there were no fixed hours; the work was exciting; and he was making a lot of money. Of course, failure meant time behind bars, but he discovered prison wasn't all bad. Wren rather enjoyed the solitude of his government-funded convalescence, welcoming the opportunity to kick back and relax with his books. He had a room of his own, three square meals a day, and the guards in his pocket.

Wren disapproved of violence as a general matter, so he gravitated toward swindling, using his likeability and charm to bilk banks, credit unions, and brokerage houses. He was good at it, too, pulling down six figures a year. His success, however, was his downfall because along with it came notoriety. As word of his scams spread throughout the financial community, every amicable fat white man in a soily suit seeking start-up money came under scrutiny.

Wren's luck ran out in Kansas City. He did three and a half years at Leavenworth after the FBI nabbed him posing as a builder planning a subdivision in an upscale area. The bank manager at Orion Savings and Loan recognized him as the guy who'd scammed a credit union where he'd worked years before. Wren was cuffed and stuffed in a squad car before the ink had dried on his loan application.

While incarcerated, Wren met Anthony Brezina, a Detroit mobster. Brezina was a third-generation Italian. He was a short, barrel-chested man with powerful arms, a fiery temper, and a shock of hair as black as his heart. Brezina was still in the first of two eleven-year terms for gunning down a pair of FBI agents. Armed with a search warrant, a team of agents showed up at his home in Royal Oak. He wasn't there, so they kicked the door in and ransacked his house, looking for evidence. When they finished, the two lead agents stayed behind to post the required legal notices.

When Brezina drove by and saw his battered front door, he thought it was a hit job or a burglary. He whipped the car around the corner and parked. Then he cut through a neighbor's backyard and snuck to his garage, where he retrieved a shotgun he kept hidden in his golf bag. The first agent was bent over the dining room table with his back to the front door. He didn't get the chance to identify himself. When he turned, Brezina fired, sending him backwards over the table and onto the floor. The second agent rushed from the bedroom, gun drawn. Brezina, who'd moved to the hallway, sprayed him with buckshot, killing him. When he discovered they were FBI agents, he fired their weapons, so it appeared they'd shot at him, and placed them in their hands.

Brezina claimed self-defense at trial, testifying he thought his home was being burglarized. He said the agents drew on him and fired without identifying themselves. Although the search warrant was in full view on the dining room table, the agents' badges were in their pockets, so Brezina beat the murder charges. He was convicted of two counts of voluntary manslaughter, though, and the judge ordered his sentences to be served consecutively.

That was back in 1963. Since then, Brezina had carved out a little niche for himself at the Big House by learning everything about every inmate who passed through its walls. He collected names, addresses, and contact information like other people collected stamps. He kept notes on inmates' personalities, behavior, quirks, and especially their crimes. Information became Brezina's currency, and he used it to match up criminals. If an inmate scheduled for release needed work or if somebody on the outside needed someone with a specific set of skills, Brezina was the man to contact. Business was good, too. He was making more money in the joint than he was out. Only one guy stiffed him, and his severed head was later discovered on a fence post on Long Island, near Ronkonkoma Beach. The rest of him wound up as chum in the Sound.

Wren folded the sports page in half and then half again before propping it up against the ketchup bottle. He took a triangular piece of toast and heaped on a forkful of potatoes, a fried egg, a sausage patty, and a folded-over strip of bacon. Then he shoved two-thirds of it in his mouth and started chewing, savoring the combination of flavors. Wren wiped a trickle of grease off his chin with his jacket sleeve and reached inside his suitcoat for a pen, sending waves of skin rolling across his body like waves on the beach. He hunched over the newspaper, making small notations in the margins while eating. Wren liked to gamble, so no matter what the season, he had bets down. Always an odd number, though, because he hated washes.

"Good morning, Mr. Marlin," Wren said, smiling good-naturedly at the identically dressed, albeit far neater, man who'd suddenly appeared at the table. He set the remaining third of his overly burdened toast on the plate, licked a driblet of gooey yolk from his thumb, and, leaning across the table, offered a handshake. Marlin ignored it. *No way am I shaking that hand.*

"Likewise, Mr. Wren."

"Grab a tray and get something to eat," Wren said, withdrawing his hand. If he was offended, he didn't show it. He cut a slice of ham in half, stabbed it with his fork, and crammed it in his mouth.

"No thanks, I never eat breakfast," Marlin said, pulling a chair from the table and sitting. He looked for room to lay his hat, but there wasn't any, so he held it in his lap.

"Most important meal of the day." Wren held up the other slice for examination before biting off a huge chunk. He started chewing, smiling as he did.

"I've watched you eat, Mr. Wren. Every meal's important."

"You're a funny man, Mr. Marlin" Wren said with genuine laughter. "You should be onstage." He wolfed down the last of the ham, followed it with a poached egg and a couple of sausage links and then turned his attention to his biscuits and gravy.

"You like baseball," Marlin said, nodding at the sports page.

"Uh-huh," Wren replied. "I was just going over my picks from yesterday." He spooned gravy over a couple of biscuits and popped them in his mouth, one at a time, and started chewing.

"Picks? You mean gambling?"

"Mm-hmm." His cheeks were full, but his teeth were working hard to empty them.

"How come I didn't know you gambled?"

"You never asked." He'd finished chewing and swallowed.

"How'd you do?"

"I hit four out of five."

"Not too shabby."

"Can't complain," Wren grudgingly acknowledged, "but I would've run the table if the White Sox hadn't blown it in the ninth." He soaked up gravy with another biscuit.

"So, what'd you make if you don't mind me asking."

"Seventy-five hundred."

"Are you kidding me?!"

"After the vig."

"After the what?"

"The vig, the vigorish." Wren laid his fork down. "It's what the bookie charges for taking the bet—usually ten percent." He wiped his chin with his sleeve again. "That's how he stays in business. He makes money off every bet, win or lose."

"I see."

"Yeah, so, if you want to win a hundred, you have to lay a hundred ten."

Marlin, his hair and eyes the color of nickel, turned in his chair and rested his arm across the backrest. He scanned the crowd, looking for anyone who seemed out of place. Satisfied nothing was amiss, he glanced at his watch and then looked back at Wren.

"So, where's Mr. Wolf?"

"He'll be here," Wren replied without looking up.

"He's already late, as usual. I don't get it with him. It's unprofessional."

"You might say that, but Mr. Wolf considers caution an aspect of professionalism. Anyway, I always factor in his tardiness, so I'm not concerned. I bet he's around here, though, and has been for a while." He crammed a forkful of his pancakes in his mouth while still chewing a biscuit. Syrup dripped off his chin and on his tie.

"What if he got nabbed? We'd be sitting here looking pretty stupid with cops swarming the place."

"Take it up with him." He loaded up a slice of toast, took a big bite, and checked the day's starting pitchers.

"No need. This is my last job."

Wren didn't say anything, but he looked up and his eyes stayed on Marlin. After what happened in Teymore, he was surprised Marlin had even shown up. He took another bite and, chewing slowly, nodded and swallowed. Then he studied the lines for the day's games.

Marlin pushed his chair from the table, hung his hat on the back, and headed for the coffee station. He poured himself a cup and added a spoonful of sugar. Then he turned and leaned against the counter, ankles crossed, stirring his coffee and eyeing the patrons. *Wolf might be around, but he's not here.*

Unfortunate circumstances forced Marlin into crime. At eighteen, he left the family farm in Brooklyn, Michigan, for the Motor City. He found a job straight away, hiring on as a non-union assembler for a Flint company that produced instrument panels for GM and Chrysler. It was a decent living for a kid fresh out of high school. He didn't have it as good as his UAW counterparts working for the Big Three, but within a few years, he'd banked enough money to marry his girlfriend, Sarah, and put a down payment on a house in the suburbs. Sarah, who was a year older than Marlin, had a bachelor's degree in education, which she put to use teaching first grade in Flint.

Eventually Marlin was promoted to shift supervisor, which meant more money as well as company benefits. After the couple's son, Casey, was born, Sarah, no longer needing health insurance through work, quit her job to be a stay-at-home mom. They did well enough for Marlin to return to dirt track racing, a sport he developed a passion for as a teenager. He bought a used race car and trailer, and the three of them spent their weekends going from track to track around the Midwest. Marlin was happy, and life was looking good.

It didn't last. When Casey was five, he was diagnosed with an aggressive form of leukemia. For the next year, it was nothing but a blur of hospitals, specialists, and test after test after test. Marlin's employer was sympathetic and allowed him time off with pay, but the company's health insurance provider proved less benevolent. After Casey's medical bills had exceeded a hundred thousand dollars, the company announced certain treatments for leukemia—the ones Casey received—would be excluded from coverage under a new plan taking effect at the end of the year. The move was completely legal since it applied to everyone, even if Casey just so happened to be the only one affected.

With no insurance to cover the mounting costs of treatment, Marlin, desperate for money, robbed a bank in nearby Farmingdale. He got away, netting seven thousand dollars, all of which went for medical bills. Not long after, six months in arrears on the mortgage and facing foreclosure, he robbed another bank and then another one after that to put food on the table, keep the utilities on, and bring his car note up to date. Marlin didn't get greedy or live ostentatiously, but every few months, when the bills piled up or the hospital sent threatening letters, he donned a ski mask, grabbed his .45, and held up a bank. These periodic heists, planned meticulously but occurring sporadically and sometimes out of state, saved his family from drowning in debt. They also baffled the FBI because they had no discernible pattern.

Neither money nor treatment slowed Casey's illness, though. He eventually had to be hospitalized, and doctors warned his parents to make final plans. Sarah couldn't bear it and turned to vodka and painkillers. Marlin had no clue. He'd taken on a part-time job in addition to his factory job. In between shifts, he visited Casey at the hospital, usually late at night because of his schedules. When he got home, supper was always ready, waiting in the oven, and Sarah was in bed. She was still there when he left for work a few hours later. Marlin just assumed she was asleep, and he was careful not to wake her.

When Casey died, Sarah quit leaning on drugs and alcohol and sank into depression. They were no longer a family. They were a couple, and this time, not a happy one. Marlin quit his part-time job and took time off at the factory. He also stopped robbing banks. He stayed at home with Sarah, making sure she got out of bed, showered, and dressed for the day. Sarah needed prodding, but she went through the motions for Marlin's sake, not an easy task with her increasingly dark mood.

Then one day Sarah spoke of teaching again, maybe going to night school to get her master's. She even mentioned having another child someday. Marlin completely bought into it, wanting to start anew. He returned to work. That first day back, he came home to find she'd overdosed on vodka and sedatives.

The EMTs were unable to revive her. The police, responding to the emergency call, showed up. A cop found the ski mask and gun. The judge, citing extenuating circumstances, gave Marlin twenty months.

Marlin served his time, but with no home, no job, and no family, picked up where he left off. He got caught again two years later and served a seven-year sentence at Leavenworth. That's when he met Brezina.

Chapter 14

Saturday, May 30, 1970

The appliance store across the street wouldn't open for another two hours, allowing the nattily clad man to discreetly keep watch on Shapiro's from beneath the dark shadows of its long green canopy. Wolf's long criminal career dated to childhood, and he'd been involved with the authorities every step of the way, drawing slaps on the wrist, stays at juvenile hall, short jail sentences, and a few stints in the state pen. But it wasn't until Wolf did hard time in a federal maximum security prison that he vowed he'd never go back, and he planned to take as many of the bastards down as he could if it came to it. Until then, though, Wolf took precautions, and one of them was making sure his partners didn't show up with a tail wagging. His methods were tedious and time-consuming, and they annoyed the hell out of Marlin, but he didn't care. There was nothing more tedious and time-consuming than sitting in prison.

Wolf watched Marlin walk to the coffee station. Satisfied the pair were clean, he stuck his half-smoked cigarette in his mouth and, squinting one-eyed from the smoke, started across the street. Approaching the curb, he took a last drag and flicked the butt toward the gutter. Inside, Wolf rolled his shoulders, throwing off the stiffness and soreness from standing for so long. He slowly surveyed the crowd. Someone at a nearby table made eye contact but quickly looked away under his icy glare. Wolf took staring as a challenge to fight.

Life's experiences have a way of shaping personalities, and Wolf's were terrible from the start. Then they got worse. He was born in the Bronx, in Spuyten Duyvil, appropriately enough, with war threatening in Europe. When his mother, Ethel, went into labor, his father, Leonard Brixton, an ex-con and wanted felon, dropped her off at the emergency room and, under the pretext of parking, skipped town. Not long after, Ethel, penniless and unemployed, was evicted from their apartment and moved south across the Harlem River for cheaper accommodations.

Harlem wasn't a bad place to raise a boy. Although most white people had moved out by the time Clayton Brixton was born, a cultural renaissance of music, art, and entertainment was taking place, and the district's transformation was in full swing.

Ethel, still a looker, found work right away at the Cotton Club, where she served cocktails and caught the attention of its owner, Owney Madden, the notorious Irish gangster. Madden, who'd fancied himself a ladies' man, was smitten with Ethel, and the two became inseparable. When he retired from racketeering, he begged her to come with him to Hot Springs, but she turned him down.

Instead, Ethel set her sights on Madden's successor, Eddie McGrath. McGrath, the leader of The Westies, controlled all criminal activity in Hell's Kitchen, including the waterfront. He bought the Cotton Club and, like his predecessor, fell for Ethel. He also took a liking to young Brixton, raising him as his son, and teaching him the trade.

While other boys went off to school to get worthless diplomas, Brixton got street smart. Under McGrath's tutelage, he learned the numbers game, and he had such a knack for it, he got his own bookmaking operation before he was a teenager. For his sixteenth birthday, McGrath gave him a prostitution ring, and then, later, his own territory, which he ruled ruthlessly. His crews hijacked trucks, dealt drugs, and shook down area business owners for protection money. Brixton drew two early stints in juvenile hall, and then a later one as a teenager, but he emerged harder and meaner each time.

Brixton committed his first murder when he was twenty, after he'd already done hard time. He'd wandered into a Bronx tavern near the river for a few drinks one bitterly cold, snowy evening between Christmas and New Year's. After sloughing off his overcoat and greeting friends and associates, he settled in at the bar and ordered a beer. Brixton looked around, tossed back some peanuts, and caught a glimpse through the mirror of a man sitting in the booth across the room behind him. The man looked vaguely familiar, and while Brixton couldn't place him, the guy made him uncomfortable. He shrugged it off and chatted up a few girls, but he couldn't shake the feeling. Brixton finally just stared straight at the mirror and watched the man over his shoulder, trying to remember. He was halfway through his second beer when it hit him, and it was the way the man kept scratching his face that did it. He was the heroin addict who'd mugged him a few years back.

Sitting at the bar, Brixton recalled how he'd doggedly pursued the most beautiful woman he'd ever seen. Her name was Carmen De Luca, and although he was smitten from the moment he saw her, she treated him frostily, making clear she wanted nothing to do with him. Brixton was confounded. He wasn't bad looking, at least from a distance, and he had plenty of money, which was all he'd ever needed before. What he didn't know was that Carmen's friends told her he was a mobster and a pimp, and that he kept a lot of girls on the side.

Brixton backed off when he found out, but sometimes when he was in a good mood, he'd flirt a little and teasingly tell her he'd be by that evening. Eventually, it became a joke they shared and occasionally, despite her best efforts, she'd smile. One day, though, she surprised them both by accepting his invitation, not to a night in, but to a night out.

It was a Saturday night. They'd gone for pizza and then taken in *The Miracle of the Bells* at the Paradise Theatre. While walking to the car, a junkie wielding a gun stepped out from a darkened entryway and robbed them, stealing his money and her jewelry. Although Brixton could've easily disarmed and pistol-whipped the punk, he let him get away, thinking Carmen would get angry if he responded with violence. Instead, she was furious that he didn't! Her necklace and earrings were family heirlooms, and now they were gone! Carmen cursed him, called him a coward, and got on a city bus bound somewhere he wasn't.

Brixton grabbed another handful of nuts and turned in his seat to get a better look. The man was still an addict by the looks of him. His pale white skin had a slight bluish tint and his cheeks, hollow and unshaven, gave him a tired, gaunt appearance. The man kept wiping his nose with his coat sleeve and fidgeting in his seat. His ghoulish eyes were wildly active, darting around as if he was in the grips of paranoia. Brixton recalled the man was short and wiry and that he'd held his gun in his left hand. He glanced in the mirror again. The man nibbled the skin at his fingers and tugged his thick, curly hair. He needed a fix, and he seemed to be looking for a mark the way he eyed people.

Feigning drunkenness, Brixton withdrew a wad of cash from his front pocket and clumsily slid off his stool, holding onto the bar for support. He stumbled toward the bathroom, fumbling the bills, and let a fifty slip through his fingers. The twitchy junkie quickly covered it with his boot and scooted it under his table. A few minutes later, Brixton returned, put on his coat and hat, and headed out the door and into the night.

Four inches of snow covered the ground, parked cars, and everything else that wasn't moving. Brixton trudged east on East 129th Street toward the less populated area near the Third Avenue Bridge. The tavern door banged open and closed. The crunch of snow beneath heavy boots followed. Brixton staggered, stopped, and groped his coat pockets, pretending to search for his cigarettes. He pulled one from the pack and let it drop in the snow.

He cursed and tapped out another. He lit it and, after inhaling, leaned back with his eyes closed and slowly blew the smoke skyward. Slurring the words to a song, Brixton toddled off toward the bridge, brushing against buildings and grabbing onto signposts for support while the junkie kept a cautious, watchful distance.

The alley was two blocks from the bridge and dead-ended at the river. Brixton kept up his drunken act until he turned the corner. Then he raced to the shadows of the fire escape and set his hat on the step nearest his height. He shrugged off his coat next, hanging it on the step below and set his cigarette on the collar. Brixton ducked beneath the fire escape just as the junkie appeared at the head of the alley, silhouetted against the glare of a solitary streetlamp. He caught the glint of a blade just before the man merged into the shadows. The junkie warily approached the cigarette's orange glow and the dark outline of the coat.

"Gimme your money, or I'll cut ya," he hissed, waving the knife back and forth.

"Cut me, motherfucker."

The junkie, moving surprisingly fast, swung the blade, expecting to slash Brixton's neck, but struck grated metal instead. He cried out in pain, but stopped mid-scream when the switchblade slid between his left fourth and fifth ribs, piercing cartilage and puncturing his heart. The man's mouth remained open, but his eyes widened as he twitched and convulsed. Brixton, clutching the front of the man's worn coat, held him upright on the blade, watching him die. The junkie collapsed to the ground. Brixton knelt beside him and casually cleaned his knife with snow. Then he plucked the fifty from the dead man's pocket, walked back to the tavern, and bought a round for the house. Everyone said he'd been there all night.

Brezina recognized Wren, Marlin, and Wolf would make formidable bank robbers, and he didn't have to tell them their jobs. Wren, the charmer, handled the tellers, while Wolf, who'd grown meaner with age, kept order. Marlin, of course, was the wheelman.

Initially, the three men worked well together, pulling a string of heists without any major hitches. Marlin felt Wolf unnecessarily bullied people, but he chalked it up to style, rationalizing that it was better to be overbearing than easygoing.

Half a dozen jobs later, though, Wolf went off on a teller who'd made an ill-advised wisecrack. After he was told to hurry up, the man, still in his early twenties, decided to show some sack and suggested they take their business elsewhere if they weren't happy with the service. Wolf, eyes narrowed, grabbed him by the windpipe, and savagely pistol-whipped him, leaving him bloody, unconscious, and barely breathing. The gang sat down for a long talk afterward.

"Look," Wren began, "bank robbery can be fun and rewarding."

"Get to the point!" Wolf interrupted.

"We don't need you drawing special attention."

"The FBI's not special, huh? Tell them."

Marlin cut in. "What Mr. Wren means is, yeah, sure, we're being chased by the FBI, but they investigate every bank robbery in the country, so we're no different than anyone else pulling jobs. They assign a couple of agents to chase us, no biggie. It's all expected. That's the game."

Wren picked back up. "Neither the bank nor its customers care about the money because it's insured by the government. They're not losing anything, see?"

"Why are you telling me this shit?" Wolf's dwindling patience was being replaced by growing hostility.

"Because everything changes once you start putting people in the hospital," Wren continued.

"Or morgue," Marlin added. The teller was on life support in a medically-induced coma.

"Suddenly it's about more than money," Wren said, jumping back in. "People get scared, and they start making noise. Well, guess what? Politicians don't like noise. It makes them look bad, and that hurts at the polls, so they put heat on the FBI to catch us."

"And that makes things hotter for us," Marlin added.

Wolf nodded without replying.

The very next job, a loan officer made the mistake of hitting the silent alarm beneath his desk. Wolf saw the man's nervousness and, suspicious, decided to investigate. When he found the alarm, he casually stepped back and shot him in the chest, toppling him over backward in his chair. DTK was born. Marlin was livid. He pounded the dashboard during their getaway.

"What the fuck were you thinking?!"

"What do you mean?" Wolf replied, baiting him.

"What do I mean? What the fuck do you think I mean?! We just got done talking about avoiding violence, and you turn around and murder someone! And you did it while committing a felony! Ever hear of the felony murder rule? That's the death penalty, you fucking dumbass!"

"Call me a fucking dumbass again, motherfucker," Wolf said from the back seat, cocking the hammer on his Colt.

"Knock it off!" Wren growled. "Focus! There's nothing we can do about it now. There's always a risk of things getting ugly, Mr. Marlin, you know that. It comes with the trade. The man hit the alarm. We're lucky Mr. Wolf noticed."

"That's right, you should be thanking me for being on top of shit. The cops would've been all over us."

"If you'd been on top of shit, he wouldn't have been able to hit the alarm! Either way, you didn't have to kill him, you fucking dumbass!"

Later, after they'd divvied up their take, Marlin appealed to Wren.

"Look, we need to cut ties to this guy. He's getting off on the violence."

"Do you know someone who can step in?"

"No, not offhand."

"That's what I thought, and I'm afraid I don't either."

"Let's take a break until we find someone then. Put the word out we're looking."

"It's not that simple," Wren replied. "Putting the word out means telling people who aren't exactly in my circle of trust. It'll also create problems we want to avoid."

"Like what?" Marlin said.

"There's going to be a big reward for us now. Suppose somebody drops a dime? And if not for the money, for reduced charges or a favorable sentence? Then there's Mr. Wolf to worry about. He's not going to like being booted out of our little club. It'd get pretty ugly pretty quick."

"We can kill him. I'll do it."

"Kill Mr. Wolf? Okay, let's mull that over, too. We'd still have to find someone else, right? Who'd want to join us knowing we murdered our last partner? Not saying you'd spill the beans, Mr. Marlin, but things like this have a way of getting around. Take Brezina, for instance. He'll want to know what happened, so we'd have to be straight with whoever he sends to get answers. That means at least two people will know we murdered Mr. Wolf, and we're still on the hook for the employee. You trust Brezina? I don't. He wants out of prison. He'd trade us in a heartbeat. No, we stay together until we disband."

"Then the violence stops, or I'm gone."

"I'll talk to him again, but I can't promise you anything."

"You don't have to promise anything. Wolf does."

DTK pulled a dozen bank jobs without incident, although there was a tense moment when a guard went for Wolf's revolver. Wren excitedly described what happened during the getaway.

"Mr. Wolf had that big, shiny Colt against the guard's forehead before I could blink. You could tell he wanted to blow the guy away, but the look on his face changed, and he released the hammer."

"Wow!" Marlin said in mock amazement while looking at Wolf in the rearview mirror. "You didn't murder someone. Are you happy or sad?"

"I've got mixed emotions."

"C'mon, Mr. Marlin," Wren said, laughing heartily, "he's making progress."

"Oh, of course, he is," Marlin said, catching Wolf's eye in the rearview mirror. "That's a big step, not murdering someone. A little early to call it a trend though, isn't it?"

DTK pulled several more jobs. Wolf didn't kill anyone, but he continued to brutalize employees and customers. Marlin only found out later on the news. Wolf just laughed and said they were exaggerating to sell newspapers or boost ratings while Wren, reluctant to spoil a good thing, shrugged unknowingly. But then Teymore, and, amazingly, Wren went to bat for Wolf again.

"He didn't have a choice, did he?"

"You always have a choice!"

"So, you would've let the guy run out the bank and yell for the cops?"

"No, I would've shot him in the leg," Marlin said, staring at Wolf through the rearview mirror.

Sticking mostly to country roads, the gang headed south, stopping in Belton where Wren directed Marlin to a strip mall parking lot. They ditched the station wagon for a blue 1968 Oldsmobile 98 with Wisconsin plates and got back on the road. Marlin took I-69 south and kept the gas-guzzling Olds near the speed limit.

"Take this exit," Wolf said as the gang approached Noblesville. Marlin wordlessly steered the car onto the ramp.

"Which way?" They were approaching the stop sign.

"Take a right. There's a Carnegie Library a few blocks down just off Tenth Street. You can let me out there."

"I never took you for a bookworm," Wren said.

"There's a lot of things you don't know about me." Marlin pulled to the curb in front of the small, two-story brick building. Wolf got out without another word and stood beneath the arched entranceway until the Fury turned the corner. Then he went inside and out the back door to his car.

Marlin got on I-465 and dropped off Wren at the Holiday Inn by the airport. Then he headed across town to Broad Ripple to eat and have a few drinks.

Wren dropped his bag on the bed. His plan was simple. Eat,

watch television, and steal a car. He settled in with two extra-large supreme pizzas, a dozen breadsticks, and a basket of onion rings from a nearby pizza parlor. He ate and watched television until the eleven o'clock news came on. Then he rolled out of bed and dressed.

The lighting in the lounge was dim. There weren't many people, maybe a half dozen. Wren chose a corner booth where he could see the parking lot. He ordered a Falstaff, two double cheeseburgers, and French fries from the kitchen.

She showed up within fifteen minutes. Her name was Karen, and she was built like a fireplug. After parking her 1969 ice blue Plymouth Fury, she got out and walked unsteadily across the parking lot on white, knee-high, faux leather boots. Hiking her red miniskirt, she climbed on a stool at the horseshoe-shaped bar. The bartender, addressing her by name, set a double gin and tonic in front of her.

Wren continued eating, allowing Karen enough time to settle in. Then he rose, beer in hand, and took a seat opposite her at the bar. He couldn't peg her age, somewhere between thirty and fifty, he guessed, but it didn't matter; she was a mess either side of forty. Her makeup, which looked to have been applied with a cement trowel, couldn't hide the garden of gin blossoms on her cheeks and nose any better than it could fill the gaps between the thousands of tight, tiny wrinkles around her red lip-sticked lips. Wren wasn't sure if it was Karen, or, possibly just her eyes, that lacked focus, but he could see the latter were bloodshot. She also smelled of cigarettes, and her gravelly voice and wet cough confirmed tobacco as her other crutch.

Wren ordered another Falstaff and returned to his booth. Karen lit a cigarette and turned, squinting at the room, looking for someone to buy her drinks. She eventually got the attention of an officious office manager with overcooked skin who was in town for the race. The unnervingly short, tubby man had salt-and-pepper hair and a matching bristle broom mustache. Wren saw him walk into the lounge from the hotel and nearly laughed at the way he self-importantly swung his arms back and forth like a pocket-sized Prussian general. If Karen noticed the band of goose-white flesh on his left ring finger, she didn't care.

For the next hour, the pair cozied up in the booth across from Wren, drinking, exchanging slobbery kisses, and pawing at each other like animals. They eventually opted for his room, so, rising unsteadily and leaning on each other for support, they staggered out of the lounge, soaked in alcohol and spit. Wren, who'd kept a discreet distance, walked by and hung a "Do Not Disturb" sign on the door handle.

Morning came too quickly, but after several sleepy taps on the snooze button, Wren finally surrendered to the oncoming day. Groping blindly in the dark, he fumbled for the telephone and mumbled his breakfast order. Then he rolled out of bed, steadied himself with one hand against the wall, and, following the room's contours, felt his way to the bathroom. There, Wren turned his head away from the door and eyes shut, reached inside and fumbled for the light switch. After flipping it on, he inched the door open, gradually letting his eyes adjust to the blindingly bright light from the bank of oversized bare bulbs above the mirror. Wren reached up and unscrewed all but one of them. He may have given in to the day, but he was its uncooperative prisoner.

Wren washed at the sink as best he could; he hadn't been able to bathe or shower in a bathtub since he was seven. Room service left four trays of food in the hallway. Naked but nimble and fat thighs chaffing, he tiptoed to the door and returned with them, one atop another. Then he climbed back beneath the covers, arranged himself comfortably against a mountain of snow white feather pillows, and dug in.

After a solid hour of fast-paced hand-to-mouth action, Wren sighed contentedly and set the last tray of plates and dishes on the bed. He laid back to allow his digestive system to kick in. After expelling obnoxious gases both north and south, he wiped down the room and dressed in the bathroom light. Then he grabbed his bag and, armed with a wire coat hanger, headed to the parking lot.

It didn't take ten seconds to unlock the Fury's door, and Wren had the motor hot-wired half a minute later. After a short test drive, he headed to a gas station, where he tipped the attendant to fill it up, top off the oil, check the radiator, and air up the tires. By seven o'clock, Wren was at Shapiro's enjoying his second breakfast.

Chapter 15

Saturday, May 30, 1970

Wolf tossed Marlin's hat across the table. It landed on a chair just as Marlin returned, coffee cup in hand.

"Mr. Wolf," he said, not as a greeting, but as an undeniable fact. He plucked his hat off the seat, smiling at Wolf's hostility, and sat in the chair. Eyeing his partner over the top of his mug, he leaned back, stretched his legs, and crossed his feet at his ankles.

Wolf removed a piece of lint from his freshly-creased black trousers and flicked it on the floor. Then he rubbed his rough hands together. "Looks like the gang's all here...finally," Wolf said.

"Yes, so happy you could join us," Marlin said with mock sincerity. "Thanks for squeezing us in."

"I see you two kissed and made up already," Wren said, chuckling. He wiped his mouth with his napkin and scooted his chair away from the table before plodding off to the bathroom with the sports page. He left no table scraps, and he was gone an awfully long time.

Wolf smoked and stared down people. Marlin sipped coffee and worked on the crossword puzzle. He'd completed it and was reading his horoscope when Wren returned.

"Shall we go over the game plan, gentlemen?"

"Two jobs in the same week and back-to-back at that," Wolf mused.

"This is the big one."

"How much?"

"A few hundred, maybe more."

"Whoa! That's retirement money." Wolf lit another cigarette, tilted his head back, and blew smoke at the ceiling.

"Where's the bank," Marlin finally spoke, "what's the route, and where're we headed?"

"Last question first—we're going to Louisville. I've got a place set up down there. The bank's on the near east side, over on New York Street, just off College. It's in a residential area. The highway's close: three long blocks east and two longer blocks north. It's all one way and four lanes wide. The entrance ramp starts out two lanes but quickly narrows to one. After a quarter mile, the road splits into I-65 north and I-70 east."

"Last time I checked, Louisville's south," Marlin said.

"Still is," Wren said, smiling. "Here's what we're doing. At the north split, we'll take I-70 east for about a mile, jump off at the Keystone exit, and then hop back on going west. When we get back to the split, we'll get on 65 south."

"Textbook getaway then?" Wolf said.

"The highway's elevated, so no one will see us go by, and, if we do it right and have a bit of luck, the cops won't figure it out until we're long gone."

"Luck, huh? Sounds fucked up to me."

"Appreciate your honesty," Wren said dryly. He turned to Marlin. "Make sure we're seen getting on the ramp. Don't do anything crazy like crash or run over somebody. Just drive fast, cut across a few lanes, that sort of thing. Then get on the highway and blend in. When the cops tie it to the bank, everyone will say we headed toward the north split."

"Go on," Marlin said.

"It's going to buy us time. The cops will focus their efforts north and east, but long before that, we'll have double-backed and headed south."

"It might work," Marlin said. "No one will expect it."

"All my plans work when executed properly."

"I still don't like it," Wolf said, "but whatever. I want out in Greenwood." He took a long pull on his cigarette.

"Why?" Marlin jumped in. He slid an ashtray toward him.

"Why do you want to know?"

"Because I'm driving, that's why, and unless you want to roll out at eighty miles an hour, you'll tell me."

"I've got to go to New York," Wolf said, staring at Marlin, annoyed. He exhaled bluish smoke and flicked his ash on the floor. He turned to Wren, cigarette between his lips. "My mother's in the hospital, so I'm flying out this afternoon." Wren shrugged and turned to Marlin, who shrugged back.

"What's traffic like around the bank?" Marlin asked.

"New York and College are both heavy during the week, but less so on weekends. Plus, it's race day, so everyone's at the track. Cops, too."

"What am I driving?"

"A '69 Plymouth Fury, four-door, of course, courtesy of one of Indy's more desperate gin queens."

"What about security?" Wolf asked.

"Light, very light. Just a senior citizen making a little on the side to supplement his retirement. I doubt he'll try to save the day. There's a security camera, though. Make sure you grab the tape."

"Is the old fart armed?" Wolf asked.

"He carries a thirty-eight on his hip, but he sets up on the left as you're walking in, so it'll be exposed."

"Think you can handle a retiree without killing him?" Marlin asked.

"I'll decide once I'm inside. Just be curbside when we come out."

Chapter 16

Saturday, May 30, 1970

We stopped for breakfast at a Howard Johnson's just north of I-465. Mrs. Wantel asked for a booth, and Darlene nudged Kent sideways and squeezed in beside me. We settled back with the menus after the waitress brought us water and then gave our orders when she returned.

"So, Tyler," Mrs. Wantel said, "you seem to be on a losing streak."

"I'll say."

"Yeah, man," Kent said, "what happened to your face?!" He scrunched-up the paper wrapper on his straw and slid it off.

"Well, uh, I fell down a hill and—"

"A hill?! More like a mountain from the looks of you. What'd you land on, a pile of razor blades?" He dipped his straw in his glass and withdrew it with his thumb over the top.

"No, thorns."

"Thorns! Dude, you're an accident looking for a place to happen." Kent dripped water on the paper, and the worm came to life, wriggling and growing before dying a soggy death mere seconds later. Paper worms have short lives, but, as a species, they're inextirpable.

"Tell me."

"What else have you been doing?" Mrs. Wantel said.

"Uh . . ." I smelled a trap and reached for my glass.

"Mom, please," Darlene said.

"I'm just making conversation, dear."

"I got home late, and my mom's boyfriend got on me good, so I left. Everything else happened after that." All true.

"Oh, my, and your grandmother's ill, too? I hope it's not serious."

"Mom!"

"Mom didn't say." Another true statement.

My interrogation was interrupted when the waitress arrived with our food. I kept my mouth busy after that, stuffing it with a mushroom, sausage, and cheese omelet, hash browns, two strips of bacon, and a short stack of blueberry pancakes smothered in maple syrup. I washed it all down with a large glass of orange juice. When I finished, I looked up. The Wantels were staring at me open-mouthed. I burped.

"Oops, excuse me," I said, embarrassed.

"Do you want my scraps?" Kent asked.

"I know, I ate like a pig. I'm sorry."

"That's all right, dear, eat while you can," Mrs. Wantel said. "I've only made two sandwiches each for you kids."

"You can have mine," Darlene said, "and there's always the concession stand." Everyone laughed at my gluttony. I snapped up the bill when the waitress returned.

"Breakfast is on me." I could afford it.

"C'mon now," Mrs. Wantel said, "I can't have you buying breakfast."

"It's okay, really. My food probably cost more than all three of yours combined. Besides, I want to show my appreciation for taking me to the race."

"Well, okay, if you put it that way, I guess it's all right. Let me get the tip, though."

Chapter 17

Saturday, May 30, 1970

At half past eight o'clock, Wendell Dertson, the balding, bespectacled branch manager of Citizens National Trust, crossed the red- and gold-flecked, black marble floor to the bank's double doors. Dertson, a frail, timid man with bookworm charm, greeted his aging security guard with a wide smile.

"Good morning, Mr. Prand."

"Good morning to you, Mr. Dertson." Merle Prand had just turned seventy-five, but he was tan and fit. Even with white hair, he looked twenty years younger. Prand taught physical education and coached high school tennis for thirty-five years.

"Oh, indeed it is, Mr. Prand," Dertson said, turning the latch on the deadbolt. "We're supposed to get some rain yet this morning, which will do the flowers out front some good." He was halfway to his office when Wren, wearing shades and his black fedora pulled low, pushed through the doors sideways.

"Good morning, sir," Prand said brightly. Wren passed by wordlessly, looking for the tellers. The guard's smile vanished. The branch couldn't compete with the larger banks downtown for the big commercial accounts, so it portrayed itself as "Your Friendly Neighborhood Bank" and focused its attention on serving the needs of individual customers. Prand, who considered himself an integral part of this marketing strategy, was friendly and greeted almost everyone by name. He wasn't accustomed to rudeness.

Wren, rolls of fat moving in all directions, reached into his suit jacket for his snub-nosed .357 Magnum as he approached the tellers. Behind him, Wolf saw the guard go for his .38 but beat him to it.

"Easy there, Quickdraw," he said, sliding the gun from Prand's holster. He jammed the barrel of his Colt against the aging guard's ribs and tucked the .38 in his front waistband. Then he reached back and threw the deadbolt. Wolf grabbed Prand by the windpipe and bull-rushed him. Prand, wide-eyed, backpedaled, struggling to keep his balance. His head smacked the limestone wall, and he slumped to the floor, unconscious. Wolf cuffed his wrist to the radiator. Dertson stood stock still staring open-mouthed.

"That's right, stay put, Mr. Bank Manager," Wolf said, training his .45 on him. "I want the surveillance tape."

Meanwhile, Wren had pushed open the swinging gate with his hip and lumbered straight to the tellers' stations. He smiled at the three women there.

"What's your name, miss?" he asked the nearest one, a short, thin woman, no more than twenty, with light brown eyes and caramel skin.

"Erica." She was staring at the gun.

"And who're these lovely ladies you're working with today?"

"That's Brenda," Erica said, nodding her head in the direction of an obviously pregnant woman in her mid-twenties. Brenda stood with her legs wide apart for balance. Her green eyes welled with tears and she held her hands protectively over her stomach.

"Your first?" Wren inquired.

"No, I have a daughter at home."

"I meant bank robbery." Wren chuckled, hoping to alleviate the tension. He didn't. He shrugged. He enjoyed his work, but he couldn't help it if others didn't. Wren turned to the third woman. "Who have we here?" he said with a smile.

"This is Tammy," Erica said, indicating the morbidly obese woman in the floor-length, floral-patterned muumuu. "She's in training."

"Perfect!" Wren said, genuinely thrilled. "Let's show Tammy what to do during a bank robbery!" Addressing Tammy, he continued, "Basically, just do as you're told, and when it's your turn, grab the bills—twenties and up—from your drawer and put them in this black bag. No coins, just bills, and don't touch your alarm, dye packs, or tracers. Pretty simple, isn't it?"

"Y-y-yes," Tammy said.

"Then let's get to it," Wren said.

The three women bumped into one another getting to their stations. Erica scooped the bills from her tray and dropped them in the bag.

"Perfect again! Your turn, Brenda." Brenda, tears streaming down her cheeks, grabbed her entire drawer and flung its contents, change and all, at the bag. Coins bounced off Wren and rattled on the marble floor. Bills fluttered in the air like flyers.

"Brenda," Wren said pleasantly, "you didn't pay attention during training."

"I'm sorry, sir. Please don't kill me."

Wren softly sighed. "I'm not going to kill anyone," he said, "but please do as I say from now on."

"Y-y-yes, sir."

"Okay, Tammy, your turn, show Brenda how it's done." Instead, Tammy shook like jelly, too frightened for any other type of movement. "Tammy!" Wren repeated, louder. He rolled his eyes. "Erica, would you help me, please?"

"TAMMY!" Erica yelled. She gripped the woman by the shoulders and gave her a good shake. Tammy dropped to her knees in tears. Erica shrugged.

"Brenda," Wren said, somewhat amused, "you get another chance. This time, twenties and up and, hey?"

"Y-y-yes sir?"

"Keep the change." He chuckled again. He liked his job.

Wolf trailed Dertson down a long, narrow hallway toward the rear of the bank, prodding him along with his Colt. They passed the bathrooms and the water cooler separating them before stopping in front of a door marked "Private."

"T t this is it," Dertson said.

Wolf turned the doorknob. It was locked. He closed his eyes. "What's your name?"

"Dertson . . . Wendell Dertson."

"Well, Dertson Wendell Dertson, you listen, and you listen good. We're robbing your fucking bank. Do you understand?"

"Y-y-yes, sir, I s-sure do."

"We need to be in and out in three minutes. Do you know why?"

"So you d-don't get c-c-caught?"

"Correct! That means I do not have time to fuck around!"

"S-s-sir?"

"UNLOCK THE GODDAMN DOOR!"

"Oh, s-s-sorry, sir, I forgot. I-i-it's just I f-f-freeze up when I g-g-g-get nervous."

"You better thaw out quick if you want to survive the day."

Dertson fumbled the keys, glanced nervously for Wolf's reaction, and then tried one key and then two more before fitting the right one in the slot. He turned the lock.

"Th-th-there you go, sir."

"No fucking shit." Wolf pressed the toe of his shoe against the door and turned the knob, popping it open. The room was dark, illuminated only by the hallway's fluorescent light. He shoved Dertson inside, sending him sprawling to the floor. Wolf flicked on the overhead light, revealing a storage room. On the left, just inside the door, stood a conference table. Atop it sat envelopes, a postage meter, and a plastic tub for outgoing mail. Two gray storage cabinets, one containing office supplies and the other filled with various forms and applications, were against the opposite wall. The center of the room was occupied by two rows of ugly, green filing cabinets, placed end to end and filled with bank records. Extra desks and chairs were stacked in the corner.

"Get up and get me the tape! Hurry up!"

Dertson scrambled to his feet and scampered to a small desk. He ejected the tape.

"H-h-here it is, sir," he said, handing it to Wolf.

"Very good, Dertson Wendell Dertson. Now turn off the recorder, and let's head to the vault. You might make it through the day after all."

Dertson turned back to the table and pushed the power button on the machine. When he turned around, he was staring at the business end of the Colt. He spent his last moment alive in horror before Wolf shot him in the forehead.

"But then again, maybe not."

Brenda had just put the bills from Tammy's drawer in the laundry bag when the gunshot echoed throughout the bank.

"Oh, my God!" she cried. "What was that?" Tammy, still on the floor, wailing, wailed louder.

"I want you in the vault," Wren said. "Let's go." His lips were a grim line.

"Is that where you're going to kill us?" Erica said.

"Look, I said I won't kill anyone, but goddamn it, I'll shoot all three of you where you stand if you don't do what I say! NOW MOVE!"

Erica clenched her jaw and turned away angrily. She stalked to the vault. Brenda nervously eyed Wren while kneeling beside Tammy.

"C'mon, Tammy," she said, helping the fat woman roll to her feet. Brenda put her arm around Tammy's shoulders, and together they waddled to the vault.

Red specks of blood dotted Wolf's face and starched white shirt. He rounded the corner, heels booming on the marble floor, just as Wren and the tellers entered the vault.

"Get the tape?"

"Right here," Wolf replied, patting the inside pocket of his suit jacket.

"How're we doing on time?"

Wolf checked his watch. "Minute-fifteen, we're good."

"All right, ladies," Wren said, "grab those bricks off the cart behind you. Again, larger bills only—twenties, fifties, and hundreds. Hurry, please!"

The three women went to work, grabbing stacks of cash encased in heavy plastic and dropping them in the bags. Tammy, spooked by the gunshot, moved noticeably slower than her co-workers, primarily because she kept throwing cautious looks at Wolf.

"You better quit eye-fucking me and focus on what you're doing, or I'll show you how this thing works." That had the opposite effect. Tammy bumped the cart and a stack of bills fell to the floor. Wolf started for her, but Wren placed his enormous bulk between them.

"Okay, time's up," he said, not knowing one way or the other, but trying to avoid further bloodshed.

The three women froze, their eyes shifting from Wren to Wolf and back again.

"Please don't kill us," Brenda begged, tears falling from her eyes. "I'm going to have a baby."

"I'm not going to do anything except leave," Wren replied.

"What about him?" Erica asked, nodding in Wolf's direction.

"What about me?" Wolf said menacingly.

"You killed Mr. Dertson, didn't you?"

"He tried to grab my gun."

"Mr. Dertson would never do that. He's afraid of his own shadow."

"Are you calling me a liar?" Wolf raised his .45.

"NO!" Wren shouted, grabbing Wolf's arm on the upswing and forcing it down. The gunshot reverberated inside the vault. The bullet ricocheted off the floor, knocking loose a half-dollar-size piece of marble before caroming off the wall and striking Brenda in the neck. She collapsed, blood spurting in time with her fading heartbeat.

Tammy, screaming, took off, wobbling faster than anyone could imagine. She crashed through the swinging gate and was halfway to the double doors when Wolf shot her in the back. She fell forward, landed hard and rolled onto her side, arms and legs askew.

"Please don't kill me." Erica had her arms extended, palms outward. She backpedaled, tripped over Brenda's body, and nearly fell. "Please," she begged.

Wolf, smiling, raised his gun and shot her in the chest, sending her crashing backward over the steel cart.

"You're sick," Wren said, thoroughly disgusted. He slung his swollen, black bag over his shoulder and headed out.

Chapter 18

Saturday, May 30, 1970

The sunlight streaming through the quivering leaves dappled the street corner. Marlin nervously drummed his fingertips on the Fury's steering wheel, feeling the low rumble of the 7.2-liter V-8 motor run through him. He revved it, testing it for the hundredth time. It growled like the previous ninety-nine.

Marlin hated the three-minute wait. It was the only time he lacked control over his fate, and it made him edgy. If things went wrong—someone hit the alarm, or a guard got the drop on his partners—he wouldn't know until the cops showed up or the gun battle spilled onto the street.

"Shit." Marlin touched the .45 holstered beneath his armpit reassuringly and glanced at his watch. *Two more minutes.* He leaned across the seat and cracked open the front and rear passenger doors.

"Hurry up," he whispered impatiently. Traffic eastbound on New York was busier than what Wren said it would be. Marlin glanced through his outside mirror, finding College clear. *100 seconds. C'mon, damn it, c'mon!*

Marlin dropped the gear shift into drive and idled to the corner. He tapped the brakes and turned east onto New York before braking curbside in front of the bank. He peered through the double doors. It was dark except for the first dozen feet of the lobby. He thought he heard a car backfire.

The last minute was the worst. If something went wrong, it usually happened in the final sixty seconds. Marlin gripped and regripped the steering wheel. He checked for traffic behind him. Nothing. Just some funny-looking kid crossing the street. He looked at the bank, squinting, trying to see what was going on. There was another backfire, and then he saw a woman running toward the door. Then the sound again and she was falling. Then another shot.

We got back on the road. Fattened to fatigue, I promptly fell asleep with my head on Darlene's shoulder and didn't wake up until Kent started fiddling with the radio station, trying to find a channel covering the pre-race festivities. We were in downtown Indianapolis.

Mrs. Wantel steered her 442 down the ramp, which became Ohio Street at the light. She made a quick right onto College Avenue.

"We're close. The bank's up ahead on New York."

"I see the street sign," Kent said a couple blocks later.

"Tyler, I'm going to let you out on College since 16th Street's north of here, okay?"

"Sure, no problem."

"We're still ahead of schedule, but try not to be too long." Mrs. Wantel caught the light at New York and pulled to the curb.

"I'll be right back." I gingerly climbed out of the car. Every muscle ached.

"See if they have any candy," Kent said, rolling down his window.

I let a box truck pass and limped across New York, cutting behind a blue car idling curbside in front of the bank. As I neared the front doors, I heard a muffled sound like someone stomping on a paper cup. The guy in the car heard it, too. We locked eyes, and I shrugged.

Wren crashed through the doors, absorbing the impact with the mountainous flesh of his back and shoulder. He swung the Magnum in a wide arc, but there was only some funny-looking kid by the walkway. He lowered his gun, came down the steps, and ambled toward the Fury with the overstuffed black bag slung over his shoulder.

Wolf emerged two beats later, catching one door with his foot and then shouldering both of them open. Breathing heavily, he reached down, lost his hat, and looped the thick, white cord around his hand a couple of times. Then, leveraging his weight, he dragged his swollen black bag across the threshold and down the steps.

Ahead, Wren effortlessly swung his sack of cash onto the rear seat and pushed it to the floorboard behind Marlin. Wolf, meanwhile, was trying to lift his bag. He grabbed it with both hands, but it was too bulky and he fumbled his grip.

"Fucking goddamn son of a bitch!" he yelled. Wren, who'd seen Wolf struggling, hurried back. He snatched the bag one handed and carried it to the car while Wolf, who'd retrieved his hat and put it on, stared wide-eyed with surprise.

Suddenly, the bank doors burst open, and an incredibly overweight man in a funeral black suit came barreling out with an enormous black bag slung over his shoulder. He wheeled around and trained a bazooka on me. I froze, half in surprise, half in fright, and raised my hands. He turned away and lowered it. Then he carefully descended the steps and toddled toward the car parked at the curb. I heard a loud commotion behind me, and I turned to see a second man, similarly dressed, but hatless, pulling an even bigger bag across the vestibule. The man had his back to me, but he seemed vaguely familiar. He stooped to lift the bag, but dropped it, and spat a string of obscenities. A chill ran down my spine. *Frank!*

"Pussypoon! What the hell are you doing here?!"

"Um, banking?" I said.

"Banking?!" Frank spied the bulge in my pocket. He jammed his hand inside and pulled out the thick wad of cash. "With my fucking money!"

"We don't have time for socializing, Mr. Wolf!" Wren yelled. He threw the bag on the seat behind Marlin.

"I knew you stole my wallet!" Frank spread the bills in his hands like a fan and slapped me back and forth in the face with them. I tried to fend him off, but he grabbed me by the throat and hammered my eye socket with the butt of his revolver, turning it into pea gravel.

"Arrrrghk!" I grabbed my eye and spun around but lost my balance and fell. Before I could scoot away, Frank grabbed my hair, jerked me to my feet, and slung me toward the car. I landed face first on the sidewalk, skinning my forehead, nose, and chin. Then he was on me again.

"Get in the fucking car, you little thief!" Frank kicked me in the ribs, oblivious to the irony. I curled into a ball. "Hurry up!" He drew back to kick me again, but I rolled away. Hunched over and clutching my side, I struggled to my feet. Shallow breaths felt like stab wounds. Blood dripped from my eye and ran down my face. I climbed onto the back seat, entering a new phase of hurt.

"What're you doing, Mr. Wolf?" Wren was standing by the front passenger door with his palms up.

"His name's Frank Beetz, not Wolf," I said, looking through my bloody fingers at the sweaty fat man. Frank jumped in the back, red-faced and seething, and punched my other eye.

"Shut the hell up!"

"Owwww! Quit hitting me!"

"You're not satisfied with murder, you want to start kidnapping kids, too?" Marlin spoke for the first time.

Wren angrily kicked the rear door shut, leaving a dent below the handle. Then he forced his considerable bulk onto the passenger seat. The car sagged under his weight and the corner of the door dug deep into the dirt bordering the curb. Wren pulled on the handle with both hands, but the door wouldn't budge.

"Go! Go! Go!" he yelled.

Marlin checked his mirror and mashed the accelerator, nearly putting his foot through the firewall. The Fury, tires screeching, found grip and shot forward, dislodging the door. Wren slammed it shut as the car rocketed east on New York.

"Everybody down!" Marlin shouted.

Wren scrunched down in his seat as far as he could, which wasn't much. Frank jammed my head against the seat and pinned it there with his elbow. The Fury covered the block to Spring Street in seconds, reaching seventy miles an hour before hitting the raised surface of the cross street and going airborne. Wren, his size eighteen shoes planted firmly on the floorboard, braced himself when he saw the Plymouth about to leave the road. Those of us in the back had no warning. The big sedan sailed through the intersection and landed heavily on the asphalt, bottoming out in an angry screech of metal and a bright spray of sparks. We banged our heads on the roof and landed on the seat in a tangle of arms and legs.

"Ow! Shit!" Frank yelled.

"Sorry, kid." Marlin punched the gas pedal, throwing us back in our seats.

Traffic picked up considerably as we approached the freeway overpass, but Marlin weaved the Fury past cars and trucks with practiced ease. He jumped into the far left lane and zoomed past one pack of cars but caught another wave within seconds. Boxed in, Marlin impatiently rode the bumper of a pickup until he suddenly jerked the car into the right lane, cutting off a Cadillac. White-knuckling the steering wheel, he got back on the gas, surged past the truck, and muscled the Fury into the small gap ahead. Brakes screeched, horns blared, and drivers swore, all of it loudly, but Marlin was too focused on the road to hear. He punched the accelerator and cut across two lanes, grabbing a gap in traffic and blowing by cars in a blur of colors.

Coming up on Fulton Street, Marlin swerved left to avoid a city bus. He stayed on the gas, though, and the car shot through the intersection, gobbling up pavement. With the needle pegged at eighty, the Fury covered the two blocks to Davidson Street in no time, rocketing along as if ignited.

Marlin had the right of way at the intersection, but that hardly mattered to the pimply-faced sixteen-year-old waiting at the stop sign in his dad's stoat white Camaro RS/SS, one of the eighty or so C-1 coded convertibles Chevrolet specially built to pace the 1967 Indianapolis 500. Spying the Fury speeding toward him, the kid floored it and spun the steering wheel, squealing the tires, fish-tailing onto New York, and leaving a dark cloud of exhaust and dual streaks of black rubber in his wake.

"Shit for brains," Marlin muttered, marveling at the number of idiots who managed to acquire a driver's license. He flipped the steering wheel to the left, tossing me against Frank, who tossed me back. We blew by the Camaro.

"What's wrong?" Frank asked, He was half on the seat, half on the floorboard.

"Nothing. Don't worry about it." Marlin guided the Fury into the center lane as we passed under the viaduct.

With Pine Street just ahead, Marlin drifted right, setting up for the left turn onto the half-mile straight north. Suddenly, the Camaro flooded his rearview mirror and, in the next moment, swung to the right and pulled alongside him. Smirking, the teenager shot past the Fury. Marlin tapped his brakes as he approached the lefthander and glanced at the Camaro, certain the kid would keep going east on New York.

Except he didn't. The kid chopped left across the Fury's front, leaving Marlin nowhere to go. He tagged the Camaro's left rear quarter panel, sending it spinning toward the curb. The kid wrestled the steering wheel like an octopus, and finally got the Chevy straightened out, bringing it to a skidding stop in a cloud of smoke, rubber, and grit.

The kid should have cut his losses at that point, or at least that's what the cop told the tow truck driver. Instead, he jumped on the gas in dogged pursuit of the Fury. He was thirty yards back, but with the big block Chevy unleashed, he closed fast, and by Vermont Street, he had the front bumper sucked up tight against the Fury's rear. The kid bumped the Fury twice and drifted left as if to pass, but quickly flicked the steering wheel back right and floored it.

Marlin had seen the move a thousand times on racetracks. He hit the brakes, leaving the kid no time to react. The Camaro's left fender crumpled against the Fury's right rear bumper and, amid crunching metal and tinkling glass, shredded the tire in a thick cloud of black, acrid smoke. Marlin kept the Fury a quarter car length ahead, so the two cars were rubbing panels and rode the Camaro closer and closer toward the row of cars parked curbside.

Trapped, the kid racked the steering wheel hard left, fighting for space, but Marlin pinned the Camaro against the cars and kept it there. The kid strangled the steering wheel. Beads of sweat dotted his forehead and the shrieking sound of metal shredding metal filled his ears. He was in over his head and had only just realized it.

Marlin, lips tight against gritted teeth, kept his eyes straight ahead, looking for the knockout punch. He found it just up the block—an old, rusted Dodge pickup with its rear jutting out into traffic. Marlin timed it perfectly, tapping the brakes and veering left just before the Camaro's right front fender smashed into the truck's left rear in a deafening explosion of buckling steel and breaking glass. The force of the impact lifted the Camaro's tail off the ground and slung it around to the front.

The kid whipped the steering wheel left and right to no benefit. The rear end of his car slammed into a blue Rambler and then rolled over the hood of a gold Torino before coming to a rest upside down on the sidewalk. The emergency room doctor told his parents he was lucky he'd suffered only a few broken bones.

"His day ain't over yet," his dad said.

Marlin checked the carnage behind him through the rearview mirror and snorted derisively. He ran the light at Michigan Street and shot up the entrance ramp and onto the freeway toward the north split.

Frank and I had been tossed around in the back like bingo balls. We untangled our arms and legs and scrunched down on the floorboard with our heads and chests on the seat. Nobody spoke; the tension was thicker than gutter mud. Marlin, lips pursed angrily, forced himself to slow the Fury to highway speed.

Marlin stayed in the right lane all the way to Keystone to hide the body damage. We passed under the overpass, caught the light, and got on the ramp for westbound I-70 and downtown Indianapolis. Moments later, an IPD car, a white Pontiac Enforcer, blew by with its lights on. It disappeared over the rise and veered off toward I-65 north. Within a minute, another IPD car, this one a blue Dodge Coronet, flew past on the other side of the highway, heading east, with just its lights flashing, too. Marlin gripped the steering wheel a little tighter and kept pace with the flow of traffic. At the north split, he steered onto I-65 south toward Louisville.

"That's a little more attention than I intended," Wren said.

"What's keeping Tyler? We're going to be late." Mrs. Wantel tapped her index finger on the steering wheel. She glanced at the intersection of College and New York through the mirror. They'd been waiting twenty minutes.

"Maybe there's a lot of customers," Darlene offered.

"This early on a holiday?"

"I'll go see what's going on," Kent volunteered, getting out the car.

"Thanks, Kent, you know how your dad gets on race day."

"We go through this every year," Darlene said.

"I know," Mrs. Wantel said, plainly annoyed.

"I'll be right back." Kent said through the open window. He looked right for traffic, crossed New York, and headed for the bank.

When he was out of view, Mrs. Wantel turned in her seat. "What's going on between you and Tyler?"

"What do you mean?"

"You know what I mean. You both climbed in the back seat and then you shoved Kent out of the way at Howard Johnson's, so you could sit beside him."

"Kent called shotgun, and I like sitting in the middle," Darlene said unconvincingly while twisting a strand of hair around her index finger.

"Sure, you do. You two were alone in the basement all night, too, and don't think I don't know what went on."

"You don't miss much, do you?"

"Don't forget, I was a teenager once."

"I like him, and he likes me. That's about it."

"So, he's your boyfriend?"

"Yeah, I guess so."

"You guess so?"

"Okay, yes, he's my boyfriend."

"And the story Kent told me about his grandmother?"

"I made it up."

"That's what I thought. Are you and Tyler . . . uh . . . having . . . uh . . . ?"

"It's not what you think, Mom," Darlene deflected. "He needed a place to stay. The part about his mom's boyfriend is true."

"You should've told me. I would've let him spend the night, but I can't have you lying to me. Do you understand?"

"I know, but I couldn't take the chance you'd say no."

"Too bad, you're grounded. One week. Now, since you have a boyfriend, I guess we need to talk about some things."

"What kind of things?"

"Well, things that happen between boys and girls."

"You mean sex?"

"That's exactly what I mean."

"It's okay, I already know everything."

"Oh, you do, do you? Just what do you know?"

"Where the parts fit, how pregnancies occur, that sort of thing."

"And just where did you learn all of that?"

"C'mon, Mom, you were a teenager once, remember?"

Suddenly, Kent, his face twisted in terror, jerked the car door open. "Mom, come quick, everybody's dead!"

"What?!"

"That's not funny!" Darlene said. "Where's Tyler?"

"I'm not joking! There're blood and bodies everywhere!"

Chapter 19

Saturday, May 30, 1970

With the flat, harmonic beat of its forty-foot blades, the Bell UH-1H Nighthawk settled onto the deck of the *USS Midway*, creating gusts of prop wash that forced nearby sailors to shield their eyes. The Marine pilot had landed in total blackout conditions. One by one, eleven members of First Force Recon Company, shouldering packs and weapons, disembarked. Crouching, hands atop their bush covers and wearing the NVA's ankle-high, green canvas boots, they followed an ensign to a spot on the flight deck beneath the aircraft carrier's bridge where a pallet containing ordnance and supplies waited. The Marines wasted no time, slicing the heavy-duty plastic with their KA-BARs and then prying open the wood packing crates.

First Force Recon had flown out of Đông Hà Combat Base under cover of darkness just after 2000 hours. Avoiding detection meant preventing the distinctive hollow thump of the Huey's twin-bladed main rotor from being heard inland, so the pilot, maintaining radio silence, navigated several miles east over the South China Sea and then banked north for the 180-mile flight where the *Midway* waited in deep waters three miles off the coast of the Thạch Hà ward of northern Hà Tĩnh Province. The ship was the squad's final staging ground for its mission into North Vietnamese territory.

1st Lt. Jack Puspoon, conferred with an ensign while the Marines distributed the crates' contents. The mission's importance made it highly secretive, so he'd delayed giving them their warning order at Da Nang, instead providing only an overview and informing them of the weapons, equipment, and clothing they'd need.

The Marines spent the rest of the day in seclusion, neither seeing nor speaking with anyone outside the unit. Puspoon inspected each man; a cough or runny nose meant the sidelines. After getting briefed on the terrain, they set about their usual preparations: going over insertion and extraction plans; reviewing order and procedures during movement; and discussing escape and evasion techniques. The last thing they did before chow was review hand signals and radio call signs.

That evening, the men test-fired their weapons and practiced ambush formations. Then they rested. When nightfall came, they boarded the Huey, curiosity piqued. Only now, aboard the *Midway*, would they learn the full nature of their task.

"How're we doing, Staff Sergeant?" Puspoon asked SSgt. Greg Silenka, his only staff NCO. Silenka, a Nevadan, was a powerfully built man whose chest, biceps, and thighs strained against his camouflage utilities. Just twenty-five years old, he was on his sixth tour in country, and each day was etched upon his face: dark eyes, cold and hard; wide forehead, deeply creased from the stress of combat; thin cheeks shorn of growth after a week in the rear. Together with his close-cropped black hair and short, neatly trimmed mustache, Silenka's features invested his face with a look of knowledge, confidence, and an intolerance of bullshit.

"We're ready, sir. Sgt. Rogers confirmed the Zodiacs are set for launch, and we've got all the ordnance for when the shit hits the fan."

"All right then, let's brief the men so we can get underway."

"Yes, sir." Silenka marched toward the team. "Fall in," he said gruffly. They got up and gathered close together in a loose formation.

"As you were," Puspoon said when he joined them. The Marines, keen on conserving energy, knelt on the flight deck or sat on their packs. They looked up expectantly. They were mostly hard-looking men, grizzled, lean, and muscular, who thought nothing of martyrizing their enemy. Puspoon squatted among them and reached inside his jungle fatigues for a map. Rogers snapped on a flashlight as he spread it on the deck.

"We're coming ashore in the Thạch Hà ward of northern Hà Tĩnh Province," Puspoon said, head down, pointing to a spot near the coast north of the DMZ, "and then we're heading to Núi Trường Sơn." He dragged his index finger across the clear plastic acetate to another spot and looked up. "We're going to ambush General Pham Tien Thanh." The men exchanged glances. A couple raised their eyebrows. Only one spoke up.

"He's th' one in th' tunnels, ain't he?" drawled Private First Class Ronald "Red" Timmons, a fair-skinned redhead.

Just nineteen, Red had never ventured out of Clinch County, Georgia before enlisting in the Marines Corps, but nine weeks later, after surviving boot camp, they put him on a plane to Southeast Asia. Upon landing in Saigon, Red, still very green, decided to do some sightseeing. Eventually, he wandered into a tea bar where he had a culturally edifying experience with Ba Muoi Ba and Vietnamese bar girls; he woke up broke, hungover, and alone.

Red wasn't the least bit homesick. The only time he even thought about home was during his first mission as a recon ranger, when he and the lieutenant reconnoitered a mangrove swamp in the Red River Delta between Haiphong and Hanoi. For Red, that was just another day on Blackjack Island in the Okefenokee Swamp. Now, however, his natural inquisitiveness was on full display.

"Wait until the Lieutenant's finished," Silenka snarled. Gritting his teeth, he gave Red a look of mean—nostrils flared, eyes narrowed, mouth set in an unhappy line.

"It's okay, Staff Sergeant," Puspoon said. "You're right, Red, Thanh's been running ops from a rabbit warren. He's got an entire city down there. He and other top generals are going to

Hanoi. They're meeting with General Giap to coordinate a big push south. Without Thanh, they'll have to scuttle the mission."

"Well, tha' makes sense," Red said good-naturedly, nodding his head.

"Glad you think so, Red," Silenka said, his voice laced with sarcasm. "Now shut the fuck up!" Everyone laughed, except Red, who fought the blood rush of embarrassment.

"We'll be coming ashore in two Zodiacs right here," Puspoon said, drawing a small circle on the map with a black grease pencil. "The jungle meets the coastline, so we'll have good cover. The schedule's tight, though, so we keep to the trails when we can." Puspoon paused. Heads nodded. "There's a small village, mainly fishermen and their families, but it's VC friendly." Puspoon looked up from the map. "We have to come ashore and get to the ambush site undetected."

Silenka jumped in, so that he, not Puspoon, gave the order. "We take out anyone we encounter—no exceptions," he growled. "Be quick and quiet. Hands or a KA-BAR. The Lieutenant and I have Hush Puppies," he said, touching the 9mm strapped to his belt.

"Gawt it," Red drawled. Silenka gave him a blistering look and then nodded to Puspoon.

Puspoon drew a large circle around western Hà Tĩnh.

"This whole area is in the foothills of the Truong Son Mountains." He drew a smaller circle. "Thanh will surface here. He'll avoid the plains and move right into the jungle where it's the thickest. His preferred route's west over the mountains into Laos and then—"

"Up th' Ho Chee Men?" It was Red again, and Silenka had all but had it.

"Right," Puspoon answered quickly, capping the volcano. "A-4 Skyhawks have been pounding this whole area." He swept the grease pencil in an arc from Đồng Lộc, a strategic junction at the beginning of the Ho Chi Minh, southwest of Núi Trường Sơn, north to Phương Mỹ.

"I see wha' they's doin'," Red mused.

"Goddamn it, Red, shut the fuck up!"

"Yesterday, the one-seven was inserted here." Puspoon pointed to the northwest of Núi Trường Sơn. Rogers followed with the light. "That means Thanh's only choice is north, and he won't be able to cross the mountains until he's past Trung Lộc. We're not going to let him get that far."

"How'd they figger out tha's whar he'll be?" Now everyone groaned.

"Begging the Lieutenant's pardon." It was Silenka, and he was seething. "Enough with the questions, Red. You're too stupid to realize it, but this war's a big fucking deal. You might even have heard about it back in the swamp before they shipped your sorry ass over here. Now, maybe you think it's just the eleven of us, but the rest of the Marine Corps is involved, and the Army, Navy, and Air Force have their small roles, too. Hell, even the CIA's in on the fun. Point is, word gets around about shit that goes down because the boys at MAC-V have a lot of sources and resources. They get information—direct observation reports, aerial photographs, captured documents, prisoner interrogations, you name it. They sift through everything, cross-check it, analyze it, and then present their findings and recommendations to General Abrams. You ever hear of him?"

"Yes, Staff Sergeant" Red said sheepishly.

"Based on the strength of that information, General Abrams will either agree or disagree with those recommendations. If he agrees, he'll issue an order, and Division HQ comes up with a mission, which gets handed down to battalion. Battalion then briefs the Lieutenant here at the company level, and then the Lieutenant tells us. So, there it is, Red. That's how we know Thanh will surface where the Lieutenant said. Real fucking complicated, isn't it? Now, for the last time, shut your suck and let the Lieutenant finish, or you're going to take a three-legged trip to the hospital."

"Huh?"

"I'll bury my foot in your ass!" The men erupted in laughter.

"Red," Puspoon said gently, "a few weeks ago, we inserted a team in the area. They were there a week. They moved around, mapped out the tunnel entrances, and ID'd several high-ranking officers coming and going. Since then, aerial photos have shown a gradual buildup of forces." Puspoon paused, eyed the rest of the men, and continued. "The trail from the tunnel goes north about a klick and then forks northeast and northwest. We don't know which route he'll take, so we'll have to grease him when he surfaces."

"You okay with that, Red?"

"Since Thanh will have to stay in country, G-2 believes he could have up to sixty men, counting an advance force and rear guard. I'm not going to bullshit you; this *will* get hairy. Questions?" Everyone looked at Red, who looked down.

"Get ready to move out," Silenka said.

Silenka and Sgt. Rogers handed out camouflage sticks and black demolition tape. The men smeared green, black, and brown grease paint wherever there was exposed skin, including eyelids, ears, lips, and fingernails. Then they taped up their dog tags and the metal on their web belts to eliminate reflection and noise. When they finished, each man turned his attention to individual preparations—cleaning his weapon, wolfing down C-rations, smoking that last cigarette, writing a loved one, collecting thoughts, praying.

"Tuna fish," PFC Slessen muttered under his breath.

"Yo, Red, you gonna eat those peaches?" L.Cpl. Morris "Mo" Goldberg flashed him a hopeful smile. "I'll give you my peanut butter and gorilla cookies for 'em."

"Wha' ails yuh gawt?"

"You want my turkey loaf?"

"Turkey loaf! Haail, no! Tha' stuff goes down 'ard an' comes out 'arder!"

Chapter 20

Saturday, May 30, 1970

Signs for I-74 and I-465 flashed overhead as we headed south on I-65. Frank and I were still huddled in the back while Wren, squeezed beneath the dash, squirmed up front.

"How far to Greenwood?" Frank asked.

"Forget Greenwood," Marlin replied, his eyes fixed on the road.

"I'm getting out there, remember?"

"Go for it, but I'm not slowing down."

"What the fuck?" Frank snarled, popping up in his seat.

"We can't chance it now," Wren jumped in.

The car grew silent while Frank fumed. He didn't have a flight to catch. He still planned to go to the race with Twyla, maybe stay another night if he could talk her into it. Tyler sure fucked that all up.

After a few minutes, Marlin spoke up. "What happened back there? And who's the kid?" He tilted the rearview mirror so he could see Frank, who'd folded his skinny frame below the seat again.

"I'd like to know that as well," Wren added.

"I know you killed somebody, but why? Did somebody sneeze without asking? Drop a nickel? What?"

"Motherfucking manager went for my gun while I was grabbing the tape," Frank replied, lifting his head to peek out the rear window.

Marlin knew he was lying, but he turned to Wren. "That right?"

"I was with the tellers, but that's what he said."

"What about that woman in the lobby you shot? Did she go for your gun, too?"

"She tried to escape. I didn't have a choice there either unless you want some bovine bitch mooing for the cops."

"All right, enough," Wren snapped. "It's over and done. Let's focus on what's next."

Marlin was just getting started, though. "How many people did you kill back there?"

"I don't know. I didn't have time to count. What the fuck kind of question is that? We're bank robbers for Christ's sake!"

"Uh-uh, I'm a bank robber. Mr. Wren's a bank robber. You're a psychopathic serial killer who robs banks. There's a difference."

"Serial killer, eh? Here's your serial killer, motherfucker." Frank, eyes narrowed, whipped out his Colt and cocked the hammer, but Marlin was quicker. He had the slide racked on his .45 and the barrel in Frank's face with the legerdemain of a magician.

"ARE YOU TWO OUT OF YOUR MINDS? PUT YOUR GUNS DOWN!" Wren shouted in a rare display of anger. Several seconds passed. "I SAID PUT 'EM DOWN!" Neither one moved.

Frank pointed the Colt at the back of Marlin's head while Marlin, whose eyes never left the road, had his gun barrel pressed hard against Frank's nose.

"If you don't lower your weapons," Wren, seething, said quietly, "I'm chucking your money out the window." Nothing. "Did you hear me? *Your* money, not mine!" Still nothing. Wren grabbed a strap of twenties and rolled down his window. Frank's finger tightened on the trigger.

"Last chance," he warned. He looked at Marlin and then at Frank. Then he shook his head and heaved the brick as far as he could. It landed in the emergency lane, bounced once, and broke apart in a swirling puff of green and white confetti. "That right there, gentlemen, cost you five thousand dollars each." Wren grabbed a band of hundreds. "Want to split twenty-five Gs?" Again, nothing. Wren shrugged and drew his arm back, but Marlin abruptly raised his .45.

"Okay, good, that's showing some sense." Wren looked over the seat back. "Your turn, Mr. Wolf." Frank worked his mouth back and forth, up and down, and nibbled on his lip, but he kept his Colt trained on Marlin.

"Fuck it," Marlin said. He flattened the accelerator against the floorboard. "Shoot me, psycho," he taunted. The speedometer zoomed to ninety-five and kept climbing. We were blowing past cars. "I won't feel a thing; it'll be over that quick, but you'll die in the crash, probably after lingering in excruciating pain." He glanced at Frank through the rearview mirror. "That's if you're lucky. If not, you'll have some major bones set, a bunch of glass plucked from your ugly puss, and a few hundred scars left over as memories. Then you'll rot in prison until they fry you."

Frank swallowed and regripped the butt of the Colt. We were going 110 miles an hour; the car was shaking like a wet dog! I braced for a crash.

"Be sensible and lower your gun, Mr. Wolf," Wren said, his voice and body vibrating in time with the car. "We've got a half a million dollars here, give or take ten grand."

Frank narrowed his eyes and flexed his trigger finger. His heart pounded. He lowered his gun. He'd deal with them later.

"Good," Wren said. "Now, do you want to tell us how you know this boy and what you plan on doing with him?"

Chapter 21

Saturday, May 30, 1970

Agent Kramer stood quietly, leaning against the wall, just inside CNT's front doors, holding a paper sack, watching the coroner make notations in a heavily scarred leather journal. She'd been there two hours already. Prand, the sole survivor, had been rushed to the hospital. He'd come to briefly in the emergency room before relapsing into unconsciousness. Kramer hoped to interview him next. *Assuming I ever get out of here.*

"What do you think?" said an IPD detective, interrupting her thoughts. He'd also been watching the coroner, although he was paying closer attention and turned away before the camera flash.

"I think ballistics will show it's DTK," Kramer replied, blinking her eyes and shaking her head. Then, muttering, "That'll make Sam go ballistic."

Sam Burroughs was the acting special agent in charge of the FBI's Indianapolis field office. He was an unexceptional man who'd been with the agency twenty-two years, mostly as an ineffectual office supervisor, but all of them as a binge drinker. His selection to temporarily head the Indianapolis office surprised everyone, including himself. Burroughs's career, devoid of achievement or any noteworthy success, had been a model of self-preservation, one in which he'd elevated unaccountability to an art form. Now, all of a sudden, he was answerable for a stalled investigation into the crime of the century, and all because Hoover equated seniority with competence.

As soon as Burroughs was put in charge, he reassigned Kramer's partner and dumped DTK—then just ordinary bank robberies—in her lap. Thereafter, he gave it the same attention he gave other cases, specifically, as much as needed to provide updates to D.C. during monthly teleconferences. That all changed after the loan officer was murdered. Suddenly, Burroughs was fielding calls from Clyde Tolson, Hoover's righthand man, who demanded results and threatened consequences when there weren't any. Burroughs' sole strategy, if it could be called that, was to say as little as possible and get off the phone. He would never admit he was in over his head, not with the debt load he carried. He needed the bump in pay, so his top priority was getting "acting" removed from his title.

Kramer, frowning, watched the coroner pack up. She was no closer to catching DTK than when she started. With no staff, or even a partner, she spent more time on paperwork than field investigation, usually staying late at the office to get as much done as she could. She suspected she was being set up to fail, and it didn't help matters standing around, like now, waiting while other law enforcement agencies investigated essentially the same thing and produced their own separate, but largely identical, reports.

The coroner followed the gurney outdoors. A moment later, Olivia Wantel and her children were ushered into the bank. Kramer, sack in hand, approached her while a uniformed policeman led Darlene and Kent to Dertson's office.

"You look like you could use a cup of coffee," Kramer said, hoisting the bag.

"Is it that obvious?"

"No, I just recognize the symptoms. My name's Carol Kramer, I'm a special agent with the FBI."

"And I'm Olivia Wantel."

"Yes, I know. I was hoping to have a chat with you."

Kramer led her into Dertson's secretary's office and then closed the inner and outer doors. She sat next to Mrs. Wantel and handed her a Styrofoam cup.

"Are you tired of talking yet?" Kramer asked, to get the conversation going.

"I'm considering a vow of silence," Mrs. Wantel laughed, lifting the lid and adding cream.

"I have just a few questions. I'll make sure to get the routine stuff from ISP."

"Fire away," Mrs. Wantel said, but the words had barely left her mouth when she wished she had them back. "Oh, I'm sorry. I didn't mean it like that."

"Of course you didn't, no problem," Kramer replied, "but tell me, did Tyler say why he wanted to go to the bank?"

"Not to me. Darlene—that's my daughter—just said he wanted to go to CNT, and we came here because it's the only branch I know of in Indianapolis."

"Do you know how much money he had?"

"No, I didn't ask. I only met him last night. Maybe you should talk to my kids. They know him better than me."

Kramer opened the door to Dertson's office and stepped inside, drawing inquisitive looks from Darlene and Kent. Mrs. Wantel poked her head around the door.

"Hey, you guys doing all right?" Darlene went back to looking scared and worried. Kent was clearly ticked off.

"Are we ever getting out of here? The race has already started."

"The police have to do their investigation," Mrs. Wantel said, stepping into the room. "Be patient."

"That means we're going to miss the race."

"I don't believe you," Darlene said disgustedly. "Tyler's been kidnapped, and four people are dead. So, shut up, okay? Just shut the fu—"

"DARLENE!" Mrs. Wantel warned. "Look, we'll be on our way soon, but both of you cool out. There's an FBI agent who needs to ask you a few questions."

"Great, more questions," Kent fumed.

"And you'll answer them without the attitude!"

"Yes, ma'am," he said glumly.

"Boy, you guys have had quite a day, haven't you?" Kramer said with an uplifting tone that brought neither a look nor reply. "Well, like your mom said, I'm an FBI agent. My name's Carol Kramer, and it's important that I talk to you, but first, are you guys hungry? Can I get you something to drink?"

"No, ma'am, I'm fine, thank you," Darlene said with a sniffle. Kramer spied a box of tissues on the credenza and brought them over.

"Thank you." Darlene took one and blew her nose.

"I'll take a double cheeseburger, fries, and a Mountain Dew," Kent said, suddenly perky.

"Of course, you will," Darlene said sarcastically. "Do you want the toy that goes with it?"

Kramer went to the door and whispered to the policeman, who frowned and left. She grabbed a chair and sat across from Kent and Darlene, forming a triangle.

"We might as well start while we wait," Kramer said, smoothing her gray, regulation-length skirt and placing her hands in her lap. "So, your friend's name is Tyler. What's his last name?"

"Puspoon," Darlene said.

"Excuse me?"

"Yeah, I know, weird name, huh?"

"Can you spell it?"

"P-u-s-p-o-o-n."

"Do you know his address?"

"No, I don't."

"I think he lives up by the high school," Kent offered.

"Do you three go to the same school?"

"Uh-huh," Darlene replied. "We'll be sophomores this fall."

"Got it, so are you two twins?"

"No, I'm a year older," she said.

"Tyler's mostly your friend, right?"

"Yeah," Darlene said, squirming a little. "We're kind of going out."

"I see," Kramer said, smiling. "How long have you been dating?"

"Not long."

"How long is not long?"

"Since yesterday," Darlene said, blushing.

"Well," Kramer said, laughing, "relationships have to start sometime. What're first dates like these days? Is it still pizza and a movie?"

"I don't know, we just hung out after school, and then he came over later."

"So, you've already had two dates. You're moving fast."

"I guess so."

"Excuse me a sec," Kramer said, spying the policeman. She went to the door, returning with two cold bottles of pop. "Food's on the way," she said, handing Kent one bottle and Darlene the other. "I ordered two of everything just in case."

"Thank you," Darlene said.

"Tell me about your second date."

"I didn't know he was coming by, but he was a mess when he got there."

"What do you mean?" Kramer made a couple of notes and then looked up at Darlene.

"His mom's boyfriend, some guy named Frank, punched him in the mouth."

"What's the boyfriend's last name?"

"I don't know, I've never met him."

"Me neither," Kent said.

"Okay, did Tyler say what happened?"

"Just that Frank went off on him because he was late getting home from school."

"That was your first date, right?"

"Right."

"Do you know why Tyler wanted to go to the bank today?"

"He said he needed to open an account."

"He said that, 'needed'?"

"Uh-huh."

"And what did you say?"

"I told him to wait, but he said he had to do it today."

"He wouldn't have been able to. Minors need an adult on the account."

"I didn't know that," Darlene said.

"Didn't even think of it," Kent said, shrugging.

"What I don't understand," Kramer began slowly, "is why he couldn't wait?"

"That's what I asked him, but he said he didn't want to carry that much money around all weekend."

"He could've left it at your house or in the car."

"I know, but his mind was made up."

"Did he say where he got it?"

"No."

"Do you know how much he had?"

"No, but it was a lot."

"How do you know?"

"I felt the bulge in his pocket."

Chapter 22

Saturday, May 30, 1970

"I'll ask you again, Mr. Wolf," Wren said. His body had settled like sand, filling every inch of space between the car door and Marlin's right leg. "Who's the boy?"

"Somebody who knows me, obviously," Frank replied sarcastically. "Does that answer your question?"

"Well, I'll grant you it's an answer, but it's an insufficient one, so tell me this: how do you know him?"

"Does it really matter?"

"That's difficult to say without knowing."

"Listen, we agreed not to reveal personal information in case one of us gets popped."

"That was before you started murdering people and kidnapping children," Marlin cut in.

"Okay, I'm banging his mom if you must know!"

I attacked, pummeling Frank with my knees and elbows. "You fucking bastard!" I got in a few good shots before he rammed his shoulder into my chest and drove me backward into the door. Frank reared back, fist balled, and swung at my head, but Marlin, lightning quick, grabbed it mid-flight, and, in a wink, let go, grabbed the front of his shirt, and jerked him back and forth before shoving him backward in his seat.

"Don't touch the kid."

"Stay the hell out of this!"

"This?!" Marlin exploded. "We already had a 'this' before you brought the kid in and started this fucking 'this'!"

Marlin's jaw tightened. Frank scowled. Wren sighed. I groaned.

The car was quiet again except for the highway sounds. We were in Bartleby County, which, from all appearances, had plenty of corn and soybeans but little else.

"So, what now?" Marlin asked, looking down at Wren and then giving Frank a quick glance in the rearview mirror.

"Good question," Wren said.

"Yeah, and I'd like a good answer."

"Then come up with one," Frank said.

"In other words, you don't know," Marlin said.

"Okay, here's one, get off at the next exit and I'll cap this little prick. Then we'll be back on plan."

"Let's stick with that 'this' thing," I suggested.

"Shut up, Pussypoon!"

"Haven't you killed enough people for one day?" Marlin stared out the windshield at the highway.

"You don't let up, do you?" Frank said, leaning forward, cocking his head toward Marlin, and resting his elbow on the passenger seatback.

Marlin lifted his chin and turned his head part way towards Frank. "Actually, you're the one who has a problem letting up." His eyes never left the road.

"Look, just drive the car. That's all you're here to do. You don't even need to talk to do it." Frank sat back in his seat.

"You want to kill the kid? That's your solution?"

"There's no other option, he knows me!"

"Oh, bullshit!" Marlin said. "Frank Beetz isn't your real name!"

"He's a loose string!"

"Then he'll have to dangle," Wren said. "We're not stopping."

Chapter 23

Saturday, May 30, 1970

The first thing Twyla did when she woke up was groan. It was also the second thing she did. She tried to go back to sleep, but it was no use. Her head felt like a speed bag. She lay there, cradling it, eyes shut, not daring to move, but the pounding continued.

"Shit," Twyla spat, summing up how she felt, what her mouth tasted like, and her outlook on the day. She tried to swallow, hoping to prime her saliva glands, but her throat was drier than a church biscuit, and she gagged on her tongue instead. Twyla, naked, slowly slid off the mattress onto the floor. She blindly felt her way to the foot of the bed. By a stroke of luck, she found her purse and rummaged inside, searching for aspirin, but, if not, cyanide. She found neither and, hopes dashed, smashed her foot against the metal bed frame as a bonus.

"Owwww!" Twyla grabbed her shredded, bleeding toes and hopped up and down before losing her balance and tumbling onto the bed. She pulled the covers over her and lay there, curled in a ball, clutching her mangled toes, fighting back tears, and, now, having to pee.

Twyla waited until her foot dulled to a defiant throb. Then she rolled out of bed and hobbled toward the bathroom, trailing the sheet, blanket, and comforter like the train of a wedding gown. She didn't get five feet before stepping on the short side of the blanket. Flailing and flapping, she latched onto the drapes just as her bladder let go, and slowly fell to the floor, one hook at a time, until she was lying naked in a pile of sodden textiles.

Chapter 24

Saturday, May 30, 1970

News of the slaughter at CNT first broke at a half past nine, shortly after the gang crossed into Jackson County, south of Columbus. WIBC-AM 1070 interrupted its coverage of the pre-race events to make the announcement. By ten o'clock, every television and radio station in the state had broadcast an alert for an ice blue 1969 Plymouth Fury with license plate number 97PF313 heading north on I-65 or east on I-70.

Karen made the first call. She woke up at eight o'clock, hoping not to awaken the small, hairy lump curled up in a ball next to her. She threw on her mini-skirt and, while looking for her white boots, made a mental note about short, tubby, stubby-fingered men. She quietly closed the door and tiptoed down the hallway to the rear exit with her bunched-up panties and boots in one hand and her car keys in the other. It took three trips around the hotel before she realized her car had been stolen.

Forty-five minutes later, the first calls to IPD came in about a hit-and-run driver on Pine Street heading toward the north split. Witnesses described the Fury, and someone reported the plate number. The police connected it to the bloodbath at CNT only after Mrs. Wantel, who'd frantically knocked on one neighborhood door after another, finally found someone who'd let her use the telephone. In the early chaos, reports of twenties swirling on the interstate drew scant interest except from the lucky motorists who stopped to collect them.

"That's just great!" Frank growled. He sat up quickly, spitting with rage, and leaned over the seatback to stare down at Wren.

"What's the matter now, Mr. Wolf?" Wren replied calmly.

"Nothing if you like being chased by the cops."

"We're not being chased by the cops." Marlin interjected. Frank turned to him.

"Weren't you listening?!"

"Were you? We're going south."

"They've still got the description and plate number!"

"The car, yes, the plate, no," Wren jumped in. "Where are we, Mr. Marlin?"

"We passed the Columbus exit about ten minutes ago."

Wren, grimacing, twisted himself around. He opened the glove box and removed a screwdriver and pliers. Then he pulled a California license plate from under the seat. Marlin watched out the corner of his eye.

"You came prepared," he said.

"I was hoping it wouldn't be necessary. There's a rest stop up ahead. Pull in."

Marlin tossed the Fury's plate in the weeds and climbed behind the steering wheel. He looked down at Wren, half of whom was on the car seat while the other half was on the floorboard, wedged beneath the dash.

"Are you stuck?"

"Just go, will you?" Wren sighed tiredly, hoping he wasn't. Marlin laughed and dropped the gear shift into drive.

"Hurry up, the cops are going to start looking south," Frank said sourly.

"You think?" Marlin said, looking at him through the rearview mirror. We were back at highway speed and climbing.

"I said from the start this plan was fucked up, but you two didn't listen."

Marlin closed his eyes for a second and then exhaled. "It's not the plan that's fucked up," he muttered.

"Get off at the Seymour exit," Wren said.

"Yeah, just find a quiet spot once we get outside of town," Frank said, looking at me and smiling. "I won't be a second."

"We're going to lay low for a few hours."

"Lay low?!" Frank angrily slapped the seatback. "Louisville's only an hour away!"

"No, I thought about it, and you're right," Wren said. "The cops will look south before long. They might even be looking now and just not saying so. We can't chance it. Every move has to be about safety now."

Marlin steered onto the exit ramp and headed west on State Road 50. Traffic was light, and he caught most of the lights, so we were on the outskirts of town in minutes. After a lot of struggling, Wren managed to extract himself from beneath the dash and arrange himself on the seat. Marlin, who'd scooted against the door to accommodate his partner's massive bulk, took as many gravel roads as he could. By the time we reached the rolling hills of Broben County, the ice blue Fury was grubby gray. Marlin flipped the wipers on and swept away the fine powder blanketing the windshield.

"Whoa, slow down," Wren said.

"What's up?" Marlin replied, braking.

"That farmhouse up ahead. Check out the sign. It's for rent."

"You're shitting me, right?" Frank said in disbelief. He was leaning on the seatback, looking out the windshield.

"No, not at all. It's perfect."

It was far from perfect. It was somewhere between dilapidated and condemned. In the middle of a large, overgrown, weed-choked yard, sat a decrepit clapboard farmhouse with a rotting wraparound porch and a partially-collapsed awning. The house sat atop a gentle hillock with a cornfield and barn on either downslope. There was an enormous oak tree shading the entire front yard and half the house, and an even bigger sycamore doing the same thing out back. On high, their limbs were knotted; gnarled old boxers in a decades long clinch. Together, they created a wooden bridge of sorts, consigning fallen leaves, twigs, and branches to the roof and awning where they lay, rotting.

"You call that perfect? In what way?" Frank stared in disbelief at the ruins.

"It's way out in the boondocks with no neighbors within shouting distance, and there's a barn to stash the car," Marlin said. "What could be better?"

"A hotel with a parking garage?"

"We're hiding out, not living it up."

"No, we're not. We're 'laying low for a few hours,' remember?" Frank said, quoting with his fingers.

"That's a difference without a difference. The object's to find a place where no one will think to look. Anything beyond that's a bonus."

"Including electricity and indoor plumbing," Frank sniped.

"Look, there's somebody on the porch," I said, scratching my neck and chest. An old man rose from a rocking chair and, shielding his eyes against the mid-morning sun, stared in our direction.

"Get down!" Wren shouted. Everyone ducked except Marlin.

"Did he see us?" Frank asked.

"Doubtful," Marlin replied. "He's looking into the sun."

"Go talk to him," Wren said, "but keep him away from the car."

Marlin braked at the edge of the road, stopping just beyond a rusty, dented mailbox sitting atop a rotting wooden post. The numbers "174" were crudely scratched on its side. He cut the motor, and the Fury's full-throated growl suddenly went quiet, replaced by the soft, metallic ticking and pinging as the exhaust manifold and pipes cooled.

Frank was spread out on the seat. I hunkered down, straddling the transmission hump and pulled the laundry bags over me. I watched through the tall, yellow stalks of dead grass and weeds and tufts of new, green shoots as the old man, eyeing the car warily, slowly descended the porch steps and leaned against the massive oak tree. He was unwashed and scruffy with an unkempt white beard stained yellow beneath his bottom lip. His thick white hair sprouted in all directions. The old man slid his hands in the pockets of his faded blue overalls and spat a long, dark stream of tobacco juice toward the car in what apparently passed as a greeting in southern Indiana.

Marlin, hoping for sensible communication, walked around to the passenger side of the car and leaned against the front door, shielding Wren's sizeable form.

"How're you doing?" Marlin asked cheerfully. The man nodded once.

"Do you own this place?" He nodded again.

"I see it's for rent." He nodded a third time.

"Ask him something that requires speaking," Wren whispered, "preferably more than one syllable." I giggled, and Frank drove his heel into my ribs. I gasped loudly and Marlin coughed louder to cover it.

"How much?" he quickly asked.

"Hunnert dollars a munt," the man said, straining his neck to look past Marlin and see in the car. Then he spat another stream of brown juice and wiped the dribble from his whiskers.

"That's reasonable enough," Marlin replied, even though it wasn't. "I'm going to be doing some fishing."

"Yuh don't look like no fisherman," the old man said, ignorant of double negatives. He pulled on his beard and squinted at Marlin.

"What does a fisherman look like?"

"He can look lots uh ways ah reckon, but he shore don't whar no fancy suit an' pointy-toed shoes."

Marlin chuckled. "I left straight from work. I've only got a week off, and I'm not wasting a moment of it."

"Ah rent by da munt."

"No problem. When can I have it?"

"Soons yuh pay."

"How about now? I've got a couple friends coming, too."

"Tha' be two hunnert then."

"For real?" Marlin said with a sardonic snort and then slowly handed over two bills. The old man slid the money in the right front pocket of his overalls and emerged with a key.

"There's water an' 'lectrissity. No gas."

"Gas another hundred, is it?"

"Tank's busted."

"Right," Marlin said. "Is that an Apache I see?" He was looking at the rear of an old pickup parked in the barn.

"Yep."

"Does it run?"

"Nope."

"What's wrong with it?"

"Dunno."

"Do you mind if I tinker with it? I've worked on cars since I was a teenager."

"Nope."

"Can I drive it if I get it running for you?

Fer 'nother hunnert." The old man coughed wetly, hawked, and spat something lumpy and gray. Marlin sighed and handed over another Benjamin.

Chapter 25

Saturday, May 30, 1970

Twyla returned from the land of the dead but had only just crossed the border. Her mangled toes pulsated, threatening to burst, but they'd stopped bleeding. The blood, although still tacky in a few places, had dried to a blackened crust. She pulled the cold, damp bedding from her face and squinted. Bright sunlight streamed through the window, breaching the narrow slits of her eyelids, making her wince. Twyla swallowed, nearly choked, and then coughed uncontrollably. She needed something wet.

"Frank?" Twyla's throat was raw, her voice barely a croak. She began a slow, torturous crawl toward the bathroom, gradually shedding the drapes, comforter, blanket, and sheet in her wake. The air conditioner was going full blast. She shivered. Twyla spied the Styrofoam cooler and angled for it. The lid was on the floor where it had been stepped on during the night. Small clumps of condensed foam dots formed a trail to the door. Twyla stuck her hand inside the cooler and swished around in the cool water before emerging with a can of Blatz. She quickly pulled the tab and took a long, thirsty drink. Beer sloshed over her lips and ran down her chest, making her tremble even more. She drained it and grabbed another.

After several wobbly attempts, Twyla pulled herself up by the countertop and braced herself with her hands on either side of the white porcelain basin. She took a hesitant look in the mirror. Her face, bloated from a night of chain drinking, was flushed and splotchy, and her bloodshot eyes had dark bags hanging beneath them. Twyla licked her lips. They were dry, cracked, and the bottom one was indented where one menthol after another had hung throughout the night.

A long, hot shower improved Twyla's appearance but did nothing for her hangover, mood, or outlook. While getting dressed, she reminded herself that Frank was an early riser and often went out for a newspaper and coffee while she slept in. Twyla dressed and slipped on her flip-flops. Then she limped the length of the hallway, and rode the elevator downstairs. The lobby was deserted. There were a few people in the restaurant, and one or two more browsed the gift shop, but none of them were Frank. The desk clerk was no help at all. His shift started at seven o'clock, so he wasn't around when the early crowd headed for the track, and he'd been too busy since then to notice anyone in particular. Twyla's puzzlement deepened when the clerk told her the race was almost over and their room was booked for another night.

Chapter 26

Saturday, May 30, 1970

The breeze mixed with the previous day's heat and humidity to produce a thick, rolling fog. Shrouded in darkness, two fifteen-foot, black rubber Zodiacs powered through the sea, bouncing over the windswept swells. Spray burst over the bows, dowsing the Marines straddling the tubes. A mile from shore, the Navy coxswains throttled back the 55-horsepower motors, and the Zodiacs' bows dropped to the ocean surface. Both crafts slowed to idle. After another half mile, the sailors killed the engines and raised the propellers. The Marines hunched behind their rucksacks to reduce their silhouettes. They kept their weapons trained on the jungle, and they kept still, except for their eyes, which continuously swept left and right through the mist.

The recon rangers traded their weapons for paddles, which they quickly put to use, knifing through the water with scarcely a ripple. Puspoon, at the bow of the lead craft, kept the Zodiacs on course with his compass. Soon, a cluster of fishing boats tied to a pier, rolling gently with the waves, faded in and out of view. Moments later, beyond the shoreline, in the scrub, the fog revealed eight thatched, candle-lit hooches.

Suddenly, Puspoon raised a closed fist. Everyone froze. Shadows danced on a wall in one of the dimly lit huts and then, just as quickly, stopped. Puspoon raised his binoculars, but saw only a candle flame flickering against the breeze. Then a fit of spasmodic coughing interrupted the night and set a dog barking a short distance off. Moments later, a small, bent figure carrying a candle appeared on the path. Puspoon couldn't see well enough to establish age or gender, but as the figure neared the beach, the fog thinned enough for him to make out the old mamasan.

Hunched over and leaning heavily on a piece of carved black bamboo worn smooth from use, the woman, head bent and mindful of her footing, took the trail in slow, measured steps. Her mouth, in contrast, moved in rapid campaign with her tongue, rolling the sliced betel nut around in her mouth, absorbing the arecoline for its stimulating, warm rush. She stopped and spat a stream of red juice into the scrub. Suddenly, she looked out to sea, craning her neck left and right. Time slowed, and still, she stared. Finally, the old woman dropped her head and hobbled off the trail. It was only when she crouched in the brush among the orchids, jasmine, and rhododendrons that Puspoon inwardly sighed his relief.

The surf breathed and sighed. Foamy water rushed up the beach, stretching for the jungle, never quite making it, instead disappearing into the sand or withdrawing to the sea for another try. Seconds seemed like minutes and then turned into them. Puspoon kept his binoculars trained where the mamasan squatted. She was taking too long, but he steeled himself to be patient. Another minute passed. Hesitantly, the old woman rose with the aid of her walking stick. Then, holding the candle and taking small, shuffling steps through the sand, she unhurriedly hobbled up the trail to her hooch.

Puspoon waited a full five minutes before giving the all clear. The Marines resumed paddling. Thirty meters from shore, he again raised his fist and signaled them to dismount. One by one, they noiselessly slipped into the sea and let the waves push them toward shore, alert to a possible ambush.

Strategic analysts at MAC-V planned First Force Recon's arrival for just after midnight, expecting the Thạch Hà villagers to be asleep since their day began before dawn. That meant higher tides, but the coxswains chosen for the mission had a high skill set, and maneuvered the Zodiacs close enough to the beach for the recon rangers to touch bottom, letting them move quickly and quietly while keeping their weapons dry and ready for use.

The wind picked up, sending swells breaking beyond the sandbars where eleven heavily armed men stood in chest-deep water. Braced against the billowing waves, they alternately scanned the undergrowth, eyed the hooches, and watched the trail. Puspoon signaled Cowboy, who pushed off the sand bank and rode several of the rolling whitecaps before emerging from the surf on the run. He sprinted across the beach, dropped in the scrub, and disappeared in the lush vegetation.

One by one, the men from the first Zodiac followed. Puspoon emerged last. No one spoke or moved. They lay quietly at jungle's edge, surveying their surroundings, letting their eyes adjust to the blackness of the dense tropical forest. Puspoon angled a small, red-lens flashlight into the sand directly behind him. He flicked it on and off, briefly creating a thin crescent of light. The men from the second Zodiac pushed off the sandy bottom and together rode the surging tide. They emerged from the shallows and crossed the beach where they dropped in the jungle and completed the team's semicircle perimeter. Puspoon flicked the light again, signaling the sailors that they had safely reached their departure point. The coxswains, having already attached oars to the Zodiacs, rowed out to sea before restarting the motors and returning to the *Midway.*

The Marines were on their own. Puspoon tapped L.Cpl. Ben Houghton, the squad's skinny radio operator, on the foot. Houghton, dubbed "Goat" because he showed up at boot camp with a long goatee, checked the frequency of the PRC-25 and quickly keyed the microphone twice, breaking the hiss of static at the other end. The ship's radio operator keyed twice in return, acknowledging the prearranged all clear signal. After Goat gave a thumbs-up, Puspoon nodded at Cowboy and pointed up the trail.

Cowboy was First Force Recon's senses. He weighed the sights, sounds, and scents of the jungle, attentive to anything that didn't belong. Combining caution with speed and stealth, he remained alert at all times for anything manmade—voices, broken branches, body odor—aware that a lapse in judgment, or a moment of inattentiveness, might trigger a booby trap or, worse, lead the unit into an ambush. Darkness, in which First Force Recon usually operated, made walking point all the more difficult, especially deep in the jungle where fog often reduced visibility to mere feet.

Raised on a cattle ranch by his widowed grandfather in Big Sky Country just outside Havre, Montana, K'oy'am'á Boyd, was nicknamed "Cowboy" while still in diapers. He was a descendant of Chief Joseph, the leader of the Nimíipuu, or The People, tribe. His ancestors were part of the Sahaptin family but were better known as the Nez Perce, which was what French Canadian fur traders called them.

Cowboy Boyd grew up on a ranch with his widowed grandfather, a full-blooded Nimíipuu. When he was a young boy, his grandfather captivated him with stories of driving cattle to the market in Big Sandy before the turn of the century. Cowboy spent his teenage years roaming the golden wheat fields and the peaks and valleys at the foot of the Bears Paw Mountains. His grandfather taught him how to live off the land of his ancestors and to respect it by taking only what he needed.

Together, no matter the season, the two men, one young, the other old, roamed the countryside, spending weeks at a time hunting, trapping, and fishing. Often, they set up camp on the terraces of Snake Creek, where the 1,300-mile running battle between the Nimíipuu and the US Cavalry culminated in the massacre that forced Chief Joseph's surrender just forty miles from the Canadian border and the freedom he sought for his people.

Cowboy was a natural woodsman, and he became an expert marksman. By the time he was a teenager, his tracking skills were well-known, attracting big-game hunters who offered him high dollar to lead expeditions for mountain lions and bears. He refused, rejecting killing as a "sport."

Cowboy wanted nothing more than to live on the ranch and off the land, but when his grandfather died, his father, an unrepentant lag who'd abandoned him after his Nimíipuu wife died during labor, returned with his eye on the ranch. With the help of a crooked lawyer who bribed an even more corrupt judge, Charlie Boyd successfully contested the will, inheriting the ranch and everything else when it was nullified. He wasted little time sending his "half-breed" son packing.

With no home and no other family, Cowboy walked into a military recruiting station in Great Falls and joined the Marine Corps on the written promise he'd be a grunt and sent to Vietnam. So, on a cold, snowy December morning, Cowboy boarded a bus for the two-day trip to the Marine Corps Recruit Depot in San Diego. Nine weeks later, he emerged from boot camp as the Series Honor Man and was awarded the stripe and crossed rifles of a lance corporal. He was ordered to the First Marine Division at Camp Pendleton, where he underwent infantry training with the First Battalion, First Marine Regiment. It was there Cowboy first heard about recon rangers. He applied, got accepted, and completed training.

Chapter 27

Saturday, May 30, 1970

Marlin threw the Plymouth in reverse and backed it into the barn, leaving just enough space to get the Apache out. He closed the double doors and squeezed past a badly rusted plow on his way out the back. I wandered around the side and met him in the corral.

"That tree has got to be over a hundred feet tall," Marlin said, closing the door and nodding up the slope.

"It's the biggest one I've ever seen that's for sure!" I walked up the embankment and parted the cloak of broad, green leaves. The tree's interior was dark, so I leaned in for a better look, but still couldn't make out much.

"Be careful." Marlin was walking up the slope toward the house, with his suit coat over his shoulder, hanging off his finger.

"Why?"

"It's a sycamore," he said, stopping at the bottom of the back porch. "Those leaves have tiny, yellow, fuzzy hairs on their underside. They'll make your eyes and skin burn."

I jumped back, brushing my face and arms. "You could've said something."

"I just did." Marlin climbed the steps and disappeared inside.

The last thing I needed to do was start itching, so I carefully backed my way out and leapt atop the porch to go wash. I flung the door open, and ran straight into the back of Marlin, who'd stopped dead in his tracks. I looked past him. Wren was sitting at the kitchen table with an expired can of mixed vegetables, an open box of stale crackers, and a bottle of clotted barbeque sauce.

"Is there anything you won't eat?" Marlin had his hands on his hips. Wren just smiled and smeared mushy, discolored vegetables on a cracker, smothered it in sauce, and popped it in his mouth. A cold shiver went down my spine.

"Pickled beets," Wren replied without looking up or disrupting his cadenced chewing. "Cooked spinach, too. The smell's enough to make me sick." He'd fixed three crackers in that time, stacked them, and shoved them in his mouth.

"Anything else is fair game I take it?"

"Pretty much," Wren mumbled, cheeks bulging, crumbs everywhere. About then, Frank returned with his review of the farmhouse.

"This place is a fucking shit hole!"

Wren swallowed. "But there's food!" He was eating crackers faster than he could fix them.

"That couch," Frank said, jerking his thumb over his shoulder toward the front room, "has at least a half dozen diseases—most of them contagious and at least one that's fatal—and the mattress in the back bedroom looks like somebody gave birth on it! Hell, there's a goddamn bird's nest in the toilet!"

"It's an abandoned farmhouse. What'd you expect?" Marlin said.

"I turned on the bathroom faucet, and do you know what came out?"

"Water?"

"Rust! Fucking rust! Can you believe it?"

"It's just oxidization from the pipes," Marlin said. "Turn the water on and let it run; it'll be fine."

"To hell with that. I can wait. We're leaving soon enough."

"About that," Wren mumbled and then swallowed.

"Don't even!" Frank said sharply, spinning to face him. "We're leaving when it gets dark!"

"I don't think that's such a good idea now."

"It sure the hell was an hour ago!"

"That was then. I've given it more thought. We have to be extra cautious."

"Meaning what?"

"Meaning we have to assume the worst; there are no safe roads right now."

"We never should've stopped in the first place!"

Marlin had kept out of it to that point. He was unbuttoning the cuffs on his shirt and rolling back his sleeves when he finally spoke. "Wrong, we had to get that car out of sight."

"Fine! It's out of sight! But it'll be dark soon, and if we stick to back roads, we can be in Louisville in a couple of hours."

"I'm not driving that car tonight, or any other night."

"I don't believe it! We're just going to sit here?! Just how many fucked-up moves do you guys want to make? Let me know because I can come up with one or two more."

"You're too modest," Marlin said.

Chapter 28

Saturday, May 30, 1970

Darkness grew beneath the canopy of sea pines and coconut trees, and the ghostly fog and vegetation thickened as well. With a nearly imperceptible nod from Puspoon, Cowboy rose and crept through the jungle, deftly parting broad leaves and hanging vines while silently weaving his way toward the trail. He tread so lightly he seemed to float in the mist.

L.Cpl. Terry Dunn, the second man in formation, moved steadily forward despite losing sight of Cowboy for anxious seconds. He emerged from heavy undergrowth to find the point man on a knee, fist raised at the edge of the trail. Dunn sent the signal down the line, and one-by-one everyone froze among the leafy plants and dwarf palms, weapons at the ready. Cowboy scoured the jungle, seeking the outline of a man or weapon. Candles flickered in the hooches. The surf was the only sound. *All clear.* He moved on, sidestepping a tangle of scrub before slinking out of the jungle and onto the sandy trail.

Cowboy had walked point in enemy territory near the DMZ at least a half dozen times a month since joining First Force Recon, but their missions were usually deeper in enemy territory. He always moved as slow and with as much caution as his senses dictated. Cowboy swept his M16 back and forth in an arc. Shapes, gray and black in the murk, were impossible to distinguish at times. He sank his heel in the sand, tentatively feeling for a twig, rock, booby trap—anything at all—with the sole of his boot before letting his toes touch the ground. He knew the Vietcong sometimes set traps at night on village trails.

A strong, stiff wind blew in from the ocean, rustling the trees and cooling the night. The Marines, wet clothes stuck to their skin, followed the trail away from the coast. They moved in single file through the shifting fog, maintaining five meters between them in case all hell broke loose. First Force Recon's mission was projected for no more than thirty hours. If all went as planned, they'd be back at Da Nang for breakfast the following morning.

The eleven recon rangers had the arsenal to take down a company. Nine men carried M-16s capable of firing nine hundred rounds per minute. They also carried a dozen twenty-round magazines as well as claymore mines and an assortment of smoke, concussion, and fragmentation grenades. Two men shouldered M60 machine guns: Double D, who, at six foot six and 220 pounds, was the unit's largest man, and Dunn, a similarly built oil worker from Houston. Along with their M60s, the pair packed spare barrels and fifteen hundred rounds, nearly twice that of an ordinary machine gunner. Four men had grenade launchers: Silenka and Rogers had M203s attached beneath their rifle barrels while Mo and PFC Slessen carried bloop guns. Cpl. Bill "Mild Bill" Devenzie, another giant of a man, but a nicer one you'd never meet, humped an ammo box filled with extra rounds for every weapon. Red had his M16, but he also carried the bolt-action Winchester .30-06 his dad used in World War II, a gift when he graduated sniper school. The neoprene sleeve inside his breast pocket contained a half dozen Sierra MatchKing hollow-tip rounds.

The ocean breeze and sound of the surf faded. Had it been daylight, the seaside mix of tropical fruit trees, lush green plants, and colorful flowers would've made a picturesque postcard, but at night, the rainforest was indistinguishable in its gloominess. As the

Marines moved further in country, the air gradually became a lifeless, humid stink of soggy, rotting vegetation. Leeches, black and slug-like, dropped from tree branches and squirmed inside their clothes to feast on their bodies. The dank jungle floor deadened their footsteps, though, so Cowboy quickened the pace, moving quietly, fully attuned to his surroundings. He hadn't misread a situation, not one, since joining First Force Recon, so Puspoon deferred to his judgment.

Cowboy slowed, then paused. The birds quit singing ahead of him, and then those around him stopped as well. His uneasiness grew. He dropped to a knee, heart pounding, eyes straining to see ahead in the fog. There was a faint crack, and he raised his fist. Dunn, behind him, relayed the signal. Everyone froze. Cowboy flashed four fingers at Dunn and pointed up the trail. The message went down the line.

Puspoon pulled out his Hush Puppy and screwed on the suppressor can while nodding for Silenka to do the same. He signaled Rogers to set up four men on the opposite side of the trail, two each for him and Silenka. Silenka, Mk 22 in hand, retraced his steps and crouched behind a papaya tree near a large cluster of plants and flowers opposite Moe and Devenzie. Puspoon backtracked ten yards further and hid opposite Slessen and Dunn while the other Marines moved off the trail and took cover in the jungle.

It was just another routine patrol. The four VC fighters had traveled the trail a dozen times since their deployment to the Thạch Hà district. They knew the route blind, so there was no excuse for making noise. It set off a spate of polytonal bickering that stopped only after they shared a laugh about all the ruckus they were raising. They weren't concerned, let alone afraid. US forces conducted daytime operations in the DMZ, but the VC controlled it at night.

The four men wore loose, black clothing similar to silk pajamas as well as conical straw hats. They walked single file: the lead man loosely cradled his rifle while the man at the rear held his weapon across his body, barrel down, with the butt beneath his armpit; the second and third men had their rifles slung over their shoulders. When the foursome passed Silenka, he rose from a crouch and shot the fourth man and then the third man, both in the back of the head. The first two soldiers, hearing the soft, metal clinks, whirled around, wide-eyed. Puspoon stepped onto the trail and dropped them with headshots. The others quickly carried the bodies deep into the jungle. Then they were on the move, making up for lost time.

Chapter 29

Saturday, May 30, 1970

Driving the Johnny Lightning Special, Al Unser dominated the race, leading all but ten laps and, at one point, lapping every car on the track. He cruised to victory over half a minute ahead of second-place finisher, Mark Donahue. Kenyon developed numbness in his hand and was forced to retire on lap 112. Roger McCluskey, whose own race ended earlier due to suspension damage, took over. On lap 172, he spun going into turn three and smacked the wall, setting off a wild, fiery multi-car crash. He wound up sixteenth.

Kent didn't see a lap. Even with the rain delay, the race was nearly over before the Wantels were free to leave. Against his pleas, Mrs. Wantel headed straight home, refusing to cross town so he could see the last few laps and keep his consecutive race streak alive.

"Not after what happened today. No way, José. We're going home." Kent didn't stop whining until they were north of Melott. That's when he launched into a graphic—and unsolicited—account of the scene at the bank.

"You should've seen it. I opened the door, and there was a woman lying on the floor in a big pool of blood. She was on her side, but she'd been shot in the back."

"Kent, please," Darlene said, "I'd rather not hear about it. It's too upsetting."

"There were two more bodies in the vault. Both women. Both shot. One of them was pregnant, too. I thought the security guard was dead, but he just got knocked out."

"Stop it, Kent."

"I didn't see the bank manager, but they blew half his head off!"

"SHUT THE HELL UP!"

"DARLENE!" Mrs. Wantel said, horrified.

"I asked politely." Darlene leaned forward, whispering, "One more word about the bank and I'll claw your eyes out."

"Okay, okay, geez," Kent said, jerking his head away, "you don't have to be so nasty about it."

The rest of the trip was brutally long. Kent went back to brooding while Darlene stared out the window, worrying about Tyler. Mrs. Wantel gave up trying to start a conversation. It was just as well. Her heart wasn't in it anyway.

As soon as they got home, Kent grabbed the telephone, stretched the cord from the hallway to his room, and started calling his friends to give them all the gory details. Darlene grabbed the phone book from the hallway table and, after looking up Puspoon, walked to the kitchen. Her mother was putting dishes in the cabinet, so she grabbed a towel and dried the silverware.

"Mom, I'm scared," she said, putting the knives in the drawer.

"I know you are, dear, but there's nothing we can do except pray and be strong." She was worried, too, but tried not to show it for her daughter's sake.

"Why would they take Tyler?" Darlene asked.

"I don't know, and it doesn't do us any good to speculate. What it does tell us, though, is that they wanted him alive, and that's better than how they left those other poor people."

"I guess so."

"No, dear, you know so."

"You're right, but I'm still scared." Darlene reached for the spoons.

"I think Agent Kramer will find him."

"You do?"

"Yes, I do. I've got a good feeling about her. I don't know what she was thinking, but I could see her mind working. Now, why don't you get some rest?"

"I'd rather wait up to see if she finds Tyler."

"It's getting late. I'll tell you what, you can stay up a little while longer and then it's off to bed. I'll wake you if I hear anything, okay?"

"Okay, but make Kent get off the phone. He's tying up the line."

Chapter 30

Saturday, May 30, 1970

Escaping was my top thought, but I had to the clean the bathroom first, the last of a long list of jobs Frank assigned me. I thought Marlin would intercede on my behalf, but he just shrugged his shoulders. The bird's nest fit nicely in the hollow of the oak tree.

Wren won a coin flip and took one of the two bedrooms down the hall. Frank was already ensconced in the other one. Marlin and I shared the living room.

"You take the couch, kid. I'll sleep on the floor," he said, removing his suit jacket.

"Uh-uh, no way. Frank's right, that couch looks deadly."

Marlin shrugged. "Okay, but that floor looks hard. Let me know if you want to switch up." He walked out the room and poked around inside the hallway closet across from the bathroom for a minute before emerging with three thin, musty blankets and a couple of lumpy, feather-clotted pillows. He brushed off the mouse droppings from the top blanket and threw it on the couch. Then he dropped one of the pillows and the other two blankets at my feet.

"Use your T-shirt as a pillow case," he said, tossing the other pillow on the couch, "and fold the blankets up, so you can lie on top of them." He removed his white button-down shirt and laid it over the back of the chair. "You can cover up with my jacket."

"Thanks," I muttered. Marlin spread his blanket so half of it covered the seat cushions and the other half hung over the back of the couch. Then he stretched out, shoved the pillow under his head, and pulled the top half of the blanket over him. I was already on the floor with Marlin's jacket draped over my shoulders. I yawned loudly.

"Tired, huh, kid?"

"Very."

"You'll probably sleep like a rock then."

"Probably."

"Me, I'm a light sleeper."

"Really?" *Who cares?*

"Yeah, the slightest noise wakes me up."

"Fascinating."

"Cut the sarcasm, and listen to what I'm saying."

"I'm too tired, just tell me."

"Don't get any ideas about sneaking off during the night."

"The thought never crossed my mind."

Chapter 31

Sunday, May 31, 1970

It would be another scorcher, and with all the humidity, too. First Force Recon spent several long hours navigating the jungle, often having to take cover off trails to skirt patrols. Ahead lay the narrow coastal plain, the highlands, and beyond them, dark against the deep violet sky, the Truong Son range of the Annamite Mountains.

Cowboy raised a fist and lay flat on the path ten meters from the clearing. There was no cloud cover, and the orange moon glowed bright. He crept across the hard-packed ground to the jungle's edge to study the terrain. Then he looked through his infrared M3 "snooperscope." There was nothing but low scrub to the west for five hundred meters and then acres and acres of elephant grass. Cowboy scaled a tangle of thick bamboo for a view above the grass tops through his scope. Then he checked north and south. Puspoon and Silenka crept up to join him.

"We're clear, sir," Cowboy said. He pointed where the thick jungle jutted out into the clearing south of their position. "Nothing but birds and insects."

"What about the grass?" Rogers asked.

"I scoped it. We're good."

Puspoon turned to Silenka. "Set up a skirmish line. We'll cross at five-second intervals."

"Roger, Lieutenant."

When Slessen, the last man, crossed the clearing, Puspoon signaled his point man to move out. The grass, razor-sharp and wall-like in its thickness, towered above them, blotting out the moonlight, but Cowboy moved fast, leading the others in single file on the tight trail villagers had hacked out with machetes.

The air grew stale and steadily warmer. The grass slashed the Marines' clothing, slicing clean through to their skin. The bigger men had the toughest time, having to move sideways at almost every turn to avoid serious wounds. Only Cowboy emerged unscathed. After an hour, the team arrived at a fork. The Marines, drenched in sweat, took deep breaths, filling their lungs with whatever oxygen they could pull in the dead air. Puspoon pointed the way and Cowboy took off again, this time at an even greater pace. He wanted to cover as much ground as possible while the heat and humidity were at their lowest. Sweat dripped in the men's eyes and stung their skin. They breathed heavily on the tight trail, enduring biting gnats and blood-sucking mosquitoes for hours on end. Puspoon finally ordered a break.

Sgt. Rogers established front and rear security, posting four men, two at each end, with an order to rotate after five minutes. Everyone else shed their clothes and gear and paired off to remove leeches.

"Sergeant Rogers," Puspoon said, "have the men drink a canteen of water and throw their empties off trail."

"Roger, Lieutenant."

"Give me a hand, Staff Sergeant." Puspoon took a long pull on his canteen. Then he stripped off his shirt. Silenka went to work, using his KA-BAR to pry blood-fattened leeches from his back. Puspoon rolled up his pant legs, exposing three more of the suckers. Angry, red welts marked where the parasites had fed. Puspoon took another drink and started working on his arms, chest, and stomach. By the time security rotated, he'd removed seven of the buggers.

The men dressed quickly and readjusted their equipment. A few stood with their hands clasped behind their heads, filling their lungs with as much oxygen as possible. Puspoon approached Silenka and Rogers, map in hand. Rogers flicked on his flashlight.

"Our route keeps sloping up," Puspoon said, dragging his index finger over the map toward the foothills of the highlands. "It won't take long to cross the plains."

"You're sure this grass ends?" Rogers said, eliciting a smile from Puspoon, but no reaction at all from Silenka. Silenka never smiled.

"Here's the ambush site," Puspoon said, circling a vale in the highlands, "and here's where we are." He drew another circle.

"Lots of hills to hump," Silenka said.

"Right, and they keep getting bigger the further we go. Let's saddle up."

The elephant grass eventually thinned and disappeared altogether, giving way to the patchy scrub and rolling, red clay of the plains. The Marines skirted endless rice paddies near the villages they passed through in the night. Although the ground was sloping upward, Cowboy maintained a fast pace, almost trotting. First Force Recon had reached another danger point in the mission. The vegetation, although lush in places, consisted mostly of bushy plants and scraggly jaks and firs that rarely exceeded a man's height. The Marines couldn't chance being seen; they needed to be in the lowlands before dawn.

As First Force Recon moved further west, saplings of evergreens and pines and other conifers became regular parts of the terrain. The Marines' ascents and descents steepened as well, and within hours they were traversing the ravines beneath a thick, towering forest. The early morning light barely breached the broad green leaves and colorful foliage.

Cowboy slowed the pace. They were still beneath the jungle's canopy, but nearing a ridge not far from the ambush site. Threats from patrols, booby traps, and ambushes were at their highest. Forty-five minutes later, the eleven Marines had barely gone half a klick. Cowboy suddenly raised his fist. Everyone froze, but ten pairs of eyes scanned the surrounding forest and twenty ears strained for sounds.

The limb extended over the trail, just before the fork, but it was the brief dull glint from a silver hook that drew Cowboy's attention. It was shoulder high and tied to a nearly invisible monofilament fishing line looped around the stem of a bamboo leaf. Cowboy warily approached it. He studied the spear-shaped leaf as well as the vine and then followed the limb off the trail before ducking to the other side for a different view. Cowboy separated a set of three leaves, exposing the line. Then, using his index finger, he traced it to the tree where it disappeared among the spider lilies, hibiscus, and oleanders. Stooping, he inspected the red, white, and yellow flowers before gently parting their stems and finding not only the line, but a grenade tied knee-high to a bamboo stake.

Silenka, a demolition expert, crept forward. The booby trap's proximity to the ambush site suggested it was a lethal security alarm to warn of enemy presence. He studied the trap while Cowboy started down the south fork with a keen eye. He heel-to-toe walked on the dirt trail and eyed the overhanging leaves and vines. He spotted a second trip wire straight away, and then another not long after. Both were poorly hidden, which set off an inner alert. Further on, he discovered a punji pit covered by decaying leaves. Cowboy returned, joining Silenka at the fork. Together, they scouted the northern route. It was clear. Silenka crept back to Puspoon.

"They want us going north."

"It could be an ambush. Let's backtrack half a klick and go south."

Chapter 32

Sunday, May 31, 1970

Sam Burroughs fought more hangovers than crime during his long, undistinguished FBI career, and Saturday night's tussle with vodka had left him bruised, battered, and head down on his desktop, gingerly fingering his skull, searching for fault lines. He hadn't washed or changed clothes in days, and he emitted a disturbing odor, a sickeningly sweet smell, not dissimilar to the early tang of death. Burroughs looked like death: oily skin, unshaven face, puffy, red eyes, and uncombed, greasy hair. He was quaking mad, though, and would've erupted when Kramer entered his office if not for his hammering headache. Instead, he kept quiet, and his eyes shut; noise and light were painful.

"Sit down, Kramer, and don't say a goddamn word." Burroughs' voice, always gravelly, was hoarse from three packs of smokes. His red tie was unknotted, and the top three buttons of his white dress shirt, stained yellow beneath his armpits, were unfastened. Moving very slowly, head still as a corpse, Burroughs pulled the tie from his neck and let it drop to his lap. He left it there and slowly pushed up his shirt sleeves, so they were tight on his forearms. Then he hawked something from his lungs, rolled it around with his tongue, and swallowed as if genetically programmed. Kramer shivered.

"You've been chasing DTK for months," Burroughs rasped. "and you're no closer to catching them than when you started."

"Sam, I'm as—" Kramer began, but stopped when Burroughs, wincing, lifted his palms from the desktop, imploring her with his fingers to lower her voice.

Kramer straightened her shoulders and leaned back in the government-issued chair. She crossed her legs and breathed deeply, knowing she was about to get reamed but not at all in the mood for it. She was at the short end of both sleep and patience, and feeling frustrated, jinxed even, because Merle Prand, who'd been floating in and out of consciousness, couldn't remember anything except a gunslinging horse in a white cowboy hat.

"Look, I'm as frustrated as you are," she began softly.

"THE HELL YOU ARE!" Burroughs exploded. He started to rise but grabbed his head, slumped back, and slid down in his chair. Kramer thought she heard him whimper. A long, silent moment passed. She finally stood, leaning, palms on the desktop, and looked down. Burroughs was cradling his head.

"You okay?" she whispered.

Burroughs struggled to straighten himself in his chair. "No! Tolson's hounding my ass morning, noon, and night, and he chews it to bits every time he finds it! Why can't you find them?!"

Kramer sat again and crossed her legs. "These guys are pros. They know what they're doing."

"You think?"

"They mix up the days of the week and the times of day. They wear sunglasses, and they've got their hats pulled low. There's no fingerprints because they wear gloves. If there's video, they take it. They're in and out in under three minutes. Every time."

"I'll just tell Tolson they're too good for us. He'll understand."

"I'm just waiting on that one big break."

"Maybe that's the problem, you're just waiting."

Kramer took a slow, deep breath. The man was insufferable. He'd made it clear with cool aloofness that he didn't like her on her first day of work. She suspected it was probably her gender or skin color, or, more likely, both, but she'd ignored him and focused on her casework. That changed when Burroughs was named "the acting" and assigned her the DTK case. Ever since then, Kramer had worked nights and weekends without a day off, and she was only getting further behind. Now, after Teymore and CNT, she was swamped. She'd barely slept the last two days, and, having lost her appetite from all the stress, she'd eaten only sparingly. So, remaining calm wasn't easy, but she managed it.

"Look, Sam, I've been putting in twenty-hour days ever since you assigned DTK to me. I don't have a partner, and if I'm not in the field, I'm here doing paperwork or taking calls."

"And what have you come up with? Nothing!"

"That's not true! If ballistics show it's the same gun—and it will—I think we may have a serial killer."

"Serial killer?! Are you serious? Serial killers act alone, or didn't they teach you that in school?"

"That's one-oh-one. One-oh-two covers those who don't."

"Doesn't make sense. He could've murdered fifty people by now, but, instead it's only what, how many? I've forgotten."

"Only?"

"You know what I mean."

"There's a conflict."

"What do you mean, conflict?"

"Struggle. Something, or someone, is holding him back. Probably the latter."

"Why do you say that?"

"The broken bundle of twenties."

"What about it?"

"That money didn't jump out the window. It was thrown, and not long into their getaway, so somebody wasn't happy. It has to be the murders; it's the only thing that fits."

"Anything else?"

"I don't know how much you know about the stolen Fury, but the call was logged shortly after eight yesterday morning. Half hour later, it was in a hit-and-run a few blocks from the bank.

Someone got the license number. They headed for the north split, but then IPD started fielding calls about money blowing around on 65 north of Greenwood."

"They turned around."

"That's what I think. We've had reports of a blue Fury near Columbus. ISP's looking south now."

"What else?"

"The desk clerk and a bartender at the hotel lounge ID'd the big man from sketches. He registered under the name Harvey Baxter, paid with a credit card, and listed his address as 5328 Charlotte Street in Kansas City. KC checked it out. The address is legit, but there's no Harvey Baxter. The credit card's bogus."

"What'd you find in his room?"

"Nothing. Either he wiped it or the Holiday Inn has great maid service."

"No prints?"

"Not even a smudge.

"Phone calls?"

"Just to room service and a nearby pizzeria. Food was left at the door both times, and he slid a ten-spot under the door for the pizzas."

"Damn it! What's the story on the boy?"

"His name's Tyler Puspoon. I believe the gang still has him."

"Why in the hell would they kidnap someone?"

"It's definitely a twist."

"Your serial killer just murdered a bunch of people, but balked at killing him. Why, because he's a teenager?

"I don't think so. He just killed a pregnant woman and a nineteen-year-old girl."

"Hostage?"

"Maybe, but I doubt it. There was no need. Why grab someone you'd have to babysit?"

"All right, what're you thinking then?" Burroughs was baffled.

"What if Tyler recognized one of them?"

"That's your theory?! No wonder you can't catch these guys!"

Kramer again let her irritation pass before speaking. "I can't think of any other reason that makes sense, can you? Why all of a sudden is he treated special?"

"Hmm, I don't know if I can sell that to Tolson."

"Wait, what? Whatever, Sam, we've got bigger problems."

"What's that?"

"What if they can't afford to let him go?"

Chapter 33

Sunday, May 31, 1970

It was early afternoon, hot and suffocatingly humid. The sun had crept over the mountaintops. There was scarcely light enough to distinguish the array of colors from a few feet away. Hidden on the hill in a thicket of bamboo, among the candle-like leaves of a yellow mimosa, Puspoon and SSgt. Silenka studied the clearing. Sgt. Rogers joined them, emerging on his stomach from a tangle of flame vines and golden showers. He sheathed his KA-BAR and wiped perspiration from his brow.

"There's the tunnel," Puspoon whispered. He was pointing to the southern end of a clearing where palm fronds and other broad-leafed plants were in the early stages of decay. "And that's our kill zone." His finger swept left to right. "Twenty meters wide, forty meters long."

The three men studied the area for several moments.

"Set up an L," Puspoon finally whispered. Nodding to Silenka, "You, Cowboy, Mo, and Dunn are the short line north of the clearing. I want six claymores facing west and another six to your south. Leave the clackers and drop your comm line on the way down."

"Roger, Lieutenant" Silenka said.

"Red's taking his first clear shot, so expect it right after Than emerges. I'll hit the clackers when he drops and we'll light it up. Then I'll signal your withdrawal. Acknowledge it and head for the northeast fork. There's a dry creek bed. Follow it for a quarter klick and wait. When we let it rip again, head straight south for the hill. If you're not there in five minutes, sit tight. We'll find you."

"We'll be there, Lieutenant."

"We'll cover your withdraw and climb. The code's 'black' and 'magic.' We assemble at the top and take the same way back."

"Got it, sir." Silenka crawled off, disappearing in the forest.

"Set up the long end," Puspoon said, turning to Rogers. "Red's on the elbow."

"Aye-aye, sir."

The Marines, heavily camouflaged, crawled cautiously through the jungle, scarcely moving at times and stopping altogether for long periods. The ever darkening jungle with all its night noises gave them the cover necessary to get in position undetected. Puspoon was taking up the slack in the lines to the short end when Rogers returned.

"We're ready, sir," he set the comm line next to Puspoon.

"Now we wait." As Rogers snaked away, Puspoon separated the clackers into two pairs. He turned to Red, who was sighting in his snooperscope.

"You've got one shot. Put him in the past tense."

Chapter 34

Sunday, May 31, 1970

I wasn't exactly feeling festive when I woke up. The hard floor and nightmares about my imminent demise kept me awake most of the night, and even when I managed to squeeze in a few winks, I awoke to the symphonic sounds of Wren's frequent bathroom breaks. Frank also got up, at least that's who I think kicked me. Marlin, the light sleeper, snored through it all.

Now was my chance. Chucks in hand, I snuck out of the living room, quiet as stone, and laced up at the kitchen table. I slowly eased the back door open.

"Don't run off," Marlin called from the couch.

"I won't." *Shit.*

The tree limbs extended so far out I walked off the porch and right onto one. I pinched off a huge, dark green leaf. Marlin was right. It was covered with tiny, yellow fibers on the underside. I pulled my T-shirt over my head and climbed onto a limb as big around as my forearm. I pushed past the branches, working my way inward. Warped, twisted limbs and branches extended in a thousand different directions, all of them tracing to a trunk the size of a Buick.

I started climbing, choosing my route one limb at a time, hopping from side to side, and stopping when I got where only monkeys dare. I stood on a heavy bough and grabbed onto a limb to steady myself, so I could enjoy the view, but there was nothing but short stalks of corn, which reminded me of the hot, humid twelve-hour days I spent detasseling for migrant wages. I didn't want any more nightmares, so I climbed down.

The breakfast menu featured the same hardtack, vegetable sludge, and coagulated sauce that only Wren dared eat the day before. Frank and Marlin chose to continue their hunger strike, but my fear of botulism had faded overnight, so I gagged down a small bite and chased it with well water that tasted like someone had washed his socks in it. Afterward, the four of us sat there, unwashed, unkempt, and unpleasantly odoriferous.

"We've got to get some real food today," Frank said irritably, pushing himself away from the table. "I can't eat this shit."

"Me neither," Marlin agreed, after cautiously smelling the can.

Wren, on the other hand, treated the disgusting swill like sweetmeat, blissfully spooning the dark mush onto one cracker after another, and decorating each one with intricate brown designs. Wren popped a cracker in his mouth that looked like the family crest.

"Go get some then," he said. He sniffed the water, shrugged, and took a gulp. "May as well get some other stuff, too. Soap, toothpaste, toothbrushes, deodorant."

"Some of us need toothpaste and deodorant more than others," I said, looking at Frank.

"Shut up, Pussypoon. If I want your opinion, I'll tell you what it is!"

"Get clothes, too," Wren continued. "Oh, and a camp stove, so I can cook!"

"Damn it! This isn't a Boy Scout jamboree! Just get some bread and cold meat, and we'll leave when it's dark!"

"You'll have to go to town, Mr. Marlin," Wren said, ignoring Frank. "You're the only one who hasn't been sketched."

"No problem, but not in that car. I'll get the Apache running. C'mon, kid," Marlin said, giving me a nudge, "you can help."

"I don't believe it," Frank complained, looking at Wren. "You plan on homesteading, don't you?"

I was three steps inside the barn when the urine and manure lit my lungs like napalm. I turned, retinas scorched, and blindly fumbled for the door, but kept bumping into Marlin, who was blocking my exit. Frantic, desperate seconds passed before I finally got past him and burst outdoors, coughing, choking, and gulping lungfuls of air. Tears streamed down my cheeks. Marlin's too, but he was laughing.

"When you're done playing around, we can get to work." He was leaning against the doorjamb with a big smile. I was bent over with my hands on my knees, chest heaving in and out, hacking up solid matter.

"Work?" I said, coughing and rubbing my eyes. "I can't work in there! I can't see or breathe!"

"I'll open up the doors and get a breeze going. You'll get used to it."

"How about I wait right here while you do that?" I said, squinting wetly.

Marlin laughed and disappeared inside, but he'd no sooner done so when he popped his head back out.

"Go on, I'm too close to death to run off." I was still on one knee, panting.

There was rustling followed by scraping and then a jarring vibration. A slice of sunlight ran the length of the barn floor, splitting the darkness before extinguishing it entirely. I waited for the breeze Marlin promised and headed inside. The stalls were a fetid swamp of filthy, soggy, rotting straw and bushels and bushels of road apples. Dark clouds of flies buzzed about. Barn swallows had shit everywhere.

"It's a horse farm in case you haven't noticed," Marlin said and raised his arms to invite a look around. There was tack all over: bridles, halters, and cinch straps hung off bent, rusty nails; reins and bits lay on a cluttered workbench; and two saddles with blankets sat atop a pair of nervous looking sawhorses.

"I saw three horses out back," I said. A small cyclone of dirt, dust, and bits of straw blew through the barn.

"That brown one's a Norfolk Trotter. The one with all the colors is an Appaloosa. The other's a Quarter Horse. She's just a filly."

"You know your horses, huh?"

"Yeah, I guess so. Mom and dad were farmers. We raised dairy cows and chickens. Grew crops, too. We each had a horse. Mine was a Palomino. Beautiful horse. This place brings it all back," he said wistfully. Then he smiled. "I've got to get that truck going."

The rusty, old Chevy had seen a few paint schemes since its original black. It had bald tires, a cracked windshield, and a front bumper held fast with baling wire. A dirty, green ball cap with "Anderson Corn" embroidered on it hung over the stick shift. Mice had eaten through the seats and made a nest in the stuffing. They'd shit everywhere, too.

"I'm going to swap out the battery and poke around under the hood, give things a look. Grab that pitchfork and the wheelbarrow from out back and clean out the stalls. You can dump the straw behind the barn, but not too close." I started muttering something about Soviet gulags, but he cut me off.

"Look, kid, you can help out or get out, but if you get out, get inside. Up to you."

Cleaning stalls was backbreaking work. Sweat dripped from my brow, streaking my glasses and stinging the cuts, abrasions, and punctures mapping my face. My shirt was sopping wet after the first load. My hands blistered after the second. The horses got curious and sauntered over. Shaded by the barn, they nickered and chuffed while swishing their tails and rolling their heads to drive off biting horseflies.

By the time I wheeled the third load out back, my eyes had cleared enough to see the farm to the south. It was a working farm, unlike this one, and in good shape, unlike this one. The house, a two-story, was white with black trim and red shutters. The barn, which, like the house, was ringed with flowers, appeared to have been freshly painted to match. A chip-seal road fronted the farm and ended at a gravel road running east and west. I hatched a plan.

Chapter 35

Sunday, May 31, 1970

Kramer stared at the Indiana map hanging on the pale green wall behind her desk until it was a complete blur. She was running on fumes after another short night of tossing and turning. She gave her head a quick shake. When her vision cleared, she was still staring at the map. *Twenty-two pins on a map.* Eighteen had a red bulb for bank robberies. Three yellow ones—the teller died, having never emerged from the coma—denoted robberies and murders. The twenty-second pin, the one for CNT, was orange and represented robbery, murder, and kidnapping. *Why Indiana? What's the connection?*

The light blue U.S. Government telephone book, surprisingly thin, was buried in the bottom desk drawer. Kramer telephoned the Defense Department in Washington, D.C. and got an operator who had no idea how to route her call. She ended up explaining the situation to a succession of Marine Corps officers, each one a rank higher than the last. Finally, a brigadier general promised to get word to the Commandant as soon as he got off the line.

Kramer struggled to keep her eyes open. She got up from her chair and stood at the window, yawning loudly. Then she headed to the breakroom for another cup of coffee. She heard her telephone ringing from the hallway and ran back to it.

"Kramer."

"Hey, Agent Kramer, it's Detective Reed."

"Hey."

"I wasn't expecting to catch you at work. I was going to leave word to call me. How's it going?"

"With me or DTK?"

"Both, actually, but let's hear about you first."

"Bushed, but I'm okay."

"What about DTK?"

"Not so great."

"Haven't gotten that big break yet, have you?"

"Not yet."

"You will."

"Have you got it for me?"

"I wish. ISP found the station wagon, though."

"Where?"

"Near the Burger Chef in the Belton strip mall. It's a '68 Ford Country Squire. It was stolen from a home in Gerhart over in Holt County late Thursday or early Friday."

"Did they get any prints?"

"Haven't heard, but I'll let you know. Oh, ballistics came back, too, and guess what? It was a hol—"

"Hold on, somebody's knocking at the door." Kramer cupped her palm over the mouthpiece. "Yeah?" The door opened part way and Agent Sanchez poked his head inside. "Hey, Andy, what's up?

"Just got a call from IPD. Twyla Puspoon's downtown filling out a 'Missing Person' report on a guy named 'Frank Beetz.'"

"I've got to go." Kramer hung up.

"—low point forty-five."

Chapter 36

Sunday, May 31, 1970

The moldy, wet straw and dry, biscuit-like turds slid out of the wheelbarrow just as a white Chevy C10 pickup barreled out of the east ahead of a rooster tail of dust. The truck slowed at the stop sign, turned south, and disappeared momentarily within its chalky cloud before reappearing with the brake lights on. The truck swung into the driveway, and a young man, trim and muscular and wearing a dark maroon sleeveless T-shirt, blue jeans, and white ball cap, got out and jogged across the ankle-deep grass to the back of the house. He effortlessly hopped the railing onto the porch, unlocked the door, and went inside.

"What're you looking at?"

I nearly snapped my neck. Marlin stood in the doorway, holding a can of oil. He had a dark smudge beneath his eye that smacked of a bruise. He was smiling, though, so if he was checking to see if I ran off, he was relieved to find me loafing.

"The horses," I lied, lifting the wheelbarrow. I'd been lying a lot since Friday, but it was hard telling which ones were believed. I herded Marlin back in the barn with a couple runs at him with the wheelbarrow and then pushed on past him to the stalls.

My hands burned like fire where the blisters popped, but I grabbed the pitchfork and quickly filled the wheelbarrow. Marlin's head was buried somewhere in the engine compartment. He lifted it to watch me, presumably for amusement. I wheeled past, pretending to struggle, but once outside, I took off running.

Marlin turned the nut on the crankshaft, just a fraction; he could only guess when the truck last ran. Then he removed the plugs and scrubbed them with a wire brush and took off the distributor cap and reset the points. After he hooked the electrical back up, he checked the fluids. Marlin occasionally glanced at the kid, smiling as he forked dank, smelly hay into the wheelbarrow. He shut the hood and looked for something to wipe his hands on before heading out back to wash up. He saw the wheelbarrow first. Then he spotted Tyler booking across the field.

"Damn it, kid!" Marlin jumped astride the Quarter Horse, clicked his tongue and shook her mane. She responded, kicking up dirt and going to a full gallop in seconds. Marlin locked his knees against her flanks and brought his elbows in. The filly's powerful muscles tensed and exploded, and he moved in time with her.

Hoofbeats! Loud and getting louder, too! I looked over my shoulder. The Quarter Horse, Marlin atop her, was thundering after me!

"Heeyah!" he yelled. She surged in response, closing fast, but I could see the rust on the barbwire fence. I was going to make it, and I would've, too, if not for tripping over a dirt clod and sliding headlong through a fresh pile of horse shit. A tick later, rapid-fire hoofbeats filled my ears. The filly swept past and Marlin circled her back, arriving at a trot before stopping beside me. He let loose of the horse's mane and leaned forward, scowling.

"What do you think you're doing?"

"Escaping, what's it look like?" I sat up and wiped a thick chunk of warm crap from my face and flung it to the ground. Marlin dismounted and walked over. I looked up. "Frank's going to kill me if I don't."

"No, he won't. I've got you covered." He extended his hand.

"Yeah, but I—"

"Trust me."

I looked at him, thinking it couldn't hurt, but then realized, well, actually, yeah, it could. I agreed anyway.

"Okay." I took his hand and he pulled me to my feet.

"Good, now go hose off. You're not going to town smelling like that." He slapped the horse on the rump and sent her trotting while we walked back to the barn.

Chapter 37

Sunday, May 31, 1970

Every year more than half a million people packed the Indianapolis Motor Speedway to watch the "Greatest Spectacle in Racing," the largest single-day sporting event in the world. People from all over the planet descended on Speedway, Indiana, arriving on commercial airliners, private jets, and helicopters, or in the massive caravan of cars, trucks, limousines, buses, motorcycles, and RVs that flooded the town. Traffic on the interstates near IMS was backed up for miles in both directions. Main routes suffered gridlock. Secondary roads and side streets were the worst. Entire neighborhoods were swamped with vehicles and people and beer. Lots of beer.

The day after? Nothing. It was a ghost town. The teams—owners, drivers, crews—sponsors, vendors, media, and fans all vanished. Packed up and gone. Locals couldn't be found; they were recovering. Downtown Indianapolis was just as desolate, and, although giddy about it, Kramer found it eerie having the entire stretch of Meridian Street to herself. She caught green lights nearly all the way and ran the few she didn't. She turned onto Ohio and then Alabama. Just past Market street, Kramer pulled into the last of a long line of empty parking spaces marked "Police

Vehicles Only." She tossed the gray placard stamped "FBI" on the dashboard and took the steps two at a time to the IPD building.

Inside an aging desk sergeant sipped black coffee high up on a mahogany bench salvaged a decade earlier when the county's courtrooms underwent remodeling. The bench had been transformed into a command and control center, although the boredom reigning over the skeleton crew suggested there was no need for either.

The old sergeant had been calculating his retirement pay, but when he saw Kramer over the top of his reading glasses, he put his pen on his notepad, folded his hands, and arched his eyebrows questioningly. It had been a long time since he'd gotten excited about anything.

"I'm Special Agent Kramer of the FBI." Kramer held up her badge. "I'm looking for Twyla Puspoon. She filled out a missing person report . . . ." The sergeant's long, bony index finger was pointing over her shoulder at an anxious-looking woman with a bandaged foot sitting on an oak pew, another relic from the renovation.

"Thanks," Kramer said, turning back with a bright smile. "Can I get a copy of the report?" The sergeant's unintelligible grunt indicated inconvenience, but acquiescence. Meanwhile, Twyla, who'd been watching the exchange, struggled to her feet and hobbled over.

"Excuse me. I'm Twyla Puspoon. Have you found my boyfriend?"

Kramer turned back to the sergeant. "Is there somewhere Ms. Puspoon and I can speak privately?"

"Down the hall, first door on the left," he said tiredly.

Kramer looked at Twyla. "Would you please come with me? It's urgent."

"What is it? Has something happened to Frank?"

"Please, not here."

The hinges creaked on the frost-paned door. Kramer flipped on the light switch, and eight tubes of fluorescent bulbs buzzed and flickered before lighting up the small room. There was a rectangular table with four chairs, all fashioned from blond ash and scarred from years of use.

"Have a seat," she said, stepping behind the door so Twyla could limp inside.

"Thank you." Twyla took the nearest chair. She put her hands in her lap, one over the other. "Are you a police officer?"

"FBI. I'm Special Agent Kramer."

"FBI!" Twyla straightened, tense. "Is Frank okay?"

"I'd like to talk to you about your son first."

"Tyler?" Twyla said, alarmed. "What'd he do wrong? Has he been hurt? Is he all right?"

"When did you last see him?"

"Early Friday evening. We talked on the phone after that, though. What's going on?"

"Where was he when he called you?"

"I'm not sure," Twyla said, growing irritated. "We had other things to discuss. Now, please, tell me what's going on!"

Kramer looked down at the table before raising her eyes to meet Twyla's. "We think he's been kidnapped."

Chapter 38

Sunday, May 31, 1970

Darkness arrived in the jungle well before sunset, and now, hours later, it was blacker than octopus ink. Long hours of lying motionless in the sweltering heat left the Marines wracked with numbness and pain. Clouds of gnats and hungry mosquitoes swarmed them, but the boredom was the worst, and each man steeled his mind to remain alert. Through it all, they were still, only blinking their eyes.

First Force Recon went to high alert when Than's advance team of twenty VC fighters surfaced. With no ambient light and only two snooperscopes, most of the men marked their departure by sound. Red shouldered the steel butt plate of his .30-06 and slid his hand beneath the rifle's smooth, maple forestock. He eyed them through the M3 mounted on his rifle while Puspoon, looking through a handheld model, watched as well.

First Force Recon was always outnumbered, but they swung the odds decidedly in their favor with superior firepower and the element of surprise. What seemed like the end of the world to a startled and exposed enemy was a disciplined, coordinated attack with overlapping fields of fire. In those critical first seconds, the enemy—especially inexperienced fighters—panicked or made poor decisions. That's what the Marines counted on, and they inflicted quick and certain death.

Time slowed. The eleven recon rangers were dialed in, ready to throw a surprise party. All living things—animals, birds, insects—suddenly went quiet. Cowboy jerked the line twice. *Enemy!* Puspoon immediately relayed the message along the hillside. A soft rustle of leaves signaled the unknowing attendees arrival. The VC fighters, some uniformed but most wearing black pajamas, crawled from the collage of vegetation at the tunnel's entrance. They fanned out in a defensive perimeter, but as their numbers swelled, they reformed as left and right echelons.

Several silent, eerie minutes passed. Then there was another flurry of activity and Puspoon watched eight men, larger than the others and heavily armed, emerge from the tunnel. Ten more minutes passed before the guest of honor showed. The eight VC fighters, two to a side, quickly boxed Than in. Puspoon tapped out the distance and slant range on Red's arm. There was no wind or drop, so Red's calibrations were for lead and bullet spin. Then he eased his index finger onto the trigger and put the general in his crosshairs.

Chapter 39

Sunday, May 31, 1970

The hose had been lying in the sun all day, so when the scalding water hit my face, it seared my already ravaged skin and covered the few unblemished areas with fresh new burns. My entire head was scorched. I let go the hose and hit the ground about the same time it did, hands covering my face and writhing in pain. I heard someone screaming. It turned out to be me.

I was thoroughly soaked by the time I finished washing. Dripping wet, I squish-squashed to the barn. Marlin was wedged under the dashboard, sorting out the wiring. The butt of his .45 was at the small of his back. I could've grabbed it, but there was no point since I couldn't shoot him. Frank, yes. Wren, maybe. Marlin, no.

"Are you ready?" I said. Marlin, startled, smacked his head on the underside of the dash.

"Ow! Don't sneak up on me like that!"

"How should I sneak up on you?"

"How about not at all?" he said, smiling. "What happened to your face?"

"Don't ask. You really think this thing's going to run?"

"Let's find out." Marlin climbed onto the driver's seat. A couple of seconds later, a whirring noise came from the engine compartment.

"We've got action," he said with a wink and a smile.

"It didn't start."

"It will." Marlin raised the hood. The hinges, stiff with rust, groaned like a dying cow. He unscrewed the wing nut on the air filter cover and removed the vacuum hose. The filter was stuck to the base, sealed there by years of heat, rubber, and grease. Marlin popped it loose with a screwdriver.

"See how much crud you can get out of it," he said, handing me the filter. "Don't break it."

"Okay." I sloshed over to the workbench, rapping the filter against the palm of my hand. Bits of grime rattled inside and small wisps of soot puffed out.

"It's an air filter, not a tambourine."

Marlin was back under the hood when I finished.

"No telling when this thing was driven last, but the hoses and belts aren't original." He put the air filter back. "They're in too good of shape."

I swished the gas around in the red metal can. "Not much left."

"Not much might be enough," Marlin said, winking at me. He took the can and dribbled gas inside the carburetor, replaced the cover, and tightened the wingnut.

"Okay, go spark 'em." Marlin lowered the hood and firmly shut it.

"Sure thing," I said excitedly and climbed in the cab. I leaned down and grabbed the wires beneath the dash, one in each hand, and put them together. The motor coughed, the truck lurched forward, and twin lightning bolts shot up my arms, all at the same time.

I howled and then my face slammed into the steering wheel. Marlin howled, too, with laughter. My arms felt like burnt matchsticks.

"Try it again," he said, wiping tears from his eyes, "but grab the plastic this time and take her out of gear."

"You could've said something." I shifted into neutral and put my foot on the brake. Then I touched the wires together. The Apache whirred, coughed, caught, sputtered, and finally kicked to life. Then it died.

"We got it!" Marlin slapped the fender.

"We do?"

"Didn't you hear it?"

"Yeah, for a second, but it cut out."

"There's no gas in the line." He grabbed the can and emptied what was left in the tank.

"Pump the pedal twenty times and let off."

I counted silently. "Okay!"

"Step on the brake."

"Got it!"

"Spark 'em!"

I hooked the wires together, and the Apache roared.

"Yeah!" I yelled, revving the motor a couple times.

"Hey, hey, ease off there, Mario!" Marlin yelled. "Let's not blow the engine on the parade lap!" I let off the gas pedal. The motor cleared its throat before evening out with the occasional hiccup.

"All right, back it out."

"Really?"

"You know how to drive, don't you?"

"Sure," I lied. I tortured the gearbox with horribly mistimed hand and feet movements before finally sorting out the pattern and finding reverse. I backed the truck out, herking and jerking, stopping and starting, but somehow kept the motor running. I got the truck facing the road and unhooked the wires. The motor coughed, wheezed, and died.

"You'll get a feel for it. Just takes practice."

"This truck's too cool!" I backed away and looked it over.

"Yeah, I know, I've always liked them. Now, listen, I'm going to wash up, so while I'm doing that, I want you to take care of the horses."

"Sure!" I said excitedly, still pumped about driving for the first time ever.

"Give them each a half bucket of oats and a half bucket of corn," Marlin said, nodding toward the two metal bins by the stalls. Then, pointing up, he added, "There's hay in the loft. Split up a bale and put it in their troughs."

"Sure thing!!"

"Go ahead and toss down a few bales while you're up there, but be careful, those planks aren't nailed down."

"Got it!"

"When you're done, you can clean the tank. Grab that crescent wrench off the workbench and put the plug in your pocket, so you don't lose it. Drain it and hose it down good. Grab a brush and scrub the muck off the bottom and sides. Get all that gunk out. Then rinse it out, snug the plug, and refill it."

"So, Frank has me working like a maid and you're making me the stable boy?"

"Why not?" Marlin leaned in, sniffing. "You smell like one. I thought I told you to clean up."

After taking care of the horses, I got naked and gave my clothes a good hosing down. After I beat them against the barn's cinderblock foundation, I hung them on the fence to dry and headed over to the tank. It was half full and half of that was algae. There were even a few tadpoles swimming around. After I drained the tank, I scooped out the slime and scum that was left and gave it a good hosing. Then I scrubbed, rinsed, and refilled it with fresh water. It was a long way from new, but it was clean.

My clothes were more wet than damp, but I dressed anyway. I was zipping up when the back door banged open and shut. I came around the back of the barn, expecting Marlin, but it was Frank, and he was heading down the embankment in his suit pants and wife-beater. He didn't look happy.

"What're you doing out here?"

"Frontiersmen called them chores."

"Frontier—what? Get in the damn house, you!"

"He's coming with me," Marlin announced from the back porch. "Saddle up, kid."

"That's not happening," Frank said, shaking his head. "He'll take off running first chance he gets."

"No, he won't," Marlin said dismissively. He came down the steps. "You'll stick with me, right, kid?"

"Yep," I said, smiling at Frank.

"What if people ask about his face?"

"Fistfight at school, right, kid?"

"You should see the other guy." Marlin chuckled.

"He's not going!" Frank reached to grab me, but Marlin seized his arm and twisted it behind his back, wrenching it upward until he was bent at the waist.

"Ow!" Frank squawked. "Let go, damn you!" Marlin's forearm was braced against the back of his neck, immobilizing him.

"You two need a referee, no, make that a babysitter." Wren was on the back porch in his rumpled, dirty suit, hat, and shades.

"He wants to take this little prick into town!" Frank said, face contorted in pain. Wren teeter-tottered down the steps and stopped at the top of the rise.

"Mr. Marlin, please free Mr. Wolf if you would be so kind." He walked down the slope. Marlin let Frank loose but gave him a good, hard shove that left him sprawled face down in the grass.

"He's not taking him!" Frank rose to a knee, rubbing his shoulder.

"Yes, he is," Wren replied.

"What? Why?!"

"I told him to. People in this town know each other, Mr. Wolf, but they don't know us. A stranger, more so two strangers, generates curiosity, questions, even suspicion. A boy and his dad, not so much. Curiosity, maybe, but nobody's going to suspect anything. They're a family, so they must be honest and trustworthy, get it?"

"You just make this shit up as you go along, don't you?"

"I actually read that, but in the end, it's a judgment call."

"Bad judgment call, you mean."

"So noted, Mr. Wolf. You're absolved of responsibility for whatever happens."

"But not the consequences."

Chapter 40

Sunday, May 31, 1970

"Kidnapped?!"

"I'm afraid so. Have you been following the rash of bank robberies around the state?"

"You mean the DTK gang?" Twyla asked, surprised. Then, alarmed, "You think DTK kidnapped Tyler?!"

"They robbed a CNT branch on the near east side yesterday morning. Your son was nearby, and now he's missing."

"Wait a minute, why was he in Indianapolis?"

"He was going to the 500 with the Wantels. Didn't you know?"

"No, and I don't know them either."

"Your son is classmates with Kent and Darlene Wantel. He and Darlene are dating."

"This is all news to me."

"Tyler was going to open a savings account."

"Why would he...." *Frank's wallet.*

"Although we haven't ruled out the possibility that he ran off."

"Well, you can. Tyler wouldn't run away."

"Why do you say that?"

"He had no reason to, and, besides if there's trouble, he's usually caught up in it."

"What about the fight with your boyfriend?"

"What fight? He got yelled at for getting home late."

"According to Darlene, your boyfriend punched him."

"They both told me he fell." Twyla angrily set her jaw and narrowed her eyes. Kramer noticed and backed off.

"Either way, I don't think he ran off either."

"Can I have a moment, Agent Kramer?"

"Of course, I'll grab some coffee. You want some?"

"Yes, please, I really need it."

The old desk sergeant looked blankly at Kramer when she said the pot of coffee behind him "sure smells good." Shaking her head, she walked out the building and headed west on Market Street toward Monument Circle, looking for an open restaurant. It was overcast, and the temperature had suddenly dropped about fifteen degrees. Thunder off to the west reminded her she'd left her umbrella propped against the wall by the front door where she wouldn't forget it. She crossed Delaware Street against the light, eyes searching for an open café or coffee shop. Downtown Indy looked like a ghost town, but she eventually found an open diner next to a newsstand west of the Circle.

Dark rain clouds moved in while Kramer waited at the counter. She placed her order and reviewed her notes while the waitress, a bashful teen with braces, filled two Styrofoam cups with hot, steaming coffee, bagged them, and tossed cream, sugar, and two plastic spoons inside. Kramer, dodging raindrops all the way back to the IPD building, ducked inside just before the clouds let go. She smiled and raised the white bag triumphantly as she passed the desk sergeant.

Twyla was standing at the window, favoring her bandaged foot when Kramer returned.

"I'm back," Kramer said, quietly shutting the door. "I forgot to ask how you took your coffee, so I brought cream and sugar."

"I take it black, but thanks." Twyla limped to the chair. Kramer handed her a cup.

"Look, Mrs. Puspoon—"

"Call me Twyla."

"Okay, Twyla, I just want you to know that the FBI will do everything it can to find your son and bring him home safely."

"I know you will, and I appreciate it, I really do."

"Do you have a recent photo of him?"

"I'll get you one. I only have a baby picture."

"Okay, the sooner, the better. We need to get it on the wire." Kramer took a sip and looked Twyla in the eyes. "Here's what's bothering me. Your son and boyfriend have turned up missing at the same time while in Indianapolis."

"That's an odd coincidence."

"I don't believe in coincidences. How well do you know Frank Beetz?"

Chapter 41

Red's Winchester cracked like a bullwhip. The MatchKing round smacked against General Than's forehead just below his hairline, snapping his head back as if yanked. The high-velocity bullet cartwheeled through his brain, leaving a fist-sized hole at the base of his skull.

Puspoon felt Red buck from the recoil. When Than dropped, he detonated a crossfire of four thousand ball bearings. The hot steel blasted through bodies, tearing off chunks of flesh, breaking bones, and destroying organs. First Force Recon followed with a crossfire of lead. Men staggered, knocked off balance by the impact of the rounds, and fell dead or dying. Rogers shot an illumination flare that tore through the tree limbs and dappled the jungle with an eerie white light. Clouds of smoke from automatic weapons, grenades, and claymores hung in the air. The noise was deafening, the effect decimating. Thirty men died in the first five seconds of battle.

Rogers shot another flare. The few Vietcong fighters who survived the lead and steel stumbled and fell, too dazed and disoriented to do anything except crawl aimlessly. Dunn, concealed beneath a blanket of vegetation, raked them with the M60, juddering their bodies with rounds. Two fighters found cover behind a toppled tree, blackened from decay. They spotted Dunn's muzzle flash and fired back, but Silenka lobbed a grenade that detonated near its rotted stump, killing one of them instantly. The other man, bloodied and disoriented, rose on a knee. Cowboy dropped him with a three-round burst.

Up the hill, Red had his M16 shouldered and squeezed off a round at a time, putting paid to the men who were down. Puspoon had already emptied two magazines. He slammed home a third in time to take out a fighter crawling for the tunnel's entrance. As quick as the firefight began, it stopped. Every member of Than's detail was on the ground, and although some still groaned, none moved. Puspoon jerked the short end's rope. Cowboy tugged back in response and lit out for the ravine with Mo, Dunn, and Silenka trailing him.

Than's advance team doubled back to the clearing when they heard the gunfire and explosions. Their excited voices filled the night, growing louder until they suddenly fell silent, stunned by the magnitude of the slaughter. Someone lying near the tunnel moaned, and two men pushed past their comrades to render aid. A VC officer ordered the others to find General Than. Unit members slowly migrated into the clearing, searching among the dead or dying for their commander. Most members were veteran fighters whose faces were fixed with the same grim expression they reserved whenever encountering death. Others were just boys, barely into their teens. They stared in open-mouthed shock at the mutilated bodies. Just then Puspoon hit the second set of clackers, detonating another crossfire of ball bearings. The L's long end let loose, tagging everyone left standing. Puspoon jerked Rogers's comm line and felt a tug in response. He lobbed two smoke grenades to the jungle floor and scrambled after the Marines topping the hill.

Chapter 42

Sunday, May 31, 1970

The chimes on the sporting goods store's door drew the attention of the people at the cash register, including the small, odd policeman who was sweet talking the cute little checkout girl. Marlin hesitated in the doorway, but only momentarily for he quickly recovered, gave them both a friendly nod, and headed straight to the back of the store where he stayed until it was time to go.

We wasted no time, splitting up and grabbing everything Wren had scribbled on an envelope. Marlin sent me to the checkout counter with the stove and a half dozen propane bottles. After that, it was an armload of clothes. Finally, he loaded me up with fishing gear and slipped me a fresh, crisp hundred dollar bill. Marlin waited until the girl finished bagging. Then he swept passed the cop, muttered an apology, and went straight out the door, carrying the stove and everything on top of it. The cop never got a second look at his face, and, in the time it took me to pay and collect the change, he'd tossed everything in the truck bed, climbed behind the wheel, and started the motor. I looked back at the store before closing the door. The cop was on the sidewalk staring at us. I didn't say anything. Marlin was annoyed enough.

"To hell with the 'father and son' routine," he said. He glanced at the rearview mirror as if expecting the cop to come tearing around the corner. We filled up at the gas station—me paying again—before heading to the grocery store. Marlin handed me another crisp Benjie.

"I'm waiting here," he said.

"What should I get?"

"I don't know, everything except pickled beets and canned spinach, I guess."

Investigative records would later reveal that few residents remembered seeing a kid with two black eyes, a busted lip, and a face full of blisters and rashes around Bone Prairie, but, there at the grocery store, it seemed half the citizenry came to a dead stop and openly stared at me. I kept my head down, though, and did my best to avoid eye contact while hobbling up and down the aisles, grabbing something of everything. When I finally headed for the checkout counter, I was pushing one cart and pulling another, and both of them were piled high with food. I let a pregnant, barefoot teen smoking a cigarette and holding a screaming toddler cut in front of me. She had on a dirty, stained yellow tank top and a pair of too tight, hot pink shorts, both of which failed to hide her goose white belly flesh. She smiled her thanks and bought a carton of Winstons.

I rolled the carts out to the truck. Marlin was watching the pregnant teen struggle with her kid.

"Friend of yours?" I said.

"Ha-ha, real funny. Think you got enough food?" he said, climbing in the cab.

"We'll see," I said, handing him a wad of bills and a handful of change. He waved it off.

"Keep it."

"Really?"

"Yeah, why not?"

"It's stolen money, isn't it?"

"Consider it partial repayment for what Wolf stole from you."

"Okay, but I stole it from him first." I shoved the bills in my pocket.

We headed out of town. Marlin turned to me and jerked his thumb toward the bed. "I doubt even Mr. Wren can eat all that."

"He'll try."

"That he will," Marlin agreed, "that he will."

We were a mile from the farm. I was looking out the window. The corn wasn't even knee-high yet.

"Hey, kid, do you want to drive?"

"Sure!" I said eagerly. Marlin checked the rearview mirror and pulled to the side of the road. He got out, motor running, and I slid behind the wheel.

"Let's go," Marlin said, slamming the door. I ground the gears and found first. Then I revved the motor a couple of times before slowly easing off the clutch. The truck groaned and strained to break free. When I let the clutch loose, it lurched forward all of six feet and stopped, throwing me headlong into the windshield and then backward against the seat. The truck died.

"Ow!" I said, rubbing my head. "What the hell?"

"Release the emergency brake."

I side-eyed Marlin and reached for the brake handle.

"You could have said something." When I finally got the truck rolling, I threw him a glance. "Can I ask you a question?"

"Sure, go ahead."

"You're afraid I'll go to the police if you let me go, aren't you?"

"I'm not, no, but the others are."

"I wouldn't."

"Well, eventually, you would, right? You wouldn't have a choice."

"Okay, yeah, I guess so," I said, scratching my side and then my leg and then my side again. "They're looking for me, so I'd have to, but I'd let you get away first."

"You would, huh?"

"Yeah, you could dump me somewhere out in the sticks right now and tell them I escaped."

"What if someone stopped and offered you a lift?"

"I wouldn't take it. I'd give you a chance to clear out."

"Why?"

"Well, not to save Frank's ass, that's for sure. I'd do it because I'd be dead if it wasn't for you. So even though you've robbed banks and killed people, I—"

"Whoa right there, kid," Marlin said sternly. "I've never killed anyone. I just drive the car. Mr. Wolf's the killer. That doesn't matter in the eyes of the law, I know that, but it sure as hell matters to me."

"What about Mr. Wren?"

"I don't know about his past, I never asked, but he hasn't killed anyone since I've known him."

Frank was waiting by the road, hands on hips, when we rolled up, and he started yelling and banging on the truck before I turned in.

"Are you out of your goddamn mind?!" Frank shouted, running along beside us. Marlin rolled his eyes. I snickered.

"Problem?" Marlin said.

"No shit, there's a problem. Why's he driving?!"

"He had to."

"Why?!"

"I wasn't." Marlin and I burst into laughter.

"He's fourteen fucking years old!"

"Fifteen!" I said.

"Shut up, Pussypoon! If I want noise out of you, I'll beat your ass!" Frank turned to Marlin. "What if you'd gotten pulled over, huh? What then, huh? He's got no license and no learner's permit. You'd be fucked, and so would we!"

"But we didn't," Marlin said shoving the door open and forcing Frank backward with it, "so you got your nuts twisted for nothing." He shut the door and walked to the rear bumper, Frank trailing him. Crouching behind the taillight with a hand on the gate, Marlin squinted, checking out the lines to the Apache's front fender and hood.

"You and Wren won't shut up about safety, and then you go and do something completely asinine like that without even a second thought." They were close to blows until Wren stepped in and put an area code between them.

"Boys, you have got to learn to get along."

While Marlin and I unloaded the truck, Frank brooded on the front porch steps, staring across the road, smoking cigarette after cigarette. Just before we finished, he went back in the house, stomped to his bedroom, and slammed the door. During that time, Wren, manning the kitchen, had set up the camp stove, filled the fridge, and stocked the shelves. Snacked, too, if crumbs count as clues.

"I'm going to start supper, so go ahead and relax," he said.

Marlin kicked back on the couch for a nap. I stepped out on the front porch to escape the heat. A half hour later, delicious smells wafted through the open window. I went back inside just as Wren appeared in the living room with a ham and swiss sandwich and a glass of well-water iced tea.

"You two were gone an awfully long time." He looked at me, took an enormous bite and, cheeks bulging, started chewing. I didn't say anything. Neither did Marlin. His eyes were closed. Wren swallowed. "I was starting to worry you'd got caught." He took another big bite. His chomping was the only sound for a good minute. Marlin finally spoke.

"Why? You knew how much stuff we had to get."

"It just took longer than I thought it would. So, there were no problems?"

"No, none. Ran into a cop at the sporting goods store, and he gave us the once-over, but other than that, no."

"What's this about a cop?" Frank stood in the middle of the archway separating the dining and living rooms. He'd apparently smelled the food as well.

"Nothing to worry about," Marlin said. "We were in a store. Some cop was putting the moves on the cashier."

"Any problems with him?" Frank jerked his thumb in my direction.

"None."

"It was stupid to take him and stupider to let him drive."

"Let it go, Mr. Wolf," Wren said.

"No, I'm fed up with you two and your dumbass decisions. They're going to get us killed." He stomped back to his bedroom.

It was after seven o'clock when we sat down to a supper of fried chicken, mashed potatoes and gravy, buttered corn on the cob, green beans, and steamed rolls. Wren prepared everything on the two-burner stove, sampling as he cooked, of course. Frank made me set the table. Nobody spoke; we were all too hungry. I couldn't stop itching, though.

"You got crabs or something?" Frank said between mouthfuls.

"I itch everywhere."

"I don't care, stop it. It's disgusting."

"I can't!"

"Leave the kid alone!" Marlin snapped.

"Mind your own fucking business!"

"That's what I'm telling you to do, dumbass."

Chapter 43

Sunday, May 31, 1970

"Hey, Darlene!"

Kent. Shit. Darlene was wired and tired from sleepless worry, and the last thing she wanted to do was deal with her brother. Summoning her energy, she kicked off the covers and hopped out of bed. Then, after checking to make sure the coast was clear, she dashed down the hallway and slipped out the front door. On the porch, she breathed a sigh of relief and quietly scooted a chair to the near corner where she couldn't be seen. Darlene sat, hugging her knees against her chest, and rocked back and forth, tense and uneasy, worried to death about Tyler.

"Mom, have you seen Darlene?"

"She's on the front porch, dear." Darlene slumped forward as if ran through by a lance. She bolted out the chair, leapt off the porch, and darted through the yard, heading for the garage. She nearly made it.

"Oh, hey, there you are!" The storm door banged shut and Kent came down the steps. Darlene's shoulder's dropped a good six inches. She turned to face him, frowning.

"What do you want, Kent?"

"Do you want to play Frisbee?" Darlene gave him a withering look.

"No, Kent, I do not want to play Frisbee. I've got things on my mind."

"Oh, yeah, Tyler, right?"

"Yeah, 'Oh, yeah, Tyler, right.' Jesus, Kent, you're not a complete idiot, but you're pretty close and on track to make it." Darlene ducked in the garage and emerged seconds later, running alongside her forest green, three-speed. She hopped on, found the pedals, and swerved toward him, but he dove out of the way just in time. Smirking, she sped off down the street, head over handlebars. Kent, lying in the grass, watched his sister shrink from view.

Darlene darted south on Buchanan and took the right-hander onto Fourth Street, passing the Dog n Suds on her left. Coming out of the turn, she upshifted to third, lowered her head, and tucked her elbows in, finding a comfortable tempo for the long trek north. Her long, thick hair flowed over her shoulders like a black banner. As she neared downtown, she coasted, catching the light at Water Street before pedaling across Creek's Bend and the stone bridge over the twin forks of Falcon River. The Whitehaven Hotel was on her right as she rumbled over the railroad tracks. She veered toward it and onto Elmhurst for the steep climb past Huwabola High.

Darlene squeezed the hand brakes and freewheeled the corner onto Lynwood Drive. She spotted a woman up the block sweeping the walkway of a yellow house with green shutters and pedaled toward her. She braked to a stop on the sidewalk.

"Excuse me, ma'am, do you know where Tyler Puspoon lives?"

Twyla stopped sweeping and turned, smiling at the young girl straddling the bicycle. She had on an orange- and white-striped tank top, faded, cut-off jeans, and, of course, flip-flops. She'd otherwise recovered from Friday night.

"I ought to, I'm his mom. You're Darlene, aren't you?"

"Yes!" Darlene said excitedly. She toed the kickstand on her bike. "How'd you know?"

"Just a hunch."

"Have you heard anything?"

"I only found out today. Come inside, so we can talk."

"If you're sure it's not a bother. I know you have a lot on your mind."

"As do you, dear, as do you." Twyla put her arm around Darlene's shoulder and, limping, led her up the walkway to the house.

"What happened to your foot?"

"Long story."

Chapter 44

Sunday, May 31, 1970

Kramer threw the dead bolt and chain on her apartment door and leaned heavily against it. She was bushed. Not a single lead had emerged from the massacre at CNT. There were no fingerprints, no tape, and no witnesses except for Prand, who'd finally remembered who he was, but whose memory was otherwise sketchy. FBI agents had pulled Beetz's fingerprints from the Puspoon residence and they were on their way to Washington. Kramer's body craved sleep.

A cheese toasty and a cup of tomato soup sufficed for supper. After feeding Rufus, of course. Kramer flipped on the television, took off her shoes, and kicked back on the couch. There was a commercial on, but when it was over, the late night news came on and the lead story was DTK. She switched the set off and sat in the dark.

Kramer felt her way along the carpeted hallway to her small bedroom and flipped her beside lamp on. She hung her shoulder holster on the bedpost and took off her earrings and necklace. Rufus casually strolled in. He rose on his hind legs to bump her hand; his purr sounded like a rattlesnake.

Small white comets exploded against the reddish-black of Kramer's eyelids, but it felt too good to stop, so she kept on rubbing.

When she finally opened her eyes, she was staring at herself in the full-length mirror. Kramer winced at her haggard appearance and sat heavily on the bed. She lay back, just for a moment, she promised, and then she'd get undressed and take a long, hot bath. Instead, a tidal wave of fatigue washed over her, and everything went black. It wasn't the break she was hoping for, but it was welcome just the same.

Chapter 45

Sunday, May 31, 1970

Frank grabbed a greasy, chicken wing, burped, and turned to me.

"Clear the table and do the dishes, Pussypoon." He got up and nodded for Marlin and Wren to follow him to the front room. Marlin gave me an apologetic shrug, drawing my angry snort, but, by the time I finished cleaning up, I was over it, so I fixed everyone a slice of pecan pie and a cup of coffee.

"Hey, thanks, kid," Marlin said. He was in one of the arm-chairs. I smiled and threw a fork at him, testing his reflexes. He snatched it out the air and smiled back.

Wren smiled as well. "Thank you, Tyler!" He squirmed around on the couch like a family of five, trying to get comfortable. I waited until he got settled and handed him his cup and plate, so he wouldn't have to move again. Frank grunted unintelligibly when I set his coffee and dessert on the end table. I took a seat by the door and began eating.

Frank leaned forward with his hands on his knees and glared at me. "What do you think you're doing?" he snapped.

"Eating pie."

"Get back in the kitchen."

"I'll be done in a sec."

Frank glowered at me with his dissociative eyebrows.

"Oh, for fu—...can't you just let me be?!" I loudly stomped to the kitchen, but tiptoed back and sat in the darkened dining room with my back against the wall.

"I've been thinking we should leave soon," Wren said between bites.

"Oh, so *now* we need to leave." Frank had leaned back. He had a foot draped over the arm of his chair. He forked a piece of pie in his mouth. Chewing, he turned to Marlin. "Apparently we were just waiting for you to draw the law's attention."

"How soon can you get a car, Mr. Marlin?" Wren cut in, preempting another clash.

"There's a used car lot in town," Marlin said. "I'll buy one tomorrow."

"As I pointed out earlier, we've already got a car, so we can leave as soon as it gets dark."

"And I told you I'm not driving that car, and you're not either, so forget it."

"Then go steal one. We need to leave ASAP!"

"Same thing. Too risky."

"He's right," Wren said, licking his fork until it shined. "It's not a good idea to drive around in *any* stolen vehicle when you're the subject of a manhunt."

"One of you can drop me off in the morning," Marlin said. "We'll leave as soon as I get back."

"All right, that's settled," Wren jumped in. "We leave tomorrow morning. On to other matters. What about the boy?"

"I'll take him with me and let him go later," Marlin said.

"Sounds good."

"Wrong, he's coming with me. I'll deal with him."

"I wasn't asking, I was telling." Marlin had a cold, hard look to him. He stared at Frank, unblinking, emotionless. He'd never killed anyone, but I sensed that might change in the next few seconds.

"You don't get it. My fingerprints are all over their house. If the cops get me, they're just a step from you."

"I don't care, but let's pretend I do. You and the kid are missing. They won't need Interpol to figure it out."

"So, Mr. Wolf," Wren picked up, "that means you don't need to kill the boy."

"I'll give you two a day's head start," Marlin said. "I'll drop him off somewhere close to home."

"NO!" Frank erupted, reaching for his Colt. "He's coming with me, and I'll kill whoever tries to stop me." When Marlin drew his .45, I hit the floor. They were going to settle it with lead!

Chapter 46

Sunday, May 31, 1970

The television was tuned to *The Ed Sullivan Show.* The audience howled at Rich Little's impersonations of John Wayne and Richard Nixon, but not Darlene. She was staring at the fresh plaster on the wall, thinking about Tyler.

"Frank threw his briefcase," Twyla said. Then she nodded toward the door. "After he broke the window."

"Hmm, okay." Darlene scratched her arm until it stung.

"Have a seat," Twyla said on her way to the kitchen. "I'll fix some lemonade. I'll bet you're thirsty." Twyla was a bit more talkative than she was squeezed in among a carload of FBI agents. She'd spent the trip steeling herself to face Tyler's kidnapping the same way she'd handled Jack's war.

Darlene sat on the couch while Twyla busied herself in the kitchen. The walls showed where picture frames once hung.

"Where do you live?" Twyla called.

"Essie."

"That's five miles from here!"

"Yeah, probably."

"I hope it made you hungry." Twyla entered the living room carrying a tray with a pitcher of lemonade, two glasses, a plate of cookies, and several napkins. She set the tray on the coffee table and poured Darlene a glass of lemonade. Darlene took a sip.

"Mmm! This is delicious! Thank you so much!" She thirstily drank half of it.

"Have a cookie, dear. They're peanut butter, Tyler's favorite. I made them this morning, so there'd be some when he gets home."

"I hope it's soon." Darlene scratched her leg and reached for a cookie. "Have you met Agent Kramer?"

"Mm-hmm, this morning, she's the one who told me."

"I've been waiting for her to call." Darlene scratched her leg again, harder.

"The FBI searched the house and garage today. They took all of Frank's stuff and dusted for fingerprints. Agent Kramer thinks he's a member of the DTK gang."

"DTK?! She didn't tell us that!" Darlene sat back in her chair, even more worried now.

Twyla noticed and frowned.

"I'm just not used to this," she said.

"Used to what?"

"Just sitting around, doing nothing."

"What do you want to do?"

"Have a look around. Maybe the FBI missed something."

"Like what?"

"I don't know, but I ought to know what should and shouldn't be in my own house."

"Garage, too?"

"Garage, too."

"We could have a look."

"Do you want to?"

"Of course! But I should call my mom to let her know where I am."

"There's a phone in the kitchen by the refrigerator."

Chapter 47

Sunday, May 31, 1970

Although the monsoon season was late arriving, passing mountain rainstorms left the jungle hot, steamy, and shrouded in mist. The creek bed was damp, littered with tree limbs, rocks, and other debris from seasons past. It was slow going in the dark, but not as dangerous as it would be when the rain began in earnest.

Cowboy scaled a fallen teak tree and huddled with Silenka, Mo, and Dunn beneath the bank at the quarter-klick mark. Behind them, the agitated voices of Than's advance unit reached a fevered pitch and then tapered off. A few minutes later, more explosions and gunfire rocked the night. Cowboy, who'd waited for that very moment, vaulted the bank and broke for the hill, dodging branches and vines as he weaved his way through the rainforest. The others stayed tight on his heels.

Positioned atop the hill, DD, flanked by Devenzie and Slessen, watched the four white silhouettes approach through his starlight scope.

"Black," Silenka rasped when they gathered at the base of the short, but very steep hill.

"Magic," Devenzie whispered back. A few seconds later, a thick coil of rope thudded to the ground. Cowboy wrapped it around his waist a couple of times and gave it two hard tugs, pulling it taut. Then he started climbing, wedging the toe of his boot in crevices and pushing off rocks, hoisting himself hand-over-hand up the side of the hill. At the other end, Rogers, Goat, and Red worked together to haul him over the top. One by one, Dunn, Mo, and Silenka followed.

The fog thickened as the Marines followed the ridgeline's gradual descent through the mountains. Cowboy forced a fast pace despite the terrain, showing less concern for risk where he'd proceeded cautiously just hours earlier. The Marines were in a footrace with the Vietcong that would last throughout the night and into the morning, taking them from the mountain highlands to the foothills and through the plains to their extraction point.

When First Force Recon emerged over the last of the rises, they approached the elephant grass cautiously. They'd outpaced the VC and eluded the patrols that lay in wait between villages, but negotiating the tight, twisting path through the towering dark fortress of grass was time consuming. Cowboy set a blistering pace in the dark, and this time, Puspoon didn't order a break. They moved for hours on end, ignoring the leeches, biting insects, and cuts.

Dawn was still an hour away when the Marines finally emerged from the elephant grass at the edge of the clearing. They were miles from the coast, but they could taste the salty air and feel it on their skin. They set up a skirmish line on the ocean side of the clearing, just inside the jungle, taking cover behind fallen trees, brush, or bamboo thickets. The clearing was their extraction point.

The fog thinned and burned off as the temperature climbed. The air was filled with the scent of fragrant lantanas. The sun still hadn't broken the night, but it was already 86 degrees, a clear sign the day would be as hellishly hot as the one before. The Marines, however, planned to be gone before it peaked.

MAC-V closely monitored enemy communications throughout the mission. They'd picked up bursts of frantic chatter among battalions from the Second VC Regiment, Third NVA Division—Than's command. Confusion, panic, and chaos ran through the ranks. Decoded intercepts revealed Hanoi had abruptly canceled the summit. Than's assassination was an embarrassment, and General Giap wanted blood.

The Marines were ready. Anticipating a firefight, they were locked in. Puspoon stood, exploring the rising terrain through his binoculars, but could barely make out shapes in the dark haze. There was a slight rustling and Silenka emerged from the tangle of plants and flowers.

"LP says we've got gooks closing in, sir," he whispered.

"How many?"

"Five, maybe more."

"Distance?"

"Quarter klick."

"They're probably scouts. Bring the LP in. I'm going to have a look." Puspoon inserted a fresh magazine in his M16 and skirted the skirmish line before stopping at a stand of trees. He stood atop a gnarled strangler fig and wrapped his arm around a bamboo tree, looking out over the elephant grass through his M3.

He didn't like what he saw. The NVA had joined the hunt, and there were easily a hundred enemy fighters on their trail. At least twenty had already made it through the elephant grass. Puspoon returned to the skirmish line.

"Shit's about to hit the fan, huh, Lieutenant?" Silenka asked. He knew his commanding officer better than Twyla did.

"Looks like it."

"It's zero six hundred, sir," Rogers said.

"Eighteen minutes until evac. Tell the men to be ready."

"Aye-aye, sir."

Ten minutes passed. Pulses quickened. Fingers tightened on triggers. Then, the PRC-25 broke squelch twice. Puspoon grabbed the transmitter and quickly cued it once and then twice more. He waited for the response—two breaks in quick succession followed by one long pause and then two more quick ones. He signaled Rogers and Silenka on either end of the firing line and waited for them to toss yellow smoke grenades to mark the landing zone. Then he spoke.

"Dragon One, Dragon One, this is Dragon Two, do you copy?"

"Roger, Dragon Two, we copy."

"Dragon One, friendlies east... yellow 50...two twenty-four to two-twenty seven. . . mark enemy, attack at 500 to 1000 out."

"Copy, Dragon Two, friendlies east... yellow 50...two twenty-four to two-twenty seven. . . mark enemy, attack at 500 to 1000 out. Standby."

Two minutes later, three Cobra gunships flying in a V formation swooped in. Most of the NVA soldiers and Viet Cong fighters were still on the rolling, red clay hills where there was no cover other than scrub, jaks, and scraggly fir trees—terrible terrain to be caught out in. They panicked, breaking training and ranks, and ran in all directions while the attack helicopters swept past, spewing flechette rockets and raking them with 7.62 mm rounds from their twin mini-guns. The co-pilots protected the break with three hundred 40 mm grenades. The effect was devastating. No one survived.

Enemy fire poured from the grass as two UH-1H Hueys appeared above the clearing and dropped into the LZ. They hovered a few feet above ground before setting down. The main rotors' twin seesaw-shaped-blades produced a windstorm of dirt, leaves, and stalks of dead grass. The Marines broke cover alone or in pairs, sprinting toward the Hueys. Dunn, with the M60, led the way but didn't get ten yards before hearing the raggedy, metallic popping of AK-47s. He spotted a half dozen enemy soldiers firing from a stand of jak trees on the knoll, stopped, and squeezed off three short bursts. One man collapsed from a round to the thigh that nearly took his leg off. Another pitched backward from chest wounds. The other fighters dove for cover and Dunn kept them pinned down while Mo and Red boarded. He followed them in and moved to the opposite bay to join the door gunner, who, strapped in his seat, pummeled the grass with his .50 caliber machine gun.

SSgt. Silenka stood in the clearing, firing his M16 at a stand of trees where enemy fighters had taken cover. Several soldiers joined them after they emerged from the elephant grass. Silenka was side-stepping toward the first Huey when his rifle jammed. He smacked the forward assist and tried again without luck. Silenka drew his .45, and began squeezing off rounds while striding toward the helicopter. He stopped occasionally to draw a better bead or reload. Bullets zinged past him. He killed two more VC fighters and winged another. Silenka's marksmanship attracted the enemy's attention, and more bullets came with it. One of them slammed into his right shoulder just before he reached the open bay. He stumbled backward and fell. Searing hot pain shot through him. He rolled onto his good side to get up, but saw a VC sapper charging the helicopter. Silenka switched gun hands and emptied the magazine, aiming for the legs. The sapper fell, muffling the explosion, and his mangled body rose several feet in the air. Silenka struggled to his feet, fist pressed against his shoulder, trying to staunch the blood flow. Mo helped him aboard, and Red immediately went to work on his wound.

One of the door gunners exchanged fire with a handful of VC fighters. More joined them, emerging from the grass, shooting on the run. The other door gunner spotted them and opened up, sending three hundred rounds ripping through the trees and scrub, thudding into wood, dirt, and bodies.

Ten VC fighters charged from the south. Bullets whizzed through the clearing and kicked up dirt around the Marines caught out. A round smacked against the bulletproof Plexiglass windscreen, leaving a spider-web crack. Another ricocheted off an ammo box and struck Slessen's thigh. Blood gushed from the gaping wound, soaking his trousers. He swore angrily and scrambled for a dressing to staunch its flow.

Enemy fighters streamed out of the grass. They approached in groups of twos and threes, shooting on the run. Red, kneeling in the open bay, emptied the magazine of his M16 at them while DD and Devenzie, who'd also spotted them, framed them in a crossfire and sent them all scrambling for cover.

Puspoon was pinned down in the jungle. He'd found a cavity in the ground beyond a culm of bamboo outside the clearing. He hadn't been spotted, but rounds were shredding plants and splintering wood all around him. There was a lull, and Puspoon jumped to his feet and broke across the clearing. Suddenly, the first Huey lifted, exposing him to a new angle of fire. He juked and deked, never slowing, across the clearing. DD switched bays to cover him, and then Cowboy joined in. The second pilot pulled pitch as Puspoon neared. The Huey rose with a protesting groan, tail first, before leveling out at four feet. Puspoon leapt onto the rail as the single turboshaft engine roared to a deafening level and started to rise. Devenzie dragged him aboard as the Huey quickly rose and veered east, following its twin toward the coast and out to sea.

Chapter 48

Sunday, May 31, 1970

I peeked through my fingers. Frank had his Colt pointed at Marlin, who was crouched by the door, gun barrel up, peering out the front window.

"We've got company," Marlin said to Wren, nodding outdoors. "It's a cop."

Wren, trousers undone for digestive comfort, rolled to his feet with the grace of a three-legged water buffalo. Holding, his pants in one hand and his gun in the other, he toddler-walked across the floor and flattened himself against the wall, sending a heavy shudder through the farmhouse. The awning groaned.

I crawled back to the front room.

"You signaled that cop!" Frank spat.

"Leave him alone," Marlin warned. "He didn't do anything."

"Then why's a cop out front?"

"He's got no partner or backup, so he's probably bored and checking us out. Go to the kitchen, kid, and stay there. Cool out, Mr. Wolf, I'll handle this."

"You better, or I will."

Officer Phil Trotter breathed a sigh of relief when he saw the Apache. He braked gently, easing the Bone Prairie Police

Department's blue 1965 Ford Galaxie 500 to the side of the road in front of Max Terwilliger's wreckage of a farm. He cut the engine and sat for a moment, listening to the tick and ping of the cooling motor. Then he switched the key forward to get the last cold blast of air from the AC. Trotter leaned across the blue vinyl seat, but couldn't see anything except brown weeds, dried grass, and new greensward.

The heat was intense, and the humidity was at its smothering worst. Trotter, wearing a long-sleeved khaki shirt and black tie, was already perspiring. A trickle of sweat ran from his armpit over his ribs before soaking into the fabric. He opened the door and started to get out, but paused, remembering he was supposed to radio his location to Anita back at the station if he left the squad car. Trotter sat there, one foot in and one foot out, staring at the Apache, deciding what to do. He hated radioing in every dang time he left the darn car, but Chief Clory chewed his ass out but good when he didn't, and he liked that even less. Sighing, he leaned forward, reaching for the mic, but stopped.

"Oh, hail, ahm jes' gonna be uh sec." Trotter got out and closed the door. Then, muttering, he looked down and rolled his eyes. The cuff of his blue trousers was caught on his bootstrap again. Trotter wiggled his leg around, betting the cops on television didn't have this problem. He put his hand on the Galaxie's roof and gave his leg a vigorous shake. Then another. Then a third time, jerking it around as if it was demonically possessed.

"Oh, hail," Trotter said, stooping and pulling his pant leg over the strap.

The Trotters, a couple hundred or more, crossed the Ohio River from Kentucky during the Civil War. They settled in what later became Groot, an eye-blink of a town in the backwoods of Broben County. There, they kept to themselves, breeding with blind insularity until the state finally stepped in and refused to grant any more marriage licenses until the surnames were different. The first one was a Fermack, a line of short, ill-bred Hoosiers with squeezed red faces and deeply creased foreheads, who, upon learning their "cousin," Bermuda, had married a Trotter, immediately renounced her.

Phil Trotter was slight of build. He had the characteristic flushed face and tightly corded forehead of the Fermaks combined with the Trotters' distinctive beady black eyes, pelican-like jaw, and large flaccid nose.

Trotter became fascinated with police work while still in short pants, and he hung out at the station every chance he could while growing up. Chief Clory and Anita, his wife and BPPD's voluntary dispatcher, were childless, so they'd taken an interest in him. Clory gave him odd jobs, like picking up trash, mowing the yard, cleaning offices, that sort of thing, just so he'd have some walking-around money.

Most people couldn't wait to escape Bone Prairie after high school. Not Trotter. He left Groot and moved into town, scraping enough together working for Chief Clory to afford canned meals and a small, cramped apartment above the diner.

It wasn't but a few years later that a rumor circulated about Trotter attending the police academy up north. Some people laughed and others scoffed, but nobody believed it, and it faded from thought and discussion. No one noticed that Trotter hadn't been around for a while. Nor did they think twice about Chief Clory mowing the grass for a second straight summer. So, naturally, it was a complete surprise, and frankly, a bewildering one, when Clory proudly announced that Phil Trotter was BPPD's newest police officer. Hearing Trotter later boast of going through the academy four times only caused further distress.

After freeing his cuff, Trotter opened the rear door of the Ford and carefully removed his Smokey. Holding it chest high with only his palms touching the wide circular brim, he rolled his knotty shoulders and stretched his thin neck in a half dozen directions, working the kinks from his joints in a series of pops and cracks. Carefully and with precision, Trotter placed his hat atop his head in the manner of a drill instructor, brim down over his eyes. It wasn't a real Smokey—all the adult sizes were too big—but instead a passable replica from a Junior Park Ranger outfit he found in the toy department at Sears. He'd trashed the child-sized green shirt, plastic badge, and compass that came with it.

Trotter gripped either side of his black duty belt and hiked it up, relieving the pressure on his boney hips. He rubbed the deep, red creases where the sharp, thick leather—and fifteen pounds of equipment—rested, and, wincing, gently eased it back in place.

Marlin stepped onto the porch as Trotter headed up the walk. He nodded to the policeman, who nodded back while carefully picking a safe route up the rotting wood stairs.

"How yuh doin', suh?" Trotter said with a big, toothy smile. "Ahm Offsuh Trotter, BeePeePeeDee," he said, resting his right hand on his .38, the way Malloy sometimes did on *Adam-12.* Marlin instinctively reached for the .45 at the small of his back before catching himself. He shoved both hands in his back pockets instead.

"Doing all right," Marlin said. "What brings you way out here, Officer?"

"Oh, waail, ah saw yuh an' yer boy in Reelz back thar."

"Uh-huh, you were hitting on the girl at the register, weren't you?"

"Ah guess ah was," Trotter said, red face getting redder. "Ah saw yuh drivin' that 'Patchy, too." He turned and looked at the truck. "Ah've bin tryin' tuh buy it offa Max since ha' school, so ah gawt worried, thankin' maybe yuh'd bawt it." He looked at Marlin. "Didja?"

"No, but I might make him an offer," Marlin said with a chuckle. He'd sized up Trotter, so he was trying for folksy.

"Don' go doin' tha'," Trotter said, smiling back. "Ah'd half tuh uh-ress' yuh." Marlin laughed dutifully but said nothing. "Ah gawt wahhreed an' then when ah gawt hare an' saw the truck, ah was so relieved. Y'all Max's kin?"

"No, we came up here to fish and just happened on the place. Max said I could drive the truck if I got it going."

"Ah see, tha's good, tha's good," Trotter said, nodding his head over and over.

Marlin smiled, but said nothing, hoping his silence would be hint enough that the conversation had run its course. Unfortunately, it wasn't.

"Where's yer car then?"

"In the barn," Marlin said, and when that drew a blank look, he added, "I've been having trouble with the top and didn't want it to get rained on."

"Raaain?! Wha's tha'?" Trotter snorted and laughed. "Yuh mus' nawt be from 'round hare. Ain't rained in weeks!" When Marlin didn't reply, he went on, "So, yuh gawt a rag top, huh?"

"Yeah, Mustang." Marlin said it without thinking, regretting it immediately.

"No kiddin'? Wha' yare?"

"Sixty-four-and-a-half." *In for a penny.*

"Wow! Ah'd shore lak tuh see it!" Trotter said excitedly, starting down the steps.

"Some other time, Officer. My son and I are fixing supper, and I left him at the stove, so I need to get back."

"Gotcha, shore, sorry," Trotter said, carefully negotiating the last couple steps. He looked back over his shoulder. "Ah din't maain tuh intrude. Like ah said, ah jes' wanted tuh make shore 'bout the truck."

"I'll tell Max you still want it." Marlin folded his hands behind his back and watched Trotter strut to the Galaxie and drive off. He didn't go back inside until the dust on the road had settled.

Chapter 49

Sunday, May 31, 1970

The garage was hotter than summertime in the south of Hell. Twyla had barely set foot inside when the heat hit her.

"Whoa!" she said, backing out as if blown by a desert wind. "It's cooking in there!" The screen door banged shut, and Darlene, shoulders slumped, stood on the side stoop with a dejected look on her face.

"Mom wants me home before dark," she said, plopping down on the top step. "I'll have to leave soon."

"Tell you what," Twyla said, walking to the front of the garage, "Let's go ahead and search for a while. We'll put your bike in the trunk and I'll drive you home." She raised the overhead door to let the garage cool.

"Oh, thank you, thank you!" Darlene said enthusiastically, clapping her hands and jumping off the steps. She practically skipped to the garage. "You don't know how worried I've been just hanging around the house, doing nothing, waiting for the phone to ring. It's driving me crazy! Where do we start?"

"I want to check Jack's toolbox first. Frank was digging around in it. Maybe the FBI missed something." Twyla pulled the top drawer. It was locked. "The key's on the hook by the fridge. Would you mind getting it?"

"Okay, be right back."

The garage was full of hot, dead air. Twyla looked around, fanning her face. She knelt and felt around inside a bucket of dirty shop rags. She didn't find anything, but she got her fingers greasy and smudged her top.

"I know!" She mounted a step stool and felt along the top plate atop the door frame, finding splinters, grime, and mouse turds, but nothing else. When Darlene returned, she was wiping her hands on a soiled rag.

"Found 'em!" Darlene said, handing her a key ring.

"Thanks, dear."

"Not a problem. Where do you want me to start?"

"Hmm, let's see." Twyla walked to the center of the garage and nodded toward the back left corner. "Everything there belongs to Tyler, and he's always digging around for something, too. I don't think Frank would chance hiding anything back there."

"That'd be dumb."

"Same thing for the other corner; it has the lawnmower, rakes, and other stuff for the yard, and Frank doesn't do any of the work."

"What about in between?"

"Let's save that for last. Tell you what, start in the front corner over there and work your way back."

"Will do!"

"Oh, and keep your eyes peeled for a wallet. Frank lost his, but he thinks Tyler stole it." Twyla unlocked the toolbox and opened the top lid.

"Is that why he hit him?"

Twyla's eyes narrowed to hyphens. She pursed her lips. She'd forgotten. "Tyler said that?"

"He said it was a 'one-punch knockout.'"

"Right." She yanked open the top drawer of the toolbox, hotter than steam, and slammed it shut. Then she jerked open the one below it.

Darlene gave Twyla a cautious glance and quietly moved to the other side of the garage, where she buried herself in the golf bag, thankful for all its pockets. Twyla eventually simmered down, and before long, the two were chatting about boys, high school, and summer vacation. They rummaged through boxes, bags, and drawers for forty-five minutes without luck before Twyla called a halt.

"We need to get you home. It's starting to get dark."

"Yeah, okay," Darlene said disappointedly. "I was hoping we'd find something."

"Me, too, but we can look tomorrow. Just come by whenever you're ready. I'm up early." Twyla started to close the garage door, but stopped and raised it again. "Forgot the keys," she called while walking to the toolbox. She slid them in her front pocket and started back out, but stopped and cocked her head with a puzzled expression. She pulled out the keyring and held up a small gold key, worn and smudged from use. It had "11" stamped on it.

"I don't know why I haven't noticed this key before."

"What about it?"

"I've never seen it."

"Really?"

"There's supposed to be three keys, one for the house, one for the garage, and one for the toolbox. This one makes four."

Chapter 50

Monday, June 1, 1970

Dawn broke, and I was the first to rise after a fitful night of rolling around, itching and scratching on the hardwood floor. It'd been a solid week since I'd slept more than a couple hours a night, and I hadn't had a pain-free minute since Friday. Now, I was itching all over.

My housemates had kept a lookout overnight, but not without arguing first. Marlin said the cop was just checking on the Apache. Wren thought so, too, but Frank wouldn't let it go, calling them out for their earlier insistence on safety and blowing it off...again. He didn't shut up until Wren finally gave in. They did "rock, paper, scissors" for shifts; Marlin was first out, so he got stuck with the swing shift—one to four in the morning—while Wren beat Frank and choose first watch.

The kettle still had water in it, so I lit the little stove and turned the burner up. I looked through bleary eyes out the window above the sink while waiting for the water to boil. The morning sky was a fiery red tinged with blasts of yellow and orange. There was a long, green sedan parked in the driveway over at the farm. Somebody was inside, too, but with the sun glinting off the windshield, all I could see was an elbow hanging out the window. I thought about busting out the door and booking over there, but I was beat, so instead, I plunked down at the kitchen table and, between sips, felt my face. It was lumpier than yesterday.

The first cup woke me up. The second one made me twitchy, so I trudged to the barn and cleaned the stalls before it got really hot. Afterward, I put out grain and hay, and the horses, neighing and whickering, trotted over and started eating.

When I went back inside, Marlin was up, or at least he'd woken up. He sat slumped forward, arms across his knees, head atop them, eyes shut. I set the kettle to boil again, and added an extra spoonful of coffee.

"Thanks, kid," Marlin mumbled sleepily when I set the steaming cup on the end table. The smell of coffee filled the room. He brought the cup to his lip and tentatively sipped while pulling the ratty blanket over his shoulders.

"How was guard duty?" I asked.

"Pointless. Where's Wolf?"

"Sleeping."

Marlin snorted.

You'd think life on the lam with a band of murderous bank robbers would be intense, exciting, and chock full of thrills, but so far, it'd been one big drag. Farm living *isn't* the life for me.

"What's the matter?" Marlin's head was still on his arms, but he had one eye fixed on me.

"You mean besides being a kidnap victim?"

"Yeah, leave that out, what's wrong?"

"I'm bored. There's nothing to do except sleep, and I'm not even doing that."

"You're taking care of the horses."

"That stopped being fun after the first five minutes."

"I bet Mr. Wolf can find something. Want me to wake him and ask?"

"I'll manage."

"Thought you might."

"You told that old guy we're here to fish. We've got everything except bait. If I dig up some worms, can we go fishing?"

"I'll talk to Mr. Wren."

"What about horseback riding then? Just you and me. We have all the gear. Or maybe another drive? Anything except being planted here like turnips."

"We'd have to leave the farm to do all that stuff, so don't get your hopes up."

"I should've grabbed a deck of cards."

"Now there's an idea. We could play euchre or hearts."

"Or poker."

"Poker?! You're not old enough to play poker!"

"If you say so," I said with a half-moon smile. I'd been playing with friends for years.

"What do you play?"

"Five-card stud. Ever hear of it?"

"I'm familiar with the game," Marlin said with the slightest of smiles. "Mr. Wren lays a wager or two, so I bet he'd play."

"Let's go get a deck."

"In a bit, okay? Let me wake up first."

I thought I heard an avalanche in the hallway, but it turned out to be Wren in his tighty-whities. He came to a halt at the fridge. Marlin got up, still wrapped in the blanket, and shuffled to the kitchen, cup in hand. I stayed put, knowing there'd be nothing gained seeing up close what I hadn't wanted to see at all. Marlin leaned against the countertop while Wren, bathed in the yellow glow of the fridge light, squatted on the balls of his feet. I couldn't hear a thing; they spoke in hushed tones. However, Marlin finally said something that caused Wren to shake his head and shrug his shoulders. He walked back to the front room, muttering to himself. He sat on the couch.

"We'll see," was all he said.

Chapter 51

Monday, June 1, 1970

Kramer stood on the ground floor of the Minton-Capehart building waiting forever on the elevator. She wondered how much of her life she'd waste standing there if she spent her entire career in Indianapolis. She laughed. Then shuddered. Kramer was antsy, eager for the results on the fingerprints. She glanced at her watch as she boarded the lift. After an agonizingly slow ride, Kramer rushed to her office and literally danced to her desk when she saw the blinking red light on her telephone. She snatched the handset, punched in her code, and waited, still dancing. Then she abruptly stopped and slammed the receiver down. She'd had enough of Burroughs's bellowing for two careers.

Hey, something for you!" Agent Duane Bildin stood in the doorway holding a sealed, 8x12-inch, manila envelope.

"Duane! You're back!"

"Only just, my flight landed a half hour ago. They had a car waiting like I was a real bigshot."

"You are a real bigshot! Now, gimme, gimme, gimme!" Kramer said excitedly, like a kid at Christmas. She grabbed the envelope from his hands. "Did they say if there's a match?"

"They didn't tell me squat, but I hope Burroughs's transfer papers are in there." They laughed, a little too loud.

"WHAT'S SO GODDAMN FUNNY?" *Burroughs!* Kramer sighed and dropped in her chair.

"I better get going," Bildin said quickly.

"Chicken!"

"Yes, I am," he whispered.

"KRAMER! I LEFT YOU A MESSAGE! Burroughs, splotchy-faced and bed-headed, stormed into her office, stopped in front of her desk, and stood with his hands on his hips, looking down at her.

"I heard it," she explained tiredly, "but I just got here." She held up the manila envelope. "We got the lab results. Agent Bildin dropped them off. I think he deserves a commendation for getting them to DC and back overnight, don't you?"

"Yeah, yeah, yeah." Burroughs hadn't changed clothes. Bathed either.

"He did it on his day off, you know."

"So, I'll put him up for the Medal of Honor."

"A commendation would probably be enough." *Jerk.*

"Whatever. Did you put me up for getting your search warrant approved?"

"You made a phone call, and that was your job."

"Whatever. Do we have a match?"

"I haven't had time to check."

"Open it up then!" Kramer closed her eyes and breathed slowly, letting her irritation pass. She slit the top of the envelope and removed several sheets of paper. She glanced at the cover letter and shuffled it to the bottom. "Well?!" Burroughs demanded.

"YES! We got a hit!"

"Hot damn! Who is it?"

"Guy named Clayton Brixton. Ever hear of him?"

"No, why?"

"He's from New York City. Thought you might've run across him. Weren't you there once?"

"That was a long time ago."

"Hmmm, our Mr. Brixton started a long time ago. Check this out, arrested at ten for running numbers. Ten! After that, he was in and out of juvie. This guy had a prostitution ring at sixteen! Arrested for murder in 1937, charges dismissed, solid alibi. When he was twenty-two, he got sent up to Sing Sing for armed robbery."

"That's all state shit. How does a street punk from the Big Apple wind up robbing banks in the cornfield?

"Good question." Kramer flipped a page, eyed it quickly, and then flipped to the next one. "Every conviction's in New York. Rikers in '54, Attica in '58. Oh, wait, he got sent to Leavenworth in '60."

"Leavenworth's federal. What'd he do?"

"Counterfeiting."

"Apparently he wasn't too good at it," Burroughs said. "Let me see his picture."

"Here," Kramer said, handing him the 8x10 black and white mugshots.

"Never seen him. Get this on the wire ASAP."

Chapter 52

Monday, June 1, 1970

Puspoon sat on his footlocker, drying his feet. He'd just gotten out of the shower, having spent the last forty minutes with Silenka and Slessen at the base hospital.

"Excuse me, Lieutenant Puspoon," called a voice from outside his hooch, "It's Corporal Stenson. General Widdecke wants to see you right away."

"All right, thanks." Puspoon, naked except for flip-flops and a towel loosely knotted at his waist, groaned. He had the hooch to himself, a rarity, and he wanted sleep, not an "attaboy" from the commanding general.

First Force Recon had been back at Da Nang just over an hour. They'd flown first to the *Midway* where, except for Silenka, who went straight to surgery, they were kept sequestered until debriefed. Silenka's interview occurred shortly after he awoke, and the unit departed when he was cleared to travel. Slessen's wound required only a patch.

In less than five minutes, Puspoon was dressed and standing with cover in hand outside the private quarters of Major General Charles F. Widdecke.

"Lieutenant Puspoon reporting as ordered, sir!" Puspoon

announced, entering the tent and standing at attention.

"Jack, mahh boy!" the general said with his characteristic Texas twang. He was already halfway around his desk to greet Puspoon. Widdecke was pure Texan. He grew up in Texas and went to school in Texas. He joined the Marine Corps at twenty-two after graduating from the University of Texas. The general was a highly decorated combat veteran. During World War II, he earned the Navy Cross and Silver Star for valor. Widdecke had arrived in Da Nang the previous month, assuming command of the First Marine Division after his predecessor suffered a broken leg in a helicopter crash.

"Congratulations ahhn the mission," Widdecke drawled, grasping Puspoon's hand and shaking it vigorously.

"Thank you, sir."

"Sounds like ya had one helluva tahhhm!"

"Yes, sir. Evac got a little hairy, sir."

"That's whahht ahh heard. Hahhr Staff Sergeant Silenka and PFC Slessen doin'?"

"They're doing well, sir. I'm told they'll fully recover."

"That's good tuh heah, Jack, an' it's a fahhn testuhmunt tuh your leadership that ya pulled this ahhff with no more haahrm than that. C'mere an' siddown, son." Puspoon sat on the olive drab director's chair with his cover in his lap. The general sat in the chair opposite him. A small wooden table separated the two men. Widdecke reached beneath it and brought out a half bottle of Highland Park single-malt Scotch and two tumblers. He filled them and then picked up his glass, motioning for Puspoon to do the same.

"Now, ahh don't wahhnt tuh sound maain or nuthin'," the general said, leaning in and lowering his voice, "but it was a damn good ahh-dee-uh takin' out Than, and ahm shore glad he's day-id." Widdecke leaned back in his chair. "It's gahhn hep us win this war!" he roared.

"Yes, sir. I hope so, sir."

"Tell all y'all men ahhm puttin' 'em up for the Navy Cross, an' ahhm recommendin' y'all for the Bronze Star!" Widdecke raised his glass. So did Puspoon.

"Thank you, sir."

"Heah's tuh all y'all for a job wail done!" Both men downed the Scotch. The general slowly refilled their glasses. When he handed Puspoon his glass, his face was etched with concern.

"Jack, MAC-V gave me some disturbin' news."

"Sir?"

"It's 'bout your boy," Widdecke said quietly. "He's gahhn missing."

"Missing?" Puspoon straightened up and set his glass on the table.

"He was at a bank when it was being rahhbed. The FBI buhlieves the rahhbers kidnapped him." Puspoon closed his eyes and sat back.

"Ahh wahhnt tuh hep—"

"Please, sir, I need a second."

"Take yuh tahhm, Jack." Several moments passed. The general threw back his Scotch and stared at his glass.

"Sir, I have to get home," Puspoon said. He emptied the tumbler and stood. "Now."

"Ah've gahht an F-4 Phantom with two thousand gallons of jet fuel standing baahh. Major Wilson has yuh flahht suit. Go home, Jack. Good luck."

Chapter 53

Monday, June 1, 1970

"Hey, Phee-il!" Chief Carl Dean Clory shouted from his office doorway. "C'mere minute, weel yuh?" Clory, whose deeply lined face had as many crooks and crannies as a weathered cliff, had just pinned two new posters to the bulletin board. He took a step back, squinting to make sure they were straight, and shrugged. Favoring his prosthetic left leg, a souvenir the Army gave him for killing Nazis, Clory hobbled gracelessly back to his desk. He gripped the leather arm pad of his worn oak chair with stiff, sore fingers, centered his rear, and dropped, landing squarely on the donut-shaped cushion. Clory sighed, relieved to be off his leg, and blessed Anita when he saw a steaming cup of hot coffee waiting. He leaned back and swung his legs onto his desk.

"Yeah, Chief?" Trotter drawled, poking his head in the doorway.

"Ahh heard thar was uh man an' uh boy ee-in Reelz yes-tuh-daaay. Issat r'ht?" Clory, a slow talker compared to the deepest southerner, was a Bone Prairie native. He quit school and joined the Army when he was fifteen—lying about his age—so he could fight in the Great War and then rejoined—lying about his age—after the Japanese attacked Pearl Harbor. In between the two world wars, he was hired as chief of Bone Prairie's one-man police department. He'd headed its two-man force since the end of World War II. Phil Trotter was BPPD's newest number two.

"Siddown minute, Phee-il." Clory waved Trotter in and pointed to a chair opposite his desk.

"Yeah, ahh saw'm," Trotter drawled almost as slowly as the old Chief. Even simple conversations between the two men took an eternity.

"How ole d'yuh figger tha' boy was?"

"Din't ask," Trotter said.

Clory stared at him, waiting, before finally cocking his head and squinting. "Kin yuh gay-ess, Phee-il?"

"Thart-teen, fort-teen, mebbe, why?"

"Lookie 'ere, ississ hee-im?" Clory held up a flyer with Tyler's face on it.

"Uh, ahh don' know, Chief, th' kee-id at Reelz' had uh couple black eyes an' uh fat lip. He was older, too."

"Two black eyes an' uh fat lip?!"

"Uh-huh."

"Wha' th' haail issat 'bout?"

"Ah dunno, Chief."

"Didja ask?"

"No."

Clory closed his eyes. Conversations with Trotter were often frustrating. "All r'ht, waaail, try an' ignore tha' an' look agin." Clory folded the flyer in half and flung it at him. It fluttered like a dying moth and landed on the desktop. Trotter grabbed it. He studied the face for a long minute, frowning and scrunching his face up in a half dozen different ways.

Clory broke the long silence with seven long vowels. "Waaail, Phee-il, wha' d'yuh thaaank?"

"Ahh don' thank so, but it's 'ard tuh tail, so ahh don' know, mebbe." Trotter got up and handed Clory the flyer.

"Dang it, Phee-il, thas ever' ant-ser 'cept yassirno! Throw 'em in-nar and pick agin!"

Trotter, still holding the flyer, sat down and gave it another look. After a minute, he said, "Hmm."

"Which issit, Phee-il?" Clory said, impatiently.

"Ahhl say it's nawt hee-im," Trotter finally said, sounding less a policeman than game-show contestant.

"Now, hold on thar', uh minute 'go, yuh din't know, but now yuh certain?"

"Laahhk ah say-id, th' boy at Reelz is older. He's gawt lahhngur haaair an' it's dahrker, too. B'sides, they're jes' hare tuh go fishin'."

"How d'ya know tha'?"

"Ahh tawlkt tuh 'em."

"Ya tahhhlk'd tuh 'em?!" Clory asked, flummoxed.

"Waail, ahh tawlkt tuh th' man, not the boy."

"Whyyy the haail din't yuh say so?!"

"Yuh din't ask."

"Fer chrissakes, Phee-il!" Clory fumed. "So, why din't yuh ask 'bout th' boy's . . . oh, never mind. All r'ht, thar haair tuh fish, huh?"

"Thas' what th' man say-id."

"When did Bone Prairie become uh fishin' resort, Phee-il?"

"Ahh don' know, Chief, but ahh kin ask 'em. They're staayin' on Max's farm."

"He tole yuh tha', too, did he?"

"Naw, they was eein Max's 'Patchy, so ahh gawt worried, thank'n mebbe he'd bawt it, so ah wen out tuh see if'n it was thar."

"Waayduh minnit, Phee-il. Back the haail up 'ere. Yuh wen' out tuh Max's fahhrm?"

"Shore day-id," Trotter said, eagerly awaiting praise for tracking them down.

"Didja caahl it ee-in?"

"No," he said quietly.

"Why th' haaail nahhht?!" Clory asked, completely exasperated. "Thas jest ESSOPEE , ah've tole yuh tha'!"

"Ahhm sawry, Chief."

"Sawry ain't cuttin' it, Phee-il! Caahl tha' shee-it eee-in!"

"Okay, Chief, but kin ahh jes' saaay—"

"No, goddamn it, shuddup!" Clory was steaming. He sighed. Then he sighed again, long and deep.

"All r'ht, now, didja tahhlk tuh'm at Reelz or nahht?"

"Nawt."

"G'aawn then, finish wha' yuh were sayin', diddee?"

"Did who what?"

"Th' man, Pheeee-il, th' man! Did th' man buy Max's truck?!"

"No, Max tol' him he could drahhv it if'n he got it runnin'. Man, ahh was shore glad tuh haair tha'. Ahh've wanted tha' truck fer yeeerz!"

"An ahh wish Max'd sole it tuh yuh, so's yuh's shuddup 'bout it. Tard uh haairin' it."

"Ah know," Trotter laughed nervously, "air-buddy says tha'."

"All r'ht, now, didja git thar naaaims?"

"No."

"An whyyy nahht?"

"Ahh was jes' thinkin' 'bout th' 'Patchy."

"But yuh wen' out thar, r'ht?"

"Raaht."

"An yuh inter-doosed y'saailf, r'ht? Toll 'em yer a puh-lice officer an' gave yer naaaim?"

"Ahh day-id."

"But yuh din't git thar naaaims?"

"Uh-uh."

"Didja even ask?" Clory was fuming, but trying not to show it.

"Uh-uh."

"Look fuh-mill-yer?" Clory drawled, holding up a copy of Brixton's eight-by-ten mugshot.

"Uh-uh."

"Wha' kinda car thay drahhhvin'?"

"Sixty-four-and-a-half Mustang," Trotter said.

"Whar thaay from?"

"Ahh dunno."

"Lemme gay-ess, yuh din't ask, didja?"

"Nope."

"Wha' wuss on the lahhsints plaaait?"

"Ahh dunno."

"Wha' yuh maain yuh dunno? Din't yuh see it?"

"Naw, the car was eein the bahrn."

"Whyyy wuss it ee-in th' bahhhrn?"

"The top wasn't workin' an' he din't want it tuh git way-it."

"Waaay-it?! Ain't raained inna munt!"

"Ah know! Trotter said, slapping his knee and laughing. "Tha's wha' ah tole 'em!" Clory just stared at him, feeling his blood pressure rise.

"Wha'd thaay git at Reelz, Phee-il?"

"Clothes an' fishin' gayer."

"Uh li'l or uh lot?"

"Uh lot."

"D'yuh know whar' else thaay went?"

"Nope."

"Th' fillin' station an' th' gross-shree store."

"Thaay day-id?"

"Filled up and baahht gross-shrees, too. Uh lot of gross-shrees. Whaddya make of that'?"

"Ah gay-ess theys gonna stay fer a li'l while thaay-in."

"Yuh thank, d'yuh?"

"Why ailse would thaay need awl tha' food?"

"Mebbe thar's mor'n just them two. Didja thank 'bout tha'?"

"Thar wudn't anyone ailse 'round, Chief."

"Yuh maain yuh din't see anyone ailse. Didja go ee-insahhd?"

"No."

"Din't thank so. An' ahh don' know 'bout you, but ahh bring moan tackle when ahhm goin' fishin'. An' if'n ahhm stayin' a spell, ah bring moan clothes, too! D'yuh see wha' ahhm gittin' at, Phee-il?"

"Sorta, ahh gayess."

"Yuh maain 'no,' doncha?"

"Uh-huh."

"Thaay din't plan this trip. Issuh lark." Clory rubbed his smooth chin.

"Uh lark?"

"Spur th' mo-munt, Phee-il. Spon-tain-ee-us. Unplaaaanned. Had tuh be, r'ht? Thaay said thaayir haaair tuh fish, but thaay ain't gahht no fishin' gayer! Jest baahht ever' thaang bran' new! Dudn't tha' seem odd tuh yuh?"

"Naw, not ray-lee, Chief. Some folks are laahhk tha'. Thaay git some free taahm an' thaay jes' wanna pack up an' go sumwhaairz."

"Tha's wha' ahm saayin', Phee-il!" Clory laughed heartily. "Thaay did th' goin' wittout th' packin'!" Clory took his feet off the desk and swiveled in his chair. He smacked the desktop with his hands.

"Haaay, Phee-il. Wha' 'bout tha' bank job up ee-in Indunnaplis th' otha' daay? Didja hear 'bout tha'?"

"Ahh sawl tha' awn th' news!" Trotter said it slowly, awestruck. "DEETEEKAY agin, wuddent it? Kidnap't sum kee-id, too, rahht?" He was excited.

"Thas r'ht, an' thaay 'edded south."

"Waail, we'll shore naail 'em if'n thaay come 'round haair, won't we, Chief?"

"Uh-huh, but lissen haair now, 'ississ ver' im-portunt."

"What?"

"Ahh wancha tuh check wit me afore yuh go out tuh Max's agin, y'heah?"

"Shore, why?"

"Ah bin thankin' 'bout tradin' in my old deuce an' uh quartuh, so ah jest maaht wanna have a li'l look-see at tha' Mustang if'n ah've got the tahhm."

"Okaaay, Chief, waail do. Tha' it?"

"Thassit." Trotter rose, and Clory followed him to the door with his eyes.

"Phee-il?"

"Uh-huh?" Trotter turned, pausing in the doorway.

"Yer thankin' 'bout takin' tha' tayest agin, ain't yuh?"

"Th' dee-teck-tiv tayest? Shore am! Ahh thank ahhl do purty good!"

"Ahh bet yuh do, too, Phee-il, ahh bet yuh do. Fifth tahm, r'ht?"

"Yep."

"Wail, g' luck. Now, tale 'Nita c'mere minute." Clory picked up the flyer with Tyler's face on it, leaned back, and put his feet on the desk. Anita appeared in the doorway.

"'Nita, honey, be uh dear an' git me th' Eff-Bee-Eye on th' tail-uh-fone."

Chapter 54

The telephone hotline had been jammed with callers ever since going live Saturday night. Information poured in, most of it already known and discounted. Other tips were rejected out of hand, like the one from an elderly woman—a movie buff apparently—who swore Edward G. Robinson, and his gang, were holed up in her basement. Then, of course, there were the amateur sleuths, private detectives, and psychics peddling their services and theories in hopes of making a name—and quick cash—for themselves. Several solid leads were phoned in, and although a couple of them were still being checked out, neither the FBI nor ISP had found anything useful. The DTK Gang had vanished.

Public attention was riveted on the case. DTK's notoriety evoked memories of Bonnie and Clyde among the older folks, stoking fear and sending their hearts racing like they were teenagers again. People around the state talked about DTK morning, noon, and night. They eyed their local banks warily, and from a distance, too, since no one dared go inside. It was irrational, of course, since the odds of being in a bank when it was being robbed—DTK or not—were infinitesimal, but, as some folks said, "tell that to your next of kin."

The media was having a field day. Already a top story in the Midwest, the slaughter at CNT and Tyler's kidnapping made DTK go national, even international. James Duddy, the veteran police reporter for the *New York Daily News*, was all over it. He interviewed law enforcement, witnesses, and victims' relatives before penning a series of articles that the wire services picked up. Newspapers across the country carried headlines about DTK. Then Jocko Thomas, the crime reporter for the *Toronto Star* and CFRB radio, began covering the gang. His broadcast was available throughout Canada and over its borders to anyone who could pick it up. Thomas ripped the FBI and ISP for their lack of progress. He called for a joint state-federal task force.

Kramer had suggested a joint task force after the first murder, pointing out that combining forces and sharing information would save time and money and keep law enforcement from stepping on each other's toes. Burroughs, not long in his new role but already demonstrating ineptness, gruffly rejected the idea, thinking Hoover would never approve it. He wasn't about to jeopardize his job. Now, though, a boy had been kidnapped and five more people were dead, one of them a pregnant woman, so Kramer planned to go over his head to get the JTF. Turned out, she didn't have to.

Burroughs, who'd spent the entire weekend in his office, and in varying states of inebriation, had just settled in his chair when his secretary, worry lines creasing her face, handed him a cup of coffee and said Clyde Tolson had called three times while he was in the bathroom. Pale and shaking, he grimly dialed the number. Tolson picked up on the half-ring. He was yelling before the handset got to his face, and he was still yelling when he slammed it down, having raised two concerns: one, that Burroughs wasn't at his desk while DTK was still on the loose, and two, that DTK was still on the loose. Burroughs's input wasn't solicited.

That was only the start. Tolson called back for a progress report an hour later, and then every hour after that for the rest of the day, stopping only after Burroughs blurted out Brixton's name. Burroughs left the office that night, arriving home just before midnight, wanting nothing more than a quick dinner, another drink, and sleep. Instead, his wife was waiting in the foyer, outstretched hands holding the telephone, the cord taut behind her.

Burroughs took the handset as if it was radioactive and held it at arm's length, waiting for Tolson's latest meltdown. Except it wasn't Tolson. It was the Old Man himself. Mortified, Burroughs bolted to attention, bracing for orders to Butte. Instead, Hoover, addressing him as "Sam," talked to him in a fatherly manner, sharing his thoughts and advice about bank robbers and asking if he needed anything. Burroughs, so relieved he wasn't getting transferred, didn't hear. Nor did he hear the second time.

"WELL, DO YOU?" Hoover yelled. "SPEAK, MAN, SPEAK!"

"JOINT TASK FORCE!" Burroughs blurted, pouncing on the first thing that came to mind. He closed his eyes, waiting for the blowback.

"WHY DIDN'T YOU SAY SO? DO IT!" Hoover slammed the phone down.

Hoover didn't want a joint task force, but Indiana's congressional delegation were calling for hearings, and he wanted that even less. Governor Whitcomb was under mounting pressure to do something, too. The press hounded him, shoving microphones in his face and writing stories about lack of leadership and gross incompetence. Whitcomb's approval ratings tanked. He wasn't even halfway into his governorship, and he'd become so politically toxic that members of his own party shunned him. So, the governor couldn't have been happier when informed the FBI would acquiesce to a JTF if he made a formal request. He didn't need to be told twice.

"Finally!" Kramer exclaimed, standing and punching her fist in the air. She'd just gotten off the phone with ISP Colonel Brad Pickering, who was surprised she hadn't heard. Pickering had an additional twenty troopers on the interstates and highways early Saturday afternoon. By evening, he'd ordered checkpoints at all bridges crossing the Ohio River into Kentucky and notified the state police in surrounding states to be on the lookout.

"We might be too late," Pickering said dolefully. "If they stayed on the road they could be in Mexico by now. "

"News broke quick, though, I don't know the exact time, but let's say ten o'clock. Where would that put them? Columbus?"

"Probably closer to Seymour. I'll set up base ops there and dispatch twenty-five troopers to start a grid search."

"What do you think, fifty-mile radius?"

"Sounds right," Pickering said. "That'd involve eight counties. I've already talked to most of the sheriffs down there. Their deputies have been combing every mile of road since Saturday. I bet the others have, too, but I'll give them a call just the same. DTK will be just as hard to find if they've gone to ground, though."

Chapter 55

Monday, June 1, 1970

Puspoon pulled the left control handle just below the canopy sill on the F-4 Phantom's aft cockpit. Then he yanked the opposite handle. The seals deflated with a loud whoosh! Reaching overhead, he pushed open the acrylic, clam-shaped shell to the scream of the fighter jet's twin turbine engines. The pilot, Major Paul Broussard, had done the same thing moments earlier but now he had his eyes fixed on the flagman. The pair welcomed the breeze; the air-conditioning automatically switched off as soon as the F-4 dropped below 60 miles per hour.

The Phantom taxied off the runway toward the hangars. Puspoon unfastened his safety harness and disengaged his oxygen supply.

"Say, Cap, you gonna led me buduh inna hanga furst, 'r whad?" Broussard said good-naturedly in his deep, throaty growl. Broussard, who was French-Creole, grew up along the Mississippi River in Plaquemines Parish. He went on to earn degrees at "ELLESHYEW" in computational mathematics and mechanical engineering. He joined the Air Force afterward.

"Sorry, Major." Puspoon chuckled after figuring out what the pilot had said. "I'm kind of in a rush."

"I unnerstan', Cap, bud da gen'ril, he gonna bud da gris-gris on me iffa you ged hurt."

"I'd put in a good word for you, sir."

"Nuh-uh, I ain't playin' wid'ya now. Da gen'ril he gibbin me dem orduhs puhsnal." Broussard stopped the F-4 and, heeding the flagman's signal, cut the engines. Maintenance crewmen and technicians swarmed the aircraft.

"Dere ya go," Broussard said.

"Much appreciated, Major. I owe you one."

Puspoon, small duffel bag in hand, climbed from the cockpit. He tossed his bag to the deck below and stepped tailward atop the fuel cells attached to the fuselage before scooting onto the wing. Then, using one hand, he hopped to the smooth cement surface. Back on earth, Puspoon stripped off his flight suit, revealing faded Levi's and a tight-fitting, black T-shirt emblazoned with the words *Marine Recon* in gold across the front. He felt for his switchblade and opened his wallet to check for the small, circular mirror he kept on him.

"Looka dere, dat's da gen'ril's car." Broussard stood next to Puspoon and nodded toward the south end of the hangar where a new navy blue Mercury Monarch bearing the flag of an Air Force two-star general had pulled up. The driver's door opened and a lieutenant emerged wearing the braiding of an aide-de-camp. "He be comin' fur you."

"Welcome to Grissom, Major Broussard." The lieutenant snapped off a smart salute.

"Where y'at, Cap?" Broussard replied, lazily returning the salute with two fingers to his forehead.

The aide then acknowledged Puspoon with a nod. "Welcome, Lieutenant Puspoon, I'm Lieutenant Yarber. General Turner instructed me to take you wherever you need to go."

"Ain't dat sump'in now?"

"What's that, sir?" Yarber asked.

"I ain't nevah seen no gen'ril send a car 'ceptin' for 'nudder gen'ril."

"It's a first for me, too."

"See, it's like me tol' you," Broussard said to Puspoon.

"Lieutenant, I'm ready when you are."

"Okay, let's find a phone; I need to make a call." Puspoon turned to Broussard and saluted. "Major, thanks again. I appreciate the ride."

"G'luck, Cap."

Chapter 56

Monday, June 1, 1970

Calls had slowed to a trickle by late Monday afternoon, allowing ISP to catch up on all the tips that flooded the hotline through the weekend. Although no solid leads had emerged, Kramer, free from all the mind-numbing paperwork—witness interviews, evidence reports, case updates—that had hindered her for months, was finally directing a full-scale FBI investigation, and she was trying to do just that when the worst part of her job barged into her office.

"Where are we on DTK?" growled a scowling Sam Burroughs. His face was flushed, bloated, his eyes bloodshot.

"Take a seat, Sam," Kramer said with a wave, after he'd already done so. He reeked of alcohol, and its fumes trailed his every move. "You should've told me Hoover okayed the JTF, but then I didn't even know you'd requested it."

"Why, so you could get your picture in the paper?" Burroughs had cleaned up and put on a clean suit for the governor's press conference, but his streak of hangovers left him looking sweaty and pasty.

"No, that's why you were there." It slipped out, but it was true. Burroughs had arrived feeling like Melvin Purvis, but instead spent the whole time fending off questions about the FBI's failure to capture DTK. Kramer knew she was about to feel the full brunt of his frustration, but having already surpassed levels of tolerability she didn't know she had, it was time to stand her ground. "I could've been coordinating with ISP twelve hours ago!"

"Doesn't matter," Burroughs said.

"It doesn't?" Kramer asked, surprised at such a stupid assessment even from him.

"I'm taking over the investigation."

"You!?" Kramer, stunned, fell back in her chair as if hit by a truck.

"Yes, me!" Burroughs roared, offended. "Why do you say it like that?!"

Kramer tried not to laugh. "When's the last time you led a field investigation?"

"That's not the point. This one needs a fresh set of eyes to finish the job."

"You mean get the job." That didn't slip out, and it was no less true. "`Look, Sam," Kramer growled, standing. "We've just ID'd Brixton and Tyler. Every cop in America has their pictures and a sketch of the big man. This will go down quick now that I finally have the manpower I've needed."

"Yet, here we are, and they're still loose."

"That might have something to do with the fact that I've been running a one-man, wait, one-woman, no, make that, one-black-woman investigation this whole time, and I just now heard about the JTF!"

"Excuses!"

Kramer leaned forward with her hands wide apart on the desktop, so they were face-to-face and stared at him through angry eyes. "I've already coordinated with Pickering. We've got an operations center up and running in Seymour, troopers cruising the highways, and eight counties blanketed with law enforcement." Not exactly the truth, but it would be soon.

"I don't know." Burroughs stood, crossed his arms, and walked to the window. He looked across Michigan Street at the Haugh

Building, considering his options. The surest way to get "Acting" removed from his title would be to rescue the boy and capture the gang by himself, but that was an oversell for a man who couldn't solve an embezzlement from the office's sunshine club. Cracking what was blossoming into the crime of the century required skills and knowledge he lacked.

"One week," Burroughs said, "that's it." Then he stomped out.

Chapter 57

Monday, June 1, 1970

The kettle was whistling like a buzz bomb, and I was dancing around the front room, clawing at my skin like a heroin addict. Angry, red patches of blistering lesions had erupted everywhere on my body, including my face and scalp. I was scratching madly wherever my hands could reach and rubbing up against things to get where they couldn't.

"Easy there, kid. What's the matter?" Marlin switched off the camp stove when I jitterbugged into the kitchen. The kettle trailed off.

"I itch everywhere!" I scratched a spot I didn't even know existed.

"Let me see." He took my face in his hands and looked it over. Then he held my arms out and lifted them while I danced in place. "Raise your shirt . . . now turn around. Yeah, I can see why, too," he chuckled.

"What is it? Why're you laughing?!"

"You've got poison ivy," he said, stirring his coffee. "What've you been doing, rolling around in the weeds?"

"Something like that," I said, quickly thinking of Darlene and hoping she wasn't feeling as miserable as me.

"Calamine lotion and baking soda," Wren called from his familiar position, squatting in front of the fridge. "That's what my mom used on us."

"Apple cider vinegar works better," Marlin replied, "and you don't get caked in pink and white frosting."

"Embalming fluid," Frank said, entering the kitchen and the conversation, neither of which pleased anyone. The three of us exchanged looks while he took a seat at the table, spread a dish towel, and disassembled his Colt.

"Embalming fluid?" Wren said disbelievingly.

"It'll eat that shit right up."

"How do you know that?" Marlin asked. Frank started to answer, but he cut him off. "Never mind, I don't want to know."

While the three of them debated remedies, I wobbled back and forth on one leg, moaning in agony, scratching my calf with my foot and twisting my arm up my back to itch in between my shoulders. They all laughed when I fell.

"I can't stop scratching!"

"We'll run to town and get some vinegar and cotton balls," Marlin said.

"Let's go! I can't take this anymore!"

"Hop in the truck. I've got to go to the bathroom." He started down the hall.

"He's not going to town again," Frank said.

"He's going where I go," Marlin replied, turning around to face him.

"Not to the bathroom," I said, trying to be funny. Nobody laughed. I kept scratching.

"Leave him here, Mr. Marlin," Wren said, again seeing where their conversation was headed and trying to derail it. Marlin didn't say a word. He just turned and walked to the bathroom and shut the door behind him. A minute later, he emerged, zipping his fly to the sound of the toilet flushing. Marlin walked back to the kitchen and stopped at the back door. He gave Frank a long look and left.

Chapter 58

Monday, June 1, 1970

DTK had escaped without a trace. Kramer feared the gang had disbanded, dispersed, and disappeared, but her instincts said they were hiding out. If so, they'd have to surface soon, if only for food. The telephone interrupted her thoughts.

"Agent Kramer."

"G'mawn'n, Agent Kray-muh, muh naaame's Cheeef Clahhree. Ahhm down 'ere ee-in Bone Prairie. Yuh th' one ee-in charge of th' Dee-Tee-Kay case?" It took him a good thirty seconds to get that out.

"Yes, I am. What can I do for you, Chief?"

"It's more what ahh kin do fer you," he drawled. "Ahm prit shore th' gang's on a fahhrm dahhwn 'ere."

"What makes you think so?" Kramer's heart broke into a gallop. She grabbed a yellow legal pad and a black ballpoint pen and started scribbling notes, frowning throughout. Then, grim-faced, she nodded her head.

"Okay, what's your number there? Wait . . . wait a sec, start over . . . uh-huh . . . okay, got it." She started to hang up but stopped. "Right, don't do anything. I'm sending a couple agents. . . yeah, I'm coming, too. . . uh-huh, leaving now." She hung up. Her phone immediately rang again.

"Agent Kramer."

"Agent Kramer, this is Twyla Puspoon, Tyler's mother."

"Hi, how're you holding up? I meant to call you, but I've been busy, and I'm really sorry, but I don't have time to talk now either."

"I understand. Is there anything new?"

"I just got off the phone with the police chief in Bone Prairie. He thinks the gang's on a farm down there."

"What about Tyler?"

"There's a boy Tyler's age with them. He was with a man in a store, and they were tracked to a farm outside of town. I have to go now."

"Is he okay?"

Kramer hesitated. "So far as we know."

"Where's Bone Prairie? I've never heard of it."

"Just off 64 between Turlington and Pomby. I'm hanging up now."

Chapter 59

Monday, June 1, 1970

A growing crowd gathered in front of the elevator on the ground floor of the Minton-Capehart building. Puspoon had been there the longest.

"We're all assuming it works, right?" A man's voice from the rear.

"Oh, it works, but on its own schedule," someone else said. A few chuckles followed.

"It's like waiting at the pharmacy." People murmured in assent or gave knowing nods.

"One of Otis's early models," said an elderly man with stark white hair, leaning on a cane. No one doubted him given his age and the length of their wait.

Finally, there was a soft, barely audible "ding" and the doors rattled for several seconds before slowly opening. People filtered out and splintered in different directions. Puspoon, towering over the crowd, held the doors while the last few people dribbled out. Then he let all the women and the old man board before slipping inside. He pressed nine and moved to the back as people called out their floors.

"Two, please."

"Would you hit five? Thanks."

"Four, please, Destini."

"Shirley, press seven for me."

"Just hit 'em all!" The doors banged shut amid laughter.

There was a sudden jolt, and the elevator, groaning like the dead, rose sluggishly.

Nine long stops later, the doors slowly knocked apart, revealing a dark wood door with opaque glass displaying the FBI logo. The lobby was cold and unwelcoming, featuring a standing American flag in the corner, pictures of Nixon and Hoover on the wall above it, and a dozen gray metal folding chairs lining the perimeter. There was neither coffee nor tea, and no reading material except the FBI's Most Wanted List. DTK had vaulted to the top.

Puspoon stared at Brixton's face on the wanted poster. Then he crossed the room to the receptionist, a thickset, sixty-year-old former prison matron wearing an institutional gray pantsuit and a frown. She looked at Puspoon with equal parts disdain and distrust until he introduced himself.

"I'm sorry, Lieutenant," she said, now a concerned grandmother. She looked at a bank of lit buttons on a NASA-like telephone. "Agent Kramer's line's busy. Please have a seat. I'll tell her you're here."

"Thank you." Puspoon chose a chair near the flag. Suddenly, the inner-office door burst open, and Kramer rushed through it.

"Agent Kramer! That's Lieutenant—"

"I'm Tyler's dad."

"Come with me. I believe we've located your son. We'll talk in the car."

Chapter 60

Monday, June 1, 1970

I ran out the front door to remind Marlin to get a deck of cards and then watched him drive off ahead of a thick cloud of dust. I started for the barn, but a solid smack upside the head sent me reeling.

"Ow! What the hell, man!" I wheeled around, eyes brimming with tears. "What'd you do that for?"

"I don't need a reason," Frank said, turning his ring right side up. "Now get in the house. I'm not letting you out of my sight."

"I'm not done with the horses." I turned toward the barn, but he gave me a solid shove, and I hit the ground face first.

"Hey, Kentucky Derby, I said get in the fucking house!" I got to my feet, fixed him with an icy glare, and stomped upslope to the house and then up the porch steps. I slammed the door behind me. A minute later, Frank flung it open.

"I told you to stay in sight!"

"Wrong! You said I wasn't getting out of *your* sight! Frank took two steps, grabbed my shirt with both hands, and jerked me to my feet. He had his right fist cocked when Wren suddenly blotted out the background and engulfed his fist, wrist, and a good part of his forearm in his big, meaty paw.

"Don't." That was all he said. Frank let go of my shirt and shoved me to the floor. Then, cursing, he slunk off, clenching and unclenching his fingers and rubbing his sore shoulder.

Chapter 61

Monday, June 1, 1970

"Hello?" Darlene groaned into the telephone. She wore a cotton tank top and loose knit shorts, but she was wrapped in layers of thick gauze stained pink with calamine lotion. Her face and neck had fresh daubs of it overlying the dried and drying ones, creating an archipelago of pinks from Pepto to bloody steak. Darlene held her breath, body tense, and carefully eased back on the couch, trying not to irritate her very irritable skin. She had a pillow behind her head and her legs over the armrest. The base of the phone lay on her stomach. Darlene closed her eyes and twitched in agony; she'd thus far resisted the urge to rake her fingernails over the itchy blisters, but now she no longer cared about permanent scarring.

"Darlene?"

"Yeah?"

"It's Twyla, Tyler's mom. How're you doing?"

"Hey, Twyla," Darlene replied unenthusiastically. "Not too good. I wanted to come up, but I've got poison ivy really bad."

"Oh, you poor thing. How'd you get that?"

"Long story."

"Well, I've got good news! They think they found Tyler!"

"Really?! Are you serious?" Darlene shot upright, suddenly alert and energized. "Is he okay?"

"They believe so; a boy his age was seen shopping with a man."

"Where?"

"Some place called Bone Prairie. It's south of here about three hours. I'm heading there as soon as I get off the phone."

"Can I come?"

"Of course, dear, that's why I called, but check with your mother first, okay?"

"I will."

"I'm leaving now, though, so I'll be by in about ten minutes. You can let me know then."

"Okay, see you in ten!"

Darlene raced to her bedroom, pink gauze flapping behind her. "Mom?" She threw on a pair of clean shorts and a blouse from her dresser. "MOM!" she yelled, louder and with urgency.

"Yes, yes, yes, what is it?!" Mrs. Wantel said, rushing down the hallway to the bedroom.

"Tyler's mom called! They found him!" Darlene buttoned her top.

"Oh, thank goodness! Is he alright?"

"They think so!"

"Where is he?"

"Some town in southern Indiana. She wants me to go, can I? We'll be home before dark."

"Of course, finish getting ready."

"Thanks, Mom!" Darlene said, kissing her on the cheek. "You're the best!"

Chapter 62

Monday, June 1, 1970

Tugging the bill of his green ballcap over his eyes, Marlin entered the corner drug store, drawing immediate stares and glares. He dropped his head and rubbed his cheek, shielding his face, while passing the checkout counter. The store was colder than a Vegas casino, reminding him to grab a deck of cards. He lingered afterward, enjoying the chilled air while strolling up and down the aisles, keeping an eye out for vinegar and cotton balls. At the cash register, Marlin buried his face in a trashy tabloid and waited patiently in line. When it was his turn, the cashier, a sturdy, thick-boned, corn-fed woman in her mid-forties with cat glasses and dyed auburn hair permed prom-high, put her hands on the conveyer belt, leaned down, and looked up at him with a sour expression on her face. When Marlin winked at her, she pursed her lips and dressed them with a frown.

Outside, Marlin took the sloping sidewalk down to the Apache parked curbside. He stopped to look around before getting in, paying particular attention to the police station down the block. The squad car was parked beneath an elm tree in the parking lot. A woman pushed a covered pink stroller across the street. Teens did tricks with their skateboards. That was it. Marlin tossed the bag on the seat and climbed behind the wheel with a tune running through his head. The Chevy's 283 V-8 coughed to life, caught, and held steady despite an occasional miss. He checked for traffic just as a gray Polara pulled up at the curb and parked in the shade of an oak tree.

Marlin watched for a few seconds through his outside mirror. Then he switched the truck off, turned, and rested his arm on the seatback to look out the rear of the cab. A tall, fit black woman, in her mid-twenties, wearing a white top and gray jacket and slacks, got out on the driver's side. Marlin spotted the bulge beneath her right arm straightaway.

The passenger door opened a moment later, and a man emerged. Marlin couldn't see very well through the leaves and branches, but when he saw the short patch of hair covering the man's dome, he knew...*Jarhead!* Marlin got a sense of the man's immensity when the pair started up the steps. When they entered the police station, he lapped the block to check the plates. *Feds!*

Frank squirted lighter fluid on a small square he cut from a dishrag and pushed it through the bore of his Colt with a coat hanger. It emerged, blackened with the residue of carbon, copper, and lead. His movements were slow, awkward, and painful thanks to his partners. Frank eyed Wren spitefully. He picked up his cigarette, flicked the ash on the floor, and took a long drag.

"I've seen livestock with better table manners," he sneered.

"Perhaps, but I have better marbling."

"Food never goes to waste around you. It goes around your waist."

There wasn't much that could upset Wren when he ate. It was one of his greatest pleasures, and he did it well and often. He stabbed a piece of fried egg and rotated it on his fork. "I like the brown, crispy parts. Properly seasoned, they're a delicacy." He nibbled the edges, enjoying the crunchy bits.

"Not hard keeping you happy," Frank jibed.

"Burnt cheese, too." Wren cut off a glob of charred cheddar cheese and popped it in his mouth. "Tastes like Cheese Nips." He reached for a triangle of toast and, swallowing, heaped hash browns, two strips of bacon, and the rest of the egg on top. He looked at Frank and crammed it all in his mouth, pushing the last bit in with his pinkie.

"I can grab the pitchfork from the barn."

"Thagwoanbenessry."

Marlin shifted into neutral and jammed on the brakes, engulfing the truck in a big red cloud of dirt and sending the cards, vinegar, and cotton balls sliding out of the paper sack straight onto the rusted floorboard. He yanked the emergency brake and barreled out. Then, skirting the back bumper, he sprinted up the mound and leaped atop the back porch.

"We've got trouble!" Marlin announced, bursting through the door.

"Wusgonon?" Wren rose so fast he knocked his chair over and juddered the table a good three feet sideways. He swallowed and took another bite.

"It's the FBI!"

"Here?!" Wolf said. He'd assembled the Colt and started loading it.

"Whamayksoosinkso?"

"I saw a car pull up outside the police station. A black woman, maybe twenty-five, and a white guy got out. She was packing. I don't know about him, but he was big, probably six-five, six-six, solidly built—a real hard-looking dude. The car's got federal plates."

"Let's get out of here," Frank said. He put the last round in the cylinder and snapped it shut with a flip of his wrist just as I came up the hall from the bathroom. He pointed the long-barreled Colt at me.

"I've wanted to kill you for a long time."

Frank no sooner said it than Marlin hit him with a hard-knuckled, overhand right that landed on his left temple. He dropped like a lead potato.

"Let's go, kid." Marlin said, grimacing and flexing his hand. "I'll swap out the battery and then we're gone." He didn't look nervous, but the urgency in his voice was unmistakable. He walked to the front room.

"Where's the vinegar?" I asked.

"In the truck, grab it and throw it in the Fury."

"What about the horses?"

"Yeah, better feed them, but hurry up." Marlin peered out the front window and snapped the curtains shut. He turned to me. "Just be done before I am." I followed him to the kitchen.

"Might as well give them these," I said, grabbing the bag of apples off the counter.

"You coming with us?" Marlin asked Wren.

"Indeed, I am." Wren was kneeling before the open fridge again. He ripped open a package of smoked sausage and took a huge bite.

"Then it's time to go, not eat."

"Just getting a snack for the road," Wren said, swallowing. He bit off another chunk, and carefully stored the rest of the horse-shoe-shaped beef in his suit pocket. He grabbed a chicken leg.

"No, now!"

"Fine!" Wren said, perturbed. "But a man's got to eat!" He stood and bumped the fridge door shut with his hip.

Frank hadn't moved except to breathe. I hopped over him and headed out back. Marlin stepped on the porch and held the door open, giving Wren wide berth. Wren, who rarely saw his feet and never when standing, slowly waddled through the doorway.

"Can't you move any faster?"

"Not without risk." He slowly descended the porch steps, rolls of fat quivering beneath his shirt. He stopped at the bottom and took a huge bite of chicken. Marlin waited behind him impatiently and then hopped off the porch and circled him. He sprinted down the mound toward the Apache.

I stuck the hose in the tank and left the water trickling. Then I threw the apples out in the field and ran back to the barn. Marlin was still under the truck's hood, turning wrenches, so I put grain out and headed to the loft for more hay. I threw down a bale for each stall, and then tossed several more out the loft doors to the corral. I started down the ladder just as Marlin walked in, carrying the battery.

"One minute," he said, looking up at me.

"Got it," I said, spying Wren, who'd just appeared in the doorway.

"Hurry up, Mr. Wren," Marlin said. "You can eat in the car."

"Give me a second," he said between bites.

"We don't have a second!"

"You just said we had sixty of them!"

"Just get in the car, will you?!"

"In a second." Wren pushed off the door frame. I was coming down the ladder when I heard a gunshot. I looked over my shoulder. Wren was lying in the doorway, still clutching the chicken leg.

"Thas one, whooshhnext?"

Frank!

Chapter 63

Monday, June 1, 1970

The police department sat above the street half a block off the courthouse square. Kramer drove around the block and parked in the shade curbside behind a green Buick Electra 225. Special Agents Frank Lewis and Lou Bradshaw, dubbed "LuLu" by their fellow agents, were already there. Lewis, a wiry man from Phoenix, was fresh from Quantico, while Bradshaw, a divorced father of two from Seattle, was a seven-year veteran.

The pair had been at Shapiro's earlier, acting on a tip that three men matching DTK's description had eaten breakfast there early Saturday morning. Everyone remembered Wren, but recollections of the other two were hazy and inconsistent. All anyone could remember was that they were dressed like the circus-sized fat man. Then a busboy showed up for his shift and picked out Brixton from mugshots. The kid had been sitting on the kitchen stoop, waiting for the kitchen to open, when the Starfire pulled in behind the appliance store. He got up to check it out and saw Brixton at the wheel, and then saw him again sitting with the fat man. The tow-truck driver had the Olds hooked and was reeling it in when LuLu were dispatched to Bone Prairie.

The expansive, colorful painting encased in glass behind Chief Clory's desk was the work of Frances Slocum, the White Rose of the Miamis, in honor of the Indiana Territory achieving statehood. Using inks and dyes derived from local roots, berries, and ores, she sat at an overlook near Groot and painted a sky view of Slatty Creek's winding path through the hills and hollers of Broben County.

Puspoon and the three FBI agents watched as Officer Trotter, brimming with equal parts pride and ignorance, approached the painting with a rubber-tipped, wood pointer.

"Thar nawt ahhn th' maa-yup," Trotter drawled, hands on his hips, "but thar's plenty of roaaads 'round haair. Some are paaaved, some are nawt." He turned, making sure everyone was listening. "Nahhw, rahht haair," he said and smacked the pointer against the glass, shattering it. Trotter stared wide-eyed in alarm at the lightning bolt-shaped crack. Just then, there was a creak and Chief Clory, limping and coughing into a handkerchief, appeared in the doorway. He stopped when he saw Trotter, the pointer, and the broken glass. He exhaled heavily through his nostrils.

"Yuh know what ah need r'ht now, Phee-il?" Clory nodded hello to everyone while hobbling toward his desk.

"N-n-no," Trotter stammered, nervously clutching the pointer, backing away as the much older man closed in on him. He was as red-faced as any Fermak had ever been. Clory kept advancing and Trotter kept retreating, maintaining a safe distance. Neither one stopped until Clory had completely circled the room and herded Trotter to the other side of the door.

"Tuh git outta 'ere!" He snatched the pointer and kicked the door shut with a loud boom.

Clory turned to face the others.

"Sorry 'bou' tha'," he said, limping back to his desk. "He's not too braahht, but he maains waail." The Chief glanced at the long, jagged crack and, mumbling something about "bein' his own damn fault," sank in his chair and exhaled loudly. "FBI, r'ht?" He eyed the four of them.

"I'm Special Agent Kramer. We spoke on the phone. These two men to my right are Special Agents Lewis and Bradshaw."

"And I'm Lieutenant Jack Puspoon."

"Yer tha' boy's dad, ain't yuh?"

"Yes, sir, I am."

"Wail, mah naaame's Cheeef Clahhree, an ahhl hep y'all anywaaaay ah can."

"Would you go over what you told me on the phone?"

"Wail, lak ah said, ah heard thar was uh man an uh boy stayin' on the Terwilliger farm outside uh town, so ah gaaave Max a call. Now, lemme tail yuh sumpin' 'bout Max. He looks lak he's 'alf crazy, an' uh lotta folks thank he iss, but he's not. He's jes' uh li'l straaange iss ahhl."

"Okay, go on."

"Max said thar was jes' one fella—nobody else—an' he was dravin' uh dirty, blue Fury wid California plates an' uh lotta body damage. Paid fer a munt wid three bran' new hunnert dollar bills an' said he an' some friends was gonna do some fishin' this week. They din't bring no fishin'gayer, though."

"Let's get some backup," Kramer said to Lewis. "We need the roads sealed off, and make sure we have a hostage negotiator, too."

"Yuh mahht not wanna waaait fer all tha'."

"Why's that?"

"Ah drove out thar an' had a li'l looksee wid mah binoculars this mawn'n," Clory said. Then, looking at Puspoon, "It's de-fuh-nit-lee yer boy, Loo-tennet, an' he looked a might beat up, too. Couple black eyes an' a busted lip. He mahht be ee-in dayn'ger."

Chapter 64

Monday, June 1, 1970

Darlene opened the rear door of the beat-up Toyota and climbed in. She leaned forward just as Twyla turned toward her; they nearly bumped heads.

"Oops, sorry!" Darlene said, laughing.

"What're you doing in the back? C'mon up front."

"My mom wants—"

"Hang on, dear, your mother wants a word."

"Hi, Twyla, I'm Olivia." Mrs. Wantel leaned through the passenger window, hands on her knees. "I'm so sorry about what happened to Tyler. I've been worried sick. Would you mind if I came along?"

"Not at all. I'd love the company."

"Oh, good, thank you." Mrs. Wantel settled in the front seat and turned to Twyla with a smile. "Darlene said he's all right. That's such good news."

"They think so," Twyla replied, glancing quickly at Darlene and dropping the gear shift into drive. She pulled away from the curb. "He might've been spotted in a store with a man. That's about all I know." Twyla didn't say it, but she knew if it was Tyler, it wasn't Frank, and if it was Frank, it wasn't Tyler.

Chapter 65

Monday, June 1, 1970

Chief Clory cleared his desk and spread the map across it. Kramer, next to him, leaned forward with her forearms on the desktop, while Puspoon, on his other side, stood with his arms crossed. Lewis and Bradshaw sat across the desk in matching oak chairs.

"One option's this roaaad," Clory said, rubbing his clean-shaven jaw and tracing a black line with his crooked index finger. "It runs by this farm r'ht har jes' south uh Max's place. Tha's whar ah had mah looksee. It takes up tha' whole corner, an' yuh can see it from Max's kitchen winduh."

"What if we approached from the north, on this road right here?" Puspoon asked, pointing.

"Lieutenant Puspoon—" Kramer began.

"Call me Jack."

"Fine, Jack, you can't be involved in this operation."

Puspoon looked at her, perplexed. "Are you afraid I'll get hurt?"

"The other way around, but the Bureau's liable either way."

"Can I talk to you a moment?"

"Sure." Kramer followed him to a corner and looked at him. Her arched eyebrows revealed early worry lines on her forehead.

"We have to work together."

"Can't. Regulations. You know that." Neither one broke eye contact.

"That's my *son*," Puspoon said in a low voice.

"I'm fully aware of that."

"So, you invited me to come watch?"

"No, look, Lieu—Jack, I invited you because I didn't have time to talk at the office. I did it out of respect, but this is an FBI operation from here on out. I have to live by the rules if I want to keep my job."

"Your *job?* That's what's important here?"

"That's not what I meant, and you know it. You have to obey orders, and so do I."

"Let me ask you something," Puspoon said. "If Tyler was your son, would you want my help?"

Clory grabbed a felt-tipped marker from his desk drawer when the pair returned.

"Lemme show yuh the bes' way tuh Max's farm," he said, tracing the route on the map. "It's on Mong Road, mebbe fahhv mahhls from here." Clory flipped over Brixton's mugshot and drew a large box on it. "Ahhv been ee-in Max's house once ee-in all mah years. Ah had two laigs back then. This ere's the kitchen." Clory drew a smaller box inside the larger one and then sketched out the rest of the farmhouse, labeling the rooms and noting windows and doors.

"That helps a lot, Chief," Kramer said.

"Ahhl keep Phee-il haair. That'll hep even more."

Chapter 66

Monday, June 1, 1970

There was a roll of low thunder to the southwest when Kramer fired up the Polara. The 440 Magnum motor roared to life, rumbled, and then idled at a throaty growl. Foot on the brake, she dropped the gearshift and the car surged, straining to be let off its chain.

"Head east on 64 and look for Mong Road," Puspoon said. "It's a couple miles out of town." Kramer checked for traffic and pulled from the curb. Then, foot on the brake, she goosed the loud pedal and whipped the car around in a tight 180 degree arc of burnt rubber. The tires, spinning and smoking, cried like puppies, and when she let off the brake, they bit the pavement. The Polara raced out of town with Bradshaw in the Satellite, heavy on the gas, right behind. They drew plenty of honks and middle fingers.

"There's a duffel bag behind you," Kramer said, pausing while they crested a hill. The Polara landed hard, spraying sparks out the back. "Grab what you want. Bullets are in the side pockets."

"Are you using the shotgun?" Puspoon replied, looking over the seatback.

"Yeah, hand it to me."

"Riot model," Puspoon said, giving the Ithaca 37 a quick once-over.

"You've used it?"

"Just once, in the rain."

"I like it because I'm left-handed." Kramer gripped the shotgun's wood stock, eyes on the blacktop, and laid it alongside the door within easy reach. Puspoon grabbed the khaki canvas bag off the seat. He pushed aside .38s of different makes and checked out two .45s before picking out a 9mm Browning HP. The walnut grip felt good in his palm, and the thirteen-round magazine all but sealed it until Kramer nodded over her shoulder.

"There's a three fifty-seven in that black case back there." Puspoon lifted the ornamented oak box over the seat and lifted the lid, revealing a nickel-plated Combat Magnum with a three-inch barrel resting on a cushion of blue velvet.

"That's what I'd take if I didn't have my shotgun."

"I like it," Puspoon said, checking the weight and balance with a flick of his wrist. He looked inside the box. "You've got rounds, right?"

"There's a box of hollow points in the glove compartment." Kramer checked her .38 to make sure it was loaded and then stuffed a few fistfuls of shotgun shells in her jacket pockets.

"Turn right up ahead."

Mong Road started out paved but changed to chip seal after a mile. After another mile, it was all gravel.

"We'll be on a horse trail next," Puspoon said.

"If we're lucky." Wincing at the rocks pinging off the undercarriage and crunching beneath the tires, Kramer took her foot off the accelerator, allowing the car to slow on the gravel.

"The farm's beyond those trees, just past that bend."

"What're you thinking?" she asked.

"There's not much choice, quiet or loud."

"Let's take them by surprise." Kramer put two wheels in the grass and gently braked to a stop. Bradshaw eased the Satellite in behind.

Dark clouds threatened. Car doors opened. Lewis popped a fresh clip in his .45 while Bradshaw unholstered his .45 and loaded his Winchester. Kramer set out ahead, trotting toward the bend with Puspoon right behind her. LuLu followed. Suddenly, there was a gunshot. Everyone froze.

"Let's go in loud," Kramer said. She returned to the Polara and had it fired and rolling while Puspoon was getting in. Lewis pirouetted to avoid getting hit, and then got sprayed with rocks. Bradshaw slowed the Satellite alongside him, so he could get in, and was back on the gas before he got the door closed.

Chapter 67

Monday, June 1, 1970

I was still several rungs from the bottom when Wren went down. I leaped but landed awkwardly, twisting my right ankle.

"Ow! Crap!" I grabbed it, writhing in pain.

"Thassyoupsshhypoon?" *Boom!* The round smacked the barn's block foundation. Marlin, squatting behind the Fury's rear bumper, had his semi-automatic pistol in both hands, barrel up. He nodded at me and then nodded up at the loft before duck-walking between the wall and the car toward the right front fender.

"Hey, Wolf!" Marlin shouted. Frank fired, and the bullet blew a fist-sized hole through the barnwood. A sunbeam, filled with dancing dust motes, showed its trajectory. Marlin scampered to the plow.

"Marlnahmgonkeeluuu!"

Marlin looked at me, plainly annoyed that I hadn't moved. I pointed at my ankle and shrugged, but he jabbed two fingers at me and pointed to the loft. Shaking my head and trailing my foot like a funeral train, I crawled to the ladder and hopped up a rung at a time on my good leg. When I neared the top, the Colt exploded again and chunks of barnwood went flying not five feet from my head. I dove for the loose, dirty planks, landed with a groan, and scrambled on my hands and knees to the rear of the barn. I looked out the loft doors. Frank was on the slope, weaving around, looking sozzled.

"Hey, Wolf!" Marlin yelled. Another shot! The slug blasted a big hole in the barn door, spraying wood all over the Apache's hood. I took another quick peek. Frank was flat on his ass. Marlin dashed diagonally to the stall beneath me.

"I'm up here," I whispered, eyeing him through a knothole. He looked up.

"Where's Wolf?" he hissed. I looked again. Frank was on his feet, staggering toward the porch, gun in hand.

"He's headed for the house." Frank dropped heavily on the back stoop with his elbows on his knees and his chin on his chest. He didn't look too good.

"Okay, stay put." Marlin unlatched the metal door on the stall and eased it open with his shoulder. He had his .45 in both hands, chest high, barrel up, ready to step out and unload on Frank. Marlin took a deep breath and exhaled slowly. Suddenly, lightning crashed, and there was a thunder of hooves. The horses galloped in from the field, throwing off Marlin's timing. They slowed to a frisky trot when they reached the corral and then, nickering and shaking their manes, they walked toward the stalls. I looked back at Marlin. He had his gun at his chest again, ready to use the horses as a shield.

"GIDDYUP!" I didn't know what else to yell. Marlin, startled, froze, and the horses, frightened, bolted. He slowly turned his head and looked up at me with a scowl. I shrugged.

"Frank's behind the porch now."

"Thanks. Do you want to tell him where I am?"

"I'd rather we get in the car and leave."

"I can't."

"Why not? There's the car. You've got the keys. Let's go."

"No, I'm going after Wolf. Stay put. Your dad will be here soon." Then he was gone.

Chapter 68

Monday, June 1, 1970

The needle on the speedometer was at seventy and rising. A cloud of chalk-white dust billowed out the back of the Polara while Kramer worked the steering wheel to minimize its slide. Ahead, the shadowy ruin of the Terwilliger farm loomed; the house atop the mound and the faded red barn beyond and below it.

"There's the Apache," Puspoon said.

"Hold on." Kramer let off the gas and got on the brakes, locking all four tires in a straight skid. The cloud behind her swelled. She flicked the steering wheel to the right and held it, forcing the rear end to swing up and around on her left. She kept inching the wheel and tapping the brakes, until the Polara was skidding sideways within its own cloud.

The car skidded past the house, slowing on the rocks. As the dust cleared, Kramer got back on the gas. The rear tires, spinning and spitting rocks, finally bit and the car shot straight toward the barn. Puspoon, seeing nothing but faded red wood rushing at him, tucked his legs, but Kramer locked the brakes, wrenched the wheel hard right, and brought the Polara to a skidding stop. Puspoon was first out. Switchblade in hand, he scrambled to the truck and sliced the sidewall on the left rear tire. The corner sagged, tire hissing.

Kramer threw the gearshift into park and shouldered open the door. She grabbed the Ithaca and rolled out the car, landing in a puff of red dirt. She knelt, wedged in the doorjamb, and aimed the twelve-gauge over the hood toward the house.

"FBI! DROP YOUR WEAPONS AND SURRENDER!" Nobody heard her.

The white dust rolling out from beneath the Polara was like a blanket of gritty foot powder on the Satellite's windshield. The wipers whipped back and forth, badly outpaced.

"Brakes," a worried Lewis advised between coughs. He'd learned his first day as an FBI agent to brace for impact when Bradshaw slid behind the wheel. Suddenly, the Polara's taillights lit up. With the ditch on his left, Bradshaw steered right, angling for the house and pumping the brake like the pedal on a kick drum. The Satellite bounced roughly leaving the road, trampling grass and weeds and knocking down small stalks of corn, before bottoming out on the upslope and going airborne. The car landed heavily, nose first, smashing the grill, crumpling the hood, and tearing the front bumper off its mounts. The radiator hissed a mist of sea-green steam as the Satellite tore through the yard, shedding parts in its wake and throwing grass, weeds, and big chunks of dirt up on the porch. Lewis rode out the teeth-rattling ride, sustaining only minor whiplash injuries.

Bradshaw was less fortunate. The initial impact—abrupt and hard—mashed his broad, barrel chest against the steering wheel, shattering it, and cracking the column as well. The recoil snapped his head back, giving him a good look at the big—and quickly getting bigger—oak tree. Bradshaw stomped on the brakes and cranked what was left of the steering wheel as far left as it would go, causing the right rear to swing up and around. When it did, the quarter panel clipped the mighty oak, spinning the car back clockwise. Wheels locked, the Satellite skidded backward down the slope, leaving twin trails of freshly plowed dirt, and slammed into the Apache's passenger side. It sounded like the world exploded. Then there was silence.

Bradshaw, shaken and stunned, shifted into park, but the Satellite wasn't going anywhere without a tow truck. He groggily unbelted, shouldered the door open, and toppled out, landing on his forearms and knees in the clay-rich soil. He retrieved his Winchester from the back seat and scoped the fence line, making sure no one escaped. Lewis, who'd already bailed out, ran for the house, gun drawn, and leapt atop the tumbledown porch. He tried the doorknob. *Locked.* He peeked through the thin window curtains, but it was too dark inside to make out anything.

The air was thick with tension. The wind had picked up. It gradually built into a strong, stiff breeze, and the ever darkening cloudscape finally blackened, blotting out the sun like spilt ink on a page. Kramer was looking for better cover when a scowling man popped up behind the back porch and took a shot at her. She recognized Brixton and pumped off three rounds in quick succession, all of them after her window exploded.

Kramer, face bleeding and covered in small bits of glass, scrambled to the rear of the Polara, gave a quick look toward the porch, and scrambled to the Apache's front bumper. When Lewis heard the gunshots, he planted the heel of his heavy-soled shoe just below the doorknob, splintering the front door and taking the deadbolt and part of the transom with it. He entered the house low, sweeping his .45 from side to side. Puspoon, meanwhile, ran across the front yard, hopped on the porch and ducked under the sagging awning. He stopped at the corner. Angling his mirror, he checked the side of the house. It was fifteen yards to the backyard with nothing but grass and weeds for cover.

Chapter 69

Monday, June 1, 1970

Light rain fell while Brixton, hunched like Quasimodo, cradled his head in his hands, reeling from his concussion. He was getting queasy. Marlin had nailed him good, leaving a swollen blue knot on his left temple. Moaning, he dropped to his knees, gulping lungfuls of air, trying to suppress the contents of his churning stomach. It didn't help, and in fact, it made things decidedly worse.

Brixton dropped to all fours, convulsing. Up it came. The sour, lumpy mash hit the grass and splattered his hands and jacket sleeves. He stared blindly through tears, gasping for air, while a long strand of snot hung from his nose, reaching for the ground. The knot throbbed. He spat. He felt drunk and very sleepy. Brixton fought to clear his thoughts, and as he did, he vaguely recalled Marlin talking about the FBI, a car crash, and some black woman yelling something. He took a shot at her and got three in return. Brixton fumed. He should've been long gone instead of crouching behind a porch exchanging gunfire with the fucking feds. Steadying himself with one hand, he got to a knee and looked to the west. Then he looked north. Ankle-high corn in both directions, perfect if he wanted to get shot.

What he wanted was to scream. He was fucked and it was all Marlin's and Wren's fault. A gust of wind snapped a limb off the massive sycamore. It landed on the roof with a loud crash. Then the rain picked up. Brixton, groaning, flattened himself on the ground and crawled through the swirling grass, disappearing beneath the tree.

The rain started as a few sporadic drops, but quickly became a light sprinkle and then grew steadier. The dark clouds opened up and, just like that, Broben County was under a flood emergency. The ground was like cement, too dense to absorb the rain, it filled the cracks in the hard-packed ground.. The excess water found channels and rivulets and pooled in the lower areas of the farm and beyond. The runoff made the hillock a slippery-slide of mud.

Marlin dropped to a crouch, gun in hand. He'd climbed the embankment after bolting from the stall and circled around the back of the sycamore, stopping when all hell broke loose out front. He waited, letting things play out. A short while later, he heard grunts and groans from behind the house. Thinking Wolf had been shot, Marlin pressed on, determined to finish him off. Gun aimed, He edged further around the tree. A light rain muffled his footsteps. Wet leaves and branches brushed his back. He saw the porch, but Wolf was gone. Marlin angrily punched the air and headed back around the tree. The yard was a swamp. He slogged through grass and weeds toward the barn. Water filled his shoes. Marlin stopped when he saw Bradshaw, shielded by the Satellite, scoping the property lines. He slowly sank to a knee and nestled in among the tree branches, shielding himself from the wind and rain.

Lightening flashed, pulsing in energy, sustaining itself for several moments against the ink-black sky. Kramer, heart pounding, cautiously entered the barn. There was another flicker of light followed by a loud thunderclap. She ducked behind the Fury's front wheel, careful to keep her head below the fender, and inched toward the rear bumper. She peeked over the quarter panel, but couldn't see anything through the murk. Rain rat-a-tatted on the corrugated tin roof. Up the slope, moving with equal caution, Lewis cleared the living room. Lightening briefly lit up the house, and he saw the cups and plates. Also, leaks in the ceiling. He moved on. It was sweltering. Sweat trickled down his face. There was a long, low rumble overhead. He tried the light switch. *No power.* Lewis passed through the kitchen and edged down the darkened hallway. He cleared the bathroom and then, after peering in the closet, crept on to the bedrooms. His trigger finger was as tense as a mousetrap. Out front, Puspoon pointed the .357 at the rear corner of the house, still waiting for someone to round it. When he heard the retching, he slowly advanced toward the opposite corner, cautiously wading through the tall, wet, dead stalks.

Chapter 70

Monday, June 1, 1970

My Dad? No way! I had to get Wren's gun. If Marlin wound up on the wrong end of Frank's Colt, I wouldn't be able to run far or fast on my ankle. I had to look out for myself. I limped toward the ladder, but stopped when I heard the roar of a car coming up the road—quick, too, from the sound of it. Suddenly, a rolling wall of thick chalky dust appeared and a car shot out straight for the barn. I closed my eyes and braced for impact, but, instead of a crash, I heard tires skidding and doors opening. I exhaled a sigh of relief, but, a tick later, the earth shook to the sense-deadening sound of crashing cars. Then gunfire. I dove for the hay bales. A lightning bolt struck off in the distance, followed seconds later by a loud crack and a slow rumble of thunder. I waited, listening. It was very quiet apart from the wind, but then it started raining, and I couldn't hear anything else. I decided Wren's gun could wait.

Chapter 71

Monday, June 1, 1970.

It was blacker than death beneath the sycamore, and it was giving Brixton fits. He'd become disoriented almost immediately, and kept bumping his head whichever way he moved. Navigating cluelessly in the dark, he'd climbed over, ducked under, and wriggled around just about every limb and branch beneath the tree, and some of them more than once. At one point, Brixton, by then an exhibition of cuts, scrapes, and bruises, was stuck upside down, torso wedged tight in a triangle of thick boughs, with his arms and legs twisted in ways they were never meant to be and his entire body weight resting on his left cheekbone. When he finally got unraveled, he fell, ricocheting off limbs all the way down. Brixton groaned in pain, but he didn't have time to focus on its origins. The situation was dire and he was desperate. Self-preservation made him squirm on.

By stroke of luck, Brixton crawled over damp ground. He stopped and frantically swept his hands and arms back all around, searching for seepage. He found rainwater soon enough and followed it to a big puddle of mud. Brixton excitedly slapped his hands in the muck, feeling for its feeder. When he finally found it, he slithered to the sycamore's outermost branches.

The sky was dark, a mean mix of purple and black that replaced piss-poor visibility with whatever's worse. Brixton couldn't have cared less about the dark; he was just relieved to finally be out from under the tree. Gun ready, he stood and crept around the gigantic sycamore. He wasn't sure exactly where he was, so he kept close to the leaves and branches, getting as wet down his back as he was muddy down his front.

A gust of wind swept up, and Brixton had to brace himself to avoid being blown over. Something up ahead caught his eye, just for a moment, but it was gone so quick he wasn't sure if the wind and rain were playing tricks. He crept on, pausing several yards later to wipe his face with his jacket sleeve. He finally got his bearings when he made out the gray outline of the barn. Then he saw Wren, or at least that huge part of him covered by his white shirt, and beyond him, an FBI agent scoping the farm with a rifle. Fuming, he again cursed his partners.

Brixton, shielded by the tree, considered his options. Finding none he liked, he moved on, now crouching, eyes just above the tops of the grass and weeds. He stopped again. He was about as close to the barn as he'd get without getting shot. It was now or never. He was about to make a break for it when he spied Marlin squatting up ahead among the leaves and branches. Brixton wiped his face with his sleeve and looked again. Marlin was still there. His mood instantly brightened.

The wind and rain drowned out everything except the creaking boughs of the two trees. Brixton holstered his Colt and removed his belt from his pants. He wound an end around each hand and inched toward Marlin with his muddy, wet pants inching down his hips.

Marlin, oblivious to the belt about to be looped around his neck, clutched the Fury's keys in one hand and his .45 in the other. He'd heard noise from the barn, so he knew it was an FBI agent. He racked the slide on his gun, chambering a round. *I hope Tyler found a good hiding spot.* He got up and ran toward the barn while Brixton silently screamed in frustration.

Chapter 72

Monday, June 1, 1970

Puspoon, gripping the short-barreled Magnum with both hands, spun around the corner only to find vomit and a trail of bent grass leading to the sycamore. He stopped momentarily, completely soaked, and then took off, tramping through the sodden brush in long strides, ripping up long stalks of dead grass and weeds that wrapped around his shins and ankles. He rounded the back of the tree and spotted Brixton, struggling with his trousers, heading for the mound and the barn beyond.

"FREEZE!" Puspoon yelled. Brixton, startled, tripped and fell, disappearing among the yellow and brown stalks. He reached for his Colt, but a hollow-point slug buzzed past, taking half his ear and leaving a trail of burnt skin along the side of his head. Brixton, cursing, cupped his mangled ear and writhed in pain. Blood streamed through his fingers and over his hand onto his sleeve and collar. His sopping wet white shirt pinkened.

Huge gusts of wind blew in, moving the rainclouds northeast, and the storm stopped as quickly as it began. The sun searched for gaps in the sky off to the west. Kramer had jumped from the ladder when she heard the gunshot and ran across the barn to the back door. She abruptly stopped when she saw Wren face down by the corral.

"Don't move!" she yelled at the motionless big man. She aimed the Ithaca at his skull and circled him, looking for a weapon. She kicked the chicken leg from his hand and pulled the sausage from his pocket. "You all right up there?" Kramer called.

"I'm good," Puspoon yelled. "I've got Brixton. He's alive."

"I've got the big guy, but can't say the same." Kramer eyed the farm with concern. Tyler was still missing, and the wheelman was at large. The porch door banged shut. Moments later, Lewis appeared at the top of the mound.

"House's clear. You okay?"

"Yeah, I'm good, but we've got one on the run and no sign of Tyler."

Kramer knelt and felt beneath Wren. She found his .357 in his shoulder holster and tucked it in her back waistband. After putting his ham-sized forearms behind his back, she slapped a handcuff around his wrist, but couldn't get it closed. Frowning, Kramer twisted the metal bracelet around his wrist and worked it up and down, trying to find a place where she could get the clasp to lock. She sat up, frustrated and breathing hard. Suddenly, she snorted angrily and grabbed the cuff in both hands, leveraged her body weight, and squeezed the metal pieces together with all her might, pinching them, needing. . .only. . . a . . . hair . . . more . . . .

"OW!" Wren jerked his hand away. "Easy, lady, that hurts!"

"WHAT THE—" Kramer sputtered, stumbling backward. She shouldered the shotgun and jammed the barrel against Wren's fleshy neck.

"EASY, LADY!"

"GET DOWN!"

"I AM!"

"PUT YOUR HANDS BEHIND YOUR BACK!"

"THEY ARE!"

"DON'T MOVE!"

"I'M NOT!" Lewis raced back to the mound, gun drawn, and half-ran, half-slid down the muddy slope.

"Throw me your cuffs!" Kramer said when he reached the

bottom. After lassoing Wren's meaty wrists together, she told Lewis to read him his rights. Then she started up the embankment.

Upslope, Puspoon still had the .357 pointed at Brixton. "Where's Tyler?" he said when the commotion below quieted. Brixton raised up on his right elbow and looked over his shoulder. His ear was gristle and he was staring at a cannon. His pinkish shirt now had a red collar.

"So, you're Pussypoon's daddy." Brixton's grimace was fixed, unchanging, and so was his attitude. "Your wife gives good head."

Puspoon walked toward him and stopped fifteen feet away. "Ex-wife, and you're a liar. Now, where is he?"

"He's not here," Brixton bluffed, trying to buy time, "and you'll never see him again unless you let me go."

"Mm-hmm, and here I thought you might want that other ear." Puspoon thumbed the Magnum's hammer. Just then, Kramer crested the rise. Puspoon's eyes flashed her way, just for a tick, but it was enough. Brixton quickly rolled onto his back, pulled the Colt, and squeezed the trigger.

The gunshot was deafening. The slug smacked against his skull, shattering bone and tearing through his brain and out the back of his head. Brixton, wide-eyed, fell backward in the mud. Puspoon walked over, picked up the Colt, and spun the cylinder.

"Dumbass was out of bullets."

Lewis hustled up the hillock to the backyard, shoes caked in mud.

"Everybody all right?"

"He's been better," Puspoon said, nodding at Brixton.

"What happened?"

Puspoon started to answer, but Kramer cut him off. "Brixton drew and pulled the trigger, but he was out of bullets. The Lieutenant wasn't."

"I've got to find Tyler," Puspoon said.

"He's not in the house." Lewis nodded at Brixton. "Didn't he say?"

“Our conversation was cut short.”

“Radio the command post,” Kramer shouted to Bradshaw, who was at the base of the mound with Wren. “Tell them we’ve got a fugitive and we need this area blanketed.” She turned to Puspoon, “I think I know where he is.”

Chapter 73

Monday, June 1, 1970

Minutes seemed like hours. Then I heard gunshots and, curious, I crawled to the loft doors and pushed them open. Wren was wriggling on the ground like a beached manatee while a black woman was coming down the slope with . . . my Dad!

"DAD!" Everyone looked up, including Wren.

"Tyler!" Dad rushed into the corral. "Man, I'm glad to see you!"

"Same here!" Forgetting my ankle, I pushed off, aiming for the hay bales, but missed. Something snapped and, an instant later, pain exploded in my left knee.

My eyes fluttered, but my eyelids felt heavy and refused to stay open, so I stopped trying.

"He's waking up." The voice sounded far away, a different galaxy. I couldn't place it.

"How're you feeling, dear? *Mom.* My throat and mouth were drier than sawdust. I pantomimed for something to drink. A moment later, there was a Styrofoam cup filled with water at my lips. I tilted my head back and gulped greedily. "More," I rasped. The cup was back again. I drained it. "Where am I?" My throat felt raw. "What happened?"

"You don't remember?" *Dad.* He kept refilling and I kept chugging.

"Uh-uh." Bits and pieces of the last several days floated above me, out of reach.

"You're in the hospital." *Darlene.* I finally opened my eyes. She had big splotches of calamine lotion all over her face and neck and gauze everywhere else.

"You look like a pink mummy!" I said. Everybody laughed.

"I know, I've got poison ivy really bad."

"Me, too," I groaned. "Is that why I'm here?"

"No, dear,' Mom said, patting my arm, "you just got out of surgery."

"Surgery?" I was suddenly conscious of the pain in my knee.

"You ruptured your ACL," Dad said, lifting the sheet so I could see the cast. "You also fractured your ankle."

"Hoo-hoo! What're you doing? Stop that!" A craggy-faced nurse dressed in white breezed in. She gave Dad a sharp look and snatched the cup from him. "He can't have water, only ice chips. He'll get sick." She shooed everyone from the room, pulled the drapes shut, and returned bedside.

"Get some rest," she said sweetly while tucking me in. She switched off the lights and left, closing the door behind her.

I didn't get sick, but I got plenty of rest, not waking until Tuesday evening. Supper had all the flavor of cardboard and rags, but I was so hungry I ate every bite. Then I watched the news and found out Wren was in jail and Frank was dead. I didn't find out Dad had killed him until Darlene brought me the *Broben County Times.* The *Times* also had a small story in the police blotter about a pickup truck that had been stolen from a farm not far from the Terwilliger place. Police found it in nearby Mentbolt. The newspaper said there was a royal flush laid out on the seat. I smiled.

Acknowledgments

I started writing the manuscript that ultimately became this book in December 2009. My sons, Patrick Ford, Jr. and Caleb Poer, were in grade school. Now, Patrick's a college graduate with a marketing career and Caleb, who has nearly completed his degree, is combining art, entertainment, and marketing into what will eventually become—my guess, here—a business. Both of them contributed to my manuscript, sometimes simply by listening, but also by providing their thoughts on characters, dialogue, and scenes. Sadly, they get no royalties…yet. I love you two more than anything in the whole wide world. You already knew that, but now everybody else knows, too.

Special thanks goes to my sister, Deborah J. Atkins, my stepmother, Nancy A. Poer, and my friend, Lynette Johnson. They helped me get through a particularly rough patch in 2017, which got me back to writing sooner than I otherwise would. I love all three of you.

Many people, some writers themselves, but friends one and all, were curious about my manuscript, asking me how it was coming along, or when it'd be finished. I'm waiting until now to tell them how much their interest encouraged me to keep writing, so thank you to Larry and Elizabeth Mock, Rob Bremner, Steve Womble, Lonna Chew, Sandra Hermansen, Kolesa Lashley, Stephanie Echols, Kennedy Hunn, and Kathy Hutchins.

Stan Atha's probably surprised to find his name here. He's been my friend since high school, but it was years later, after I became a Marine, and I was finishing law school, when we were sitting lakeside at his house, and he said to me quite sincerely, "I really thought you were going to accomplish something." Yeah, me, too. Sorry.

Thanks to my friend, Al Velasquez, who provided advice on nailing accents. Bob Knight might not have put you in his book, but you're in mine.

When I was writing about the Marines in this book, I often thought about two fellow Marines, Master Sergeant Ray Felan (Ret.), and Gunnery Sergeant Erin Miller (Ret.). Top Felan and Gunny Miller personify the Marine Corps' core values of honor, courage, and commitment, and I was proud to serve alongside them. They've been friends of mine since we met in New Orleans.

Maureen Cutajar of gopublished.com dutifully formatted my manuscript, allowing you to read it digitally or in print, if at all. She saved me from banging my head for weeks on end, so I appreciate her excellent work and professional service.

Finally, Lesley Bolton, InkblotEditing.com's editorial director, took on the daunting task of transforming my scribbles into a novel, and her ideas, suggestions, and corrections were invaluable toward that end. Thanks for your hard work and expertise.

From Marine, writer, and lawyer Darrell V. Poer,
enter the mind of high school sophomore
Tyler Puspoon as his world is turned
upside down.

Made in the USA
Monee, IL
20 November 2021

82509354R00184